UNDER THE
ALASKAN
ICE

KAREN HARPER

UNDER THE ALASKAN ICE

mira

ISBN-13: 978-0-7783-1013-6

Under the Alaskan Ice

Mira
22 Adelaide St. West, 40th Floor
Toronto, Ontario M5H 4E3, Canada
BookClubbish.com

Printed in U.S.A.

For my brave, interesting and fun friend Mary Ann Manning.

UNDER THE ALASKAN ICE

CHAPTER ONE

Thanksgiving Day
Falls Lake, Alaska

"I'm getting really good walking in snowshoes, Mom!" Chip boasted as they plodded through the thick snow, heading toward the lake that gave the nearby town its name. His cheeks were already pink, and his freckles stood out. Their words made little white clouds. The crisp wind energized Meg, and their goggles and the massive Sitka spruce along the path muted the stark sun glare off the snow.

"You sure are walking great in those snowshoes, but you don't have to take steps that big, honey."

Since Chip was six, so many adventures were new to him. Meg had lost her husband, Chip's father, Ryan, in a plane crash nearly three years ago, and she was still barely at the place she could cope. At least Chip was doing so much better accepting his father's death. For months the boy had insisted his daddy was coming back as usual from a day of flying. At least now he didn't insist each plane that went over was Daddy buzzing to them from heaven. In this cold, snowy season, fewer bush planes headed north, taking hunters or fishermen into the wilds, leaving them and picking them up later.

"I just didn't want us to fall asleep after that big turkey dinner," she explained as they trudged along, heading out from the lodge where they lived with Meg's twin sister, Suzanne. They had greatly renovated the old place they'd inherited from their grandmother and brought it into the modern world with online advertising to attract more guests. "There's something in turkey called tryptophan that makes people sleepy," she explained.

"But the football games on TV wake them up, right?"

"They wake some people. Besides, even in this chilly weather, exercise is good for us. This walk will help us digest that big meal Aunt Suze and I fixed."

Meg both loved and dreaded the holidays since they brought back memories of happier times—not that she wasn't making a new life for herself and Chip at the Falls Lake Lodge, where she oversaw the kitchen and helped with their guests while Suze covered the business end of things. Meg had even begun to create homemade chocolate candies. She'd sold a lot of them this fall and winter to both guests at the lodge and townspeople in Falls Lake. The profits were going straight into the bank to provide for Chip's future education—hopefully, not as a pilot. Anything but that.

"Listen, Mom! I hear something—like a plane," the boy shouted, clomping along as fast as he could to the open-sky shore of the frozen lake. He pulled off his sun goggles and shaded his eyes, craning his neck to look up.

"It's probably someone cutting firewood from trees," she insisted, but she knew better. If their few and distant neighbors didn't have their winter wood cut weeks ago, it was a bad time to do that with the burden of the snow.

From the direction of the distant, snow-capped Talkeetna

Mountains, beyond the frozen pillar of the waterfall that fed the lake in warmer weather, the buzzing whine came louder. Meg knew it sounded bad—rough, as though an engine were sputtering.

Ripping off her goggles, which also snagged her knitted sock cap, she instinctively put a hand on Chip's shoulder so he didn't bolt, snowshoes or not. They squinted into the clear blue sky in the direction of the sporadic, choking sound.

"There," Chip shouted, pointing his leather mitten. His voice came back as an echo across the blinding white ice. *There…there…there…*

She saw it too. At least the plane was clear of the mountains, unlike Ryan's fatal flight.

"It's going to try to land on the lake," she told Chip. "See, it's a pontoon plane, and that will work. It might even have ski runners under there, given the lake is iced over."

"But it's all wobbly," the boy cried, his high voice breaking. "It's not coming in real good."

He was right. She inhaled sharply, and the air stung clear down into her lungs. She bit her lower lip and blinked back tears so they wouldn't fall and freeze on her cheeks. They stood together as she replayed what she knew about the day Ryan died.

In the lovely month of August, he'd picked up tourists from the Anchorage airport to drop them off for frontier salmon fishing. He'd headed back in the mist and rain when he shouldn't have because it was Chip's birthday, and he wanted to be with them. God forgive her, as much as she had loved Ryan, she was still angry with his decision to fly home in that weather. How she wished Chip had a father and she had a husband… These long nights were so lonely, even as busy as she kept and—

"Mom, it's going to land too hard!"

The plane was tilting, listing—the pilot had lost control.

She'd seen enough landings, been in enough Cessnas and Piper Cubs, floatplanes and even ones with ice runners, to know what was coming. She prayed that—

Even though the crash was at least thirty yards out on the ice, she grabbed Chip, threw him down and shielded him with her body as the plane slammed into the frozen lake, breaking the ice with a blast that sounded like dynamite. The loudest cracking she'd ever heard made her head hurt, a crunching nightmare.

"Mom, we got to save the pilot!" came muffled from beneath her puffy, down-filled parka.

Afraid to look, she did anyway. The unmarked small Piper Cherokee was tilted on its side, already being devoured by massive jaws of jagged ice into the belly of the lake. Its upward wing seemed to summon help as it sank. With the sun off the windows, she could not tell if more were onboard than a pilot.

"We've got to help!" Chip shouted as they scrambled up, trying to get to their feet with the awkward snowshoes still strapped to their boots. He was trying to take his snowshoes off, no doubt to run out on the ice.

She dove at him, pulled him back onto his knees and hugged him hard.

"We cannot go out on broken ice, Chip! It might crack more, and we'd go in. I'll call for help, get first responders here from the town or even Anchorage."

"They're gonna die!"

"We cannot run out on that ice! Maybe the plane will float or snag."

She kept one hand on her son's wrist and dug her cell phone out of her deep pocket with the other. At least they were in range of the fairly new cell tower that had brought the outside world to Falls Lake.

With her teeth, she yanked off one thermal glove and

was instantly bitten by the cold as she awkwardly punched in 9-1-1. The plane was sinking fast and, as Chip feared, going under. Terrible to be helpless like this. At least Ryan's death had been fast, into a rocky cliff in foul weather, not this sucking, freezing death under the ice.

"What is your emergency?" The woman's calm voice came so quietly that Meg could barely hear it over the crackling of the ice and the horrid gurgling noise.

"A small plane has just crashed through the ice on Falls Lake—the other end from the falls. Its engine sounded bad. It's sinking, pilot still on board, don't know about passengers. There is no direct access road but the one that goes past the lodge. This is Megan Metzler. My son and I are here but we can't go out on the shattered ice. Send help, maybe another plane! First responders on the road will have a hard time…"

She stayed on the line with the emergency operator and then with a rep at the NTSB, the National Transportation Safety Board, in Washington, DC, so far away.

The plane sank so quickly she almost couldn't believe it had been there. The two of them stared at the jagged hole in the ice, hugging each other, propping each other up.

"Ma'am—Mrs. Metzler." A new voice came on the line, a man's. "Anchorage first responders are on the way, but it could be over an hour, and we'd appreciate it if you can stay there to guide them in."

"Yes, okay, but the hole in the ice—it stands out."

"Good. Because we have been able to contact one of our NTSB pilots who was in the area, and he is going to land shortly on the lake."

"Tell him to be careful!"

"Yes, yes, of course. He's a veteran pilot and diver—"

"Scuba diver?"

"This time of year, a dry suit diver for cold water. He

tells us his ETA is about fifteen minutes. He's in his personal white Cessna 185 with red markings."

"A Skywagon," she blurted out, surprised she'd said that. "My—my husband was a pilot."

The man read off the number that would be on the plane's fuselage, as if she'd have to pick out the right aircraft landing on frozen Falls Lake today. A Skywagon was the plane Ryan would have loved to own, but it cost over a hundred thousand dollars, way beyond their means.

The man went on, "It is pontoon- and ski-equipped. The pilot is one of our most skilled search and recovery pilots, name of Bryce Saylor." He spelled the name since that wasn't quite how it sounded.

Trying to concentrate, she closed her eyes. They had put their sun goggles back on, but that did nothing to blur the horrid hole in the ice. Should she have tried to go out there, crawl on her stomach? It was not a lone swimmer going under the ice but an entire plane with no one visible, so the impact must have stunned, injured or even instantly killed the pilot and any passengers. It would have been a more merciful death if that were true.

"Bryce Saylor, I'll remember that," she promised, scanning the sunny, lovely and empty sky. "We'll be here to meet him."

But even as the man stayed on the phone, counting down the plane's estimated time of arrival, one thing she'd been told snagged in her brain. The pilot they were awaiting was an expert not in search and rescue, but in search and recovery of equipment, of bodies. Recovery—yes, she understood that. She was still working on that in her own life.

Bryce knew the basic lay of the land and water around Falls Lake. He'd actually stayed briefly at the lodge there about eight years ago, planning on some downtime after his breakup with the woman he'd thought he'd marry. It had been run by an elderly lady and her staff; he remembered that much. He'd done some hiking and fishing. But he'd received an emergency call—much like this one—for a sightseeing bush plane that had gone down near Anchorage, and he'd checked out of the lodge about as fast as he'd checked in.

He flew now by sight, though the snow and ice below would have blinded him without his pilot's sunglasses to reduce the glare. He saw the mountain peak with the waterfall. Right now it was a tower of ice, gleaming in the sun. The story was that the big waterfall had been dammed up by boulders for years, and a pioneer village had been built on the dry lakebed. Then, after a few decades, the boulders shifted in an earthquake, and the water burst forth over the cliff to bury the little settlement.

He couldn't help thinking of the lives lost. Loss of life was exactly what both kept him going and haunted him. Diving to recover bodies in wreckage, especially when in icy water, was not a task for everyone—maybe even not for him at times. He'd done it in the navy and had wanted to leave it behind, so he turned instead to diving for abandoned fishing nets off the harbor at Anchorage, then helping a friend establish a kelp-and-micro-algae farm, which he'd invested in.

But he wanted to put his skills to use for good, such as when victims needed to be recovered for their loved ones, so he'd joined the NTSB. He had soon been promoted to oversee recovery efforts as an official incident commander living in the state capital of Juneau, though his official base was Anchorage. It had made his dad, a former navy pilot, proud and his grandfather, who had flown the big flying fortresses called B-17s in World War II, even prouder. If only they could see him now, handpicked for a covert special task force for a very powerful man above the NTSB. But his father and grandfather were both gone now, his mother too, and he missed them all. At least he still had a brother and his family, though he wanted one of his own.

He flew lower as he spotted both the hole in the lake—with no sign of a plane in it—and two people waving from the shore. He dipped a wing to let them know it was him and made a tight circle back to give himself a trajectory to land away from the place that was probably some poor pilot's grave until he or she could be recovered. Strange to have assignments that made families both grieved and relieved to have their loved one's body back.

He cut his speed and coasted in, keeping away from any evidence, hoping the woman and the boy his contact said awaited weren't the ones who had lost this pilot, and especially that they had not gone out to meet the plane on Thanksgiving Day expecting a happy reunion. Whatever they had witnessed and whoever they were, he hoped he could help them and that they would be a help to him. It could be so damn lonely out here in the wilds, in the "Great Alone" of Alaska. But loneliness could occur anywhere and anytime, even on a big family holiday with people around like he'd had earlier at his brother's house in Seattle before flying back.

As he coasted a little closer to the frozen shingle shore, he felt happy to have someone here to meet him, even strangers.

CHAPTER TWO

Wearing snowshoes, the woman and the boy came to meet him along the frozen shore where he nosed the plane in. He waved once, then started tossing his diving gear out onto the snow. Though time was precious, he shook their hands and told the mother and son, "Thanks for staying around. I can use some help suiting up to get out there fast."

"Yes, anything we can do," the woman said.

She had a melodic voice, even with those few words. Well, he always sized people up too fast. She had a pretty face too, was maybe in her midthirties like him.

"Good landing!" the boy, maybe five or six years old, said.

He told them, "I need to get into my dry suit ASAP. Gonna strip down to my thermal wick underwear while you lay that bundled rubber suit out for me. Also, could you uncoil that long rope?" he added, pointing.

"Oh, yes, sure," the woman said and bent immediately to unwrap his black neoprene dry suit while he took off his down jacket and jeans. He could have done that inside the plane right now, but it would have taken longer and she wasn't looking, though the boy was. He seemed to be studying his face, his every move. It felt familiar—Bryce used to be curious about everything his grandpa did, since the old man was his boyhood hero.

He was glad he already wore what people always thought was long underwear. He pulled on his thermal insulation outfit over that, and the woman—had his contact said her name was Peg?—assisted.

She perfectly followed his orders, helping him shove his legs and arms in, tug the chest zipper closed, then check the seals at the neck, wrists and ankles. She even handed him his rubber dive booties and fins as if she'd done this before. He hefted and secured his air tank, which seemed so heavy here but would be so light underwater.

Last, she watched him adjust his hard shell helmet with his mounted light attached, then handed him his flashlight on a cord as if he'd asked for it.

She had incredible blue eyes, darker than his. She was very nervous but seemed steady.

"You're a big help," he said as she handed him his mask. "I'm Bryce," he said almost as an afterthought.

"They told me. I'm Meg—Megan Metzler, and this is my son, Chip."

"Nice to meet you. Gotta go. I'm praying the pilot or anyone inside has an air pocket. I'm going to knot the rope around my plane's pontoon so I don't get lost down there. Dark under ice where it's deep and wreckage can drift."

"And this lake water's murky even in the summer. Glacial runoff from the falls," she told him. She must live near here.

He nodded. "There should be help coming from Anchorage, hopefully soon. You two just stay back from that hole where it went in. I'm leaving my plane open so you can get in for a windbreak. There's coffee and doughnuts inside. Stay warm and safe."

"I understand. Thanks," she called after him as he bent

to tie the guide rope on the plane, then shuffled like an old man out onto the ice toward the jagged hole. From here the ice looked over two feet thick. The hole was about as big as his living room in Juneau.

He saw no sign of the sunken plane but remembered his contact had said the woman had even described the make of the plane that crashed. His contact had also said he knew who she was, the widow of a bush pilot who'd slammed into a cliff in bad weather a couple years ago.

Damn, he had to keep his mind on this possible rescue that would, sadly, probably be a recovery. He yanked the guide-line rope to be certain it was secure, then sat on the edge of the broken ice. The lake water made swirls and eddies as he put his legs in. He started breathing canned air, then let himself over the jagged edge into the dark, shifting depths.

"Mom, he said we could get in his plane. Let's go!"

Meg didn't want to even do that. Shouldn't they stand out here, watching for any sign from Bryce? What if he yanked on his rope or needed help if he brought the pilot up? But her nose and face were freezing, and she was trembling from the excitement and the cold, though she'd been sweating the whole time she helped the pilot prepare for his dive. Also, she needed to call Suze so she didn't think they were lost.

"All right," she said even as he tugged at her arm. Reluc-tantly, she climbed the steps into the plane, and Chip didn't even need a boost. She closed the door behind them to halt the cold blast of air across the expanse of lake ice. It was only the second small plane she'd been in since Ryan was lost.

The interior sat six people, but she knew that from when Ryan had talked at length about saving up for a plane like this.

"Can I sit in the pilot's seat?" Chip asked. "I won't touch anything, 'cept maybe put my hands on the yoke wheel."

"You just be very careful," she said as he sat in the pilot's place and she in the copilot seat.

The cockpit, even the passenger area behind them, looked new—immaculate except for duffel bags from which he'd yanked his diving gear.

"You keep a watch out that window," she told Chip, and took Bryce up on the offer of hot coffee and food just behind their seats. She opened the box of doughnuts and saw Bryce Saylor liked chocolate, just like Chip, for half of the eight left from the dozen were iced with dark brown frosting.

Keeping her gaze riveted on the crash site, she phoned Suze, told her what happened and assured her they were all right. To Meg's surprise, Suze had already learned the basics of what happened, but she pumped her for details, then explained how she'd learned about the crash.

"I got a call from the mayor. Someone in Anchorage called him. People are coming out there from town to help. I suppose it will take the rescue guys from Anchorage a while to get there. How long has the plane been down?"

"I actually don't know," she admitted. "It seems eons since it happened and especially since this recovery diver went under the ice. I'm scared it's taking him so long. I'll call you when I can, especially if something happens. We're just sitting in his plane right now to stay warm."

"You are both sitting in his small plane?" Suze repeated, which made Meg mad. Her sister worried too much about the fact she was still depressed over losing Ryan, that she didn't want to go out and about, even when a male friend had invited her. Suze tried to push her into things much too fast. Suze had never been married, never had a great love— she didn't understand.

"Gotta go," she told Suze. "Talk later."

She kept her eyes riveted to the crash site, though Chip was all eyes for the plane. She didn't mention that his father had wanted exactly this model but the cost had been pro-hibitive. She'd been told that this was Bryce's personal plane, so did that mean he had money? Strange to be sitting here, worrying about him, feeling she knew him when she really didn't. It even smelled good in here, kind of—masculine.

The man himself, best as she could tell, had military-cut blond hair and ice-blue eyes. He had chiseled features and was a head taller than her, probably a little over six feet. He was muscular—that she'd noted when he was down to his thermal wear.

She made Chip take his hands off the yoke and just sit there, so he started to read all the dials out loud. Time crawled. What if something had happened to Bryce down there? Should she get out and make sure the jagged edge of the ice hole had not cut his guide rope? No, it looked as taut as before, straight as an arrow across to the gaping hole.

"That pilot who crashed might be dead or Mr. Bryce would be back up by now with him," Chip said.

How could this boy sound so grown-up? As young as he was, as little as he must really recall his father, sometimes he sounded just like him. And here they were sitting in a plane, when one of her goals in life after losing Ryan was to keep Chip away from planes, at least small, propeller-driven ones.

"You may be right," she admitted. "But Bryce said there could be a pocket of air."

"He's a hero, isn't he?" Chip asked, looking toward her at last.

"He risks his life to help others," she said. "Yes, that's one of the most important definitions of a hero."

"I'd say as good as Han Solo and Luke Skywalker, even if his diving suit and mask made him look like Darth Vader."

Reality slammed in. This was still a mere boy, a child. Yet he knew the difference between good and evil even if in make-believe—and this tragedy and this hero risking his life were the real deal.

"Mom, look! There's a man peeking out from the pine trees," Chip said, pointing. "He's watching."

She saw who he meant. The man was wrapped in a warm woolen blanket, a white one that blended with the snow, but surely he had on a coat under that. But no wonder they didn't notice him before, partly secreted and wrapped in white.

"Maybe someone out for a walk like us," she said. "Maybe he heard or saw the crash."

"But it's kind of like he's hiding, like he didn't want us to see him, so maybe he's spying on us."

Of course, it was her imagination and she was letting all this get to her, but the man did seem to be—well, lurking. Why indeed didn't he come out to ask them what had happened, what was going on, or even volunteer to help? She'd learned Alaskans were like that, one for all and all for one.

Unless, of course, that stranger didn't want anyone to know he was here.

"Besides," Chip's voice cut into her agonizing, "there are more people down that way in snowmobiles! See?"

She tore her gaze from the vigilant stranger. "It can't just be more gawkers," she said. "It must be townspeople. You come with me. We need to tell them what's going on."

They clambered down to the ground and shouted and waved at the people streaming along the shore toward them. But she also noted that the strange watcher in the white blanket had disappeared.

CHAPTER THREE

Bryce hated to dive alone. It wasn't safe. Especially in a hostile environment, though he'd done that numerous times before. Under fire in the Middle East. In a storm. In dives a lot deeper than this. Under-ice attempted rescues that went bad.

Hell, this one was bad too. He had seen the pilot, who was definitely deceased. Plane crushed around the man like a metal pop can. The good thing: as far as Bryce could tell, there had not been any passengers. A solo flight. A fatal flight.

But the really weird thing was the fuselage had no markings, no legally mandated ID number. Maybe this was some guy who'd fixed up his own plane and took off not from an airport but his own land. In this state of loners and eccentrics, anything was possible. But Bryce knew he'd have to retrieve the body and the flight plan and manifest—if there was one—to figure all that out. The NTSB would send him a small team to help with recon and recovery if he was to remain commander of this incident—if his boss of bosses requested that—and odds were, he would. After all, this type of rescue and recovery mission wasn't typical for Bryce these days, but the lack of markings or ID were red flags he couldn't ignore. This was exactly the kind of plane the task force had been tracking.

It was eerie down here, not that it wasn't always in deep water, especially under ice. The thick, frozen roof above kept things dark, and his helmet light bounced off glass and plastic to make it seem another diver was with him, hovering, shifting.

Right now he could not access the plane past the crumpled steel and snagged body of the pilot. He hoped he didn't need the Jaws of Life or an underwater blowtorch. He played his flashlight once more over the smashed cockpit, then turned away to slowly surface, looking up for the hole in the thick ice.

Had the plane shifted while he was down here? The hole wasn't where he thought it would be, so he'd have to look for the dangling rope. Despite its length, there had not been enough of it to keep it tethered to his dive belt. Because the lake was deeper than he thought, and he knew it wouldn't take many more feet of depth before his thoughts got funny, he kept heading up.

Meg was right about the milky look of the water from glacial runoff and, no doubt, tiny rock fragments from the falls. For a moment, he felt as if he were falling instead of going up. Was he losing his steady thoughts from carbon dioxide retention? He'd been careful about that as always, but he kept having sideways ideas, not related to what he was doing and seeing.

He couldn't stop wondering why people say *falling in love*, as if it was a downer. Why not *rising in love*? *Flying in love*? *Soaring in love*? And why was he thinking of this right now?

He shook his head and popped his ears. He'd heard that this whole lake was a graveyard, with the pioneers who drowned here. Now this poor pilot in an unmarked vehicle, like the other unmarked graves. Was this guy just untrained or overconfident? Smuggling something? Running from something? Surely he wasn't blinded by the sun glare off the snow and ice and just misjudged a landing. His plane must have malfunctioned.

Bryce shifted directions toward the light above, and swam upward toward it.

Meg saw and heard the white blankness of the lake suddenly explode with people and noise. At least it was not as bad as the memory of that plane crash. Chip was waving madly as if these folks were his best friends, but she did recognize some of the people who had come out, most on snowmobiles they left on the edge of the ice, some on cross-country skis.

She hurried to meet people, to answer questions, and—she surprised herself at this—to address them in a loud, steady voice.

"Please keep off the ice and quiet down so I can explain all at once. There is a professional government rescue and recovery diver checking on the pilot and plane that went down. You can see the large hole the crash made. But we need to listen in case the diver surfaces and calls for help!"

To her amazement and satisfaction, the group of about twenty quieted and came closer to hear. She and Chip answered questions as best they could. "Yes, the National Transportation Safety Board will be sending out more help, but the diver who is here is what they call an official incident commander. I talked to NTSB in Washington, DC."

More questions, voices quieter this time. It all reminded her of an impromptu presidential news conference on the lawn of the White House.

"No, I didn't recognize the plane," she responded. "Yes, my son and I know the diver's name but little else." She cleared her throat, picturing how businesslike Bryce was, even out here in the wilds. Yet he had been kind, even protective.

"His name is Bryce Saylor," she told them. "That is his plane where we were waiting, his personal plane, not an NTSB official one. I don't know why he was in this area since he's out of Juneau, but we were glad to see him."

She glanced out again for the hundredth time at the gaping hole in the ice now greatly shadowed by the sinking sun throwing long, dark silhouettes onto the surface. But Bryce's head and shoulders were emerging from that horrid, jagged hole. She felt such a thrust of relief she nearly burst into tears.

"Chip, stay here," she said. "I'm going out a ways to see if he needs help."

She'd said that with enough authority that even the old timers and a couple of army vets she recognized in the little crowd kept quiet and followed her orders. The town had no real sheriff and the acting one was probably at a holiday meal in Anchorage. It was the mayor who had authority around here.

Walking on the ice was more treacherous than she had imagined. She took small steps, sliding along in tiny movements. Ahead of her, Bryce hauled himself completely out of the water and sat on the side of the hole, then pulled his mask off and lifted his long legs out.

Some people on the shore applauded. Meg felt so bad for the unknown pilot who had lost his life today, but she was so happy to see Bryce, stranger that he still was, emerge from the lake.

"Are you okay?" she called to him from about twenty feet away.

"Don't come closer," he ordered. "The pilot's deceased, plane's a wreck. I'll need a team. I see we have company."

"Just townspeople so far, not first responders," she shouted to him.

"I can see that, but I appreciate your being a first responder for me. Is the boy all right? Are you?"

As he got to his knees, then stood carefully, as chilled as she was, a strange warmth spread through her. Just his words and the tone of his voice made her weak in the knees even as he stood and came carefully toward her. With all that was going on, all he had to do, he was thinking of her and Chip.

"You know anybody at the lodge?" he asked to surprise her even more. "I stayed there once years ago for a couple of days but got an assignment, so I had to leave."

He kept trudging toward her. She realized how heavy his gear must be out of the water. He seemed to know this lake—and the lodge.

"You won't believe this," she told him as they struggled across the ice together toward the shore. When she carried his flippers, he put his hand on her elbow to steady her. "My sister and I run the lodge now. We have room for you—and your crew, of course."

His face looked so cold and the suction marks of his face mask were imprinted on his skin. But his eyes and smile were warm.

"Kismet," he said.

For a moment she wasn't sure what he had said, what he meant. Kiss what?

But any reply she had was drowned out by the muted applause of gloved and mittened hands and the storm of questions villagers began to shout at Bryce. Amid all that, Meg could pick out Chip's high voice saying, "I liked your plane a lot, Mr. Bryce! It was really cool—no, I mean warm—inside."

"You have to be kidding, absolutely kidding!" Suze said when a finally thawed-out Meg and Chip told her the NTSB commander and his two-man team would be staying for at least several days at the lodge.

"Thank heavens we have room," Suze said. "So, I guess we'd better put leftover turkey and the fixings on the table tonight. We went through that great pumpkin pie you made so we may have to make do with that mince pie Chip doesn't like and a plate of your chocolates."

"I like pie, really, Aunt Suze," Chip said, pulling a new warm sweatshirt over his mussed head. "But people should not put meat in pies. Maybe just tell Mr. Bryce it's a raisin pie 'cause it's got those in there. Just think, we're gonna have guests who are pilots. I bet he'll answer my questions. I was telling Mom, he looked like Darth Vader when he was in his water suit, but he's more like Han Solo—a real cool pilot like Daddy was."

That brought reality home to Meg with a thud. At least after a couple of days, once that plane and pilot had been brought to the surface to be studied, Bryce Saylor would be gone, at least as far away as Juneau. Whatever was wrong with her that she'd let her pilot avoidance rule slip with him? Everything had just happened too fast.

"What can I do to help?" she asked Suze, who, after all, had the claim of being the older sister by several minutes. They were both missing their cousin, Alex, who had lived here and had just gotten married this autumn. She and her new husband were spending the holidays in England, where Alex's parents were living now.

"Help?" Suze said, smacking her hands on her bib apron. "Says the woman who oversees the kitchen? Let's get a hot meal together for the man and figure out what we need to order for when his team arrives. Despite the fact a tragedy brings them here, it's great to have some winter guests other than a few skiers or snowmobilers. I wouldn't be surprised if some local or Anchorage media drop in to talk to you and Chip too, especially since their first responders finally showed up at the lake."

"Yes, but all were too late. And have left already," Meg added with a sigh. As exhausted as she was, she started to jot down things she'd need to do to get a good, hot leftover Thanksgiving dinner ready and fast, assuming Bryce was coming directly here from the lake scene.

She was grateful he had come along to help that poor pilot, though again she felt sad for the family of the as-yet nameless man. She more than sympathized.

"I know you," Suze whispered to Meg as Chip sat down expectantly at his place at the table. "You are upset not only at the tragedy you saw today, of course, but that you liked the pilot guy."

"I admired his work, but nothing personal, Suze," she said, keeping her voice down so Chip wouldn't hear, though he was already making buzzing sounds with his Star Wars glider, which was coming in for a landing on the table. "Besides, Bryce Saylor is more diver than pilot. That's his personal aircraft, like a hobby, not a profession and obsession."

"Okay, okay," Suze said, holding up both hands as if to ward off what was coming, though Meg knew Suze loved to have the last word. "But like I said, I know you, and those pink cheeks are not from the cold lake winds."

Meg smacked her sister's shoulder lightly and headed for the kitchen, just as Incident Commander Bryce Saylor came in, hefting a duffel bag, through the lodge's front door.

CHAPTER FOUR

Meg went to hold the door for Bryce. Strange, but the blast of air that came in with him from the darkness seemed warm.

"You didn't walk all the way through the snow with that?" she asked, eyeing his big duffel bag. A camera in a plastic case, probably an underwater one, dangled from the strap of the bag.

"Got a ride in a snowmobile from your mayor—traveling in style. Not a team but a dive partner will be here tomorrow, so I'll need to book a room for him too if you have extra space." He stepped closer to pass through the door she held open. "Thanks. I'll have to examine the wreck and recover the body, literally frozen in place. The mayor said he'd put up orange plastic barrels as a sign around the crash site warning people to stay away. We don't need someone falling in or tampering with evidence."

Standing this close to him, she saw him shudder, perhaps from a memory of seeing the corpse. Maybe that's something people never got over, one of the many hazards of his career. Or maybe it was being out in the cold so long that made him tremble.

"We may not be able to bring the wreckage up until late spring," he went on as he set his things down inside. "Out in the middle of a body of water like that, cranes and lifts won't work. We'll use float bags, but you don't need to hear all that. Just talking too much. If I sound strange it's because my lips are blue with cold."

"They're not really blue."

He turned back to her and said, "Warming up fast in here."

She followed him into the common room, thinking that at least he'd be back briefly when they lifted the plane. She wondered how long he would stay now, how much time to recover the pilot's body.

Suze came over to greet Bryce. "Glad to meet you but sorry about the circumstances," she said. Meg introduced the two of them. He took off both gloves and shook Suze's hand, then glanced around the interior of the large room from stone fireplace to group seating with the large flat screen TV on the wall and the two long wooden dining tables.

"Did Meg tell you I was here once briefly years ago? Were you related to the elderly lady in charge, or did you buy the lodge from her?"

Suze said, "Our grandmother left us the Falls Lake Lodge in her will because she knew we loved the area and had happy memories of visiting. We try to offer the same hospitality but we've pretty much redone the place itself. Let Meg show you to your room, and you can join us for a late supper of Thanksgiving leftovers—which are pretty good."

"Is your boy exhausted after today?" he asked Meg as she escorted him down the hall to the room she and Suze had decided on for him. "He's a real live wire."

"That he is, but when he's done, he's done. Goes, goes, goes, then just collapses. He was at the table, then went to play with the dogs, but I'll bet he's out cold now. You don't mind three dogs around, do you? We have a third one here for a while, a Scottie that belongs to our cousin, who used to live here but is on her extended honeymoon. They'll be living in town after they return, next-door neighbors to your new mayor friend. You know Rand Purvis has the only bank in town." She realized she was jumping topics, chattering on because she was nervous with him, and that made her even more nervous.

"So he told me. He's quite a talker, seems to have his hand in a lot of things. And, no, I don't mind dogs at all. The more the merrier at holiday time, right? Actually, since I live alone, the more the merrier in general."

She opened his room door and handed him the key that had been in the old-fashioned lock. He turned back just inside, put his duffel bag down on the floor and tossed his heavy coat on the king-sized bed.

"Meg, I really appreciate your help today to get me suited up. Especially that you came out on the ice to meet me when I resurfaced. It was great to see a beautiful face after that— after what I'd seen under the ice. So, will you be at the turkey leftovers banquet?"

He smiled, and his eyes crinkled even as they seemed to bore into her.

"I'm the chief cook and bottle washer around here—that is, I oversee meals and the kitchen, so I will be there. By the way," she added, "the rooms don't have individual showers, though each has a wash basin and toilet facilities. The private shower room in this wing is right down the hall from you—that way—and the water is hot."

"Hot sounds good after the day I've had." He smiled again. She nodded and hurried away.

"So," Suze said as she and Meg set the table together, "did he tell you what the body looked like?"

"Not really. And please don't bring it up at the meal."

Suze dropped her voice to a whisper. "Okay, on to better things. He's great-looking. He's what we used to call a hunk. What do you think?"

"I think I'd better make sure the gravy I'm reheating doesn't get that skin on it from not being stirred."

"I noticed you let Chip stay asleep in his room."

"I just checked. Out like a light. And if he came to eat with us this late, he'd never let anyone—especially Bryce Saylor—get a word in except to answer questions about flying. Oh, here he comes—Bryce. Got to get the gravy, meat and potatoes."

"I'll go, and you get him seated. I fed our other few guests while you were at the lake, so I think I can handle this," she added, rolling her eyes. "Give me that look I haven't seen for years if you want me to disappear early and leave you two alone."

"Suze! Do not make a mountain out of a molehill."

"Some molehill."

Meg sighed as Suze darted off, but Bryce was a real presence. Again, she reminded herself not to get involved, that is, more than she could help him relax here, more than she had tried to help him at the lake today.

"Hey, just set for three?" he asked.

"Suze fed our other guests earlier."

"It is pretty late. Then I doubly appreciate this and that you two are eating with me."

She pulled out a chair for him. "I know you must be exhausted."

"Actually, it gets to me mentally and emotionally as well as physically."

"I can understand that. Danger, tragedy."

"And mystery sometimes, a frustrating crime to solve. Meg, besides there being no markings whatsoever on that plane, I didn't see a flight plan, map or anything like that tied down or floating inside the cockpit, but I figure it just got slammed back into the fuselage in the crash. At least I could see far enough into that area to be sure no one else was there. As soon as I bring up the pilot's body, I've got to scour the interior of the plane for cargo, maybe contraband. Well, enough. No more talk about that tonight."

"At least you aren't missing out on a Thanksgiving dinner."

"Actually, my brother's family in Seattle had dinner a day early for reasons I won't go into. It was great to see them. I was heading home today but had to drop some things off in Anchorage, got the call en route and headed for Falls Lake. But I'm glad to stay the night, maybe a couple, here at the lodge. That was a lot of flying for one day. Needless to say, I'm bushed."

A few days sounded good to her, but she didn't say so. And where was Suze? All the covered dishes except the gravy were ready to come out and the pie was on the table.

"Would you please pour the wine?" she asked him, indicating the bottle and glasses. "I'll see if I can help Suze. I may be the kitchen maven and she handles the business, but we share duties."

"You look a lot alike. Who's older?" he asked as she popped up to head for the kitchen.

She turned back. "She is by about eight minutes. We're twins."

"I should have known. But I see differences besides length of hair."

She wasn't sure why, but that seemed an intimate comment. Even when his eyes were taking in the rustic lodge, when he admired the moose head or the back array of windows facing the now pitch-black snowy forest, she felt as if he were also looking at her.

"I'll be right back," she told him.

In the spacious kitchen, though no one else could hear, she whispered to Suze, "What are you doing?"

"Stirring your precious gravy and giving you two time to talk where you aren't out in the cold with a crashed plane and people all around—or me sitting there."

"Do not play matchmaker." Meg seized the big gravy tureen and turned off the burner. "Here, I'll pour. Hold this."

"Scold me all you want. The gravy is hot but so is the atmosphere between you two, especially for just meeting him today and under wretched circumstances. Unless he begs off early—and I bet he won't despite the day he's had—I'll be hitting the hay right after I clean up the kitchen."

"I repeat, he's a deep sea diver with a dangerous job, and he's a pilot! And he doesn't live around here anyway."

"Time for dinner and time to move on," Suze said in a singsong voice. "Meg, I know how much you loved Ryan and worry about Chip, but they'd both want the best for you."

"Which means keeping safe and careful."

Sitting before the bright-burning hearth after dinner, Bryce was pleased Meg had fixed the two of them hot chocolate "for a nightcap" when Suze went to bed. He was exhausted but he'd sleep hard and fast tonight—he hoped.

Because, even in this warm, well-lit place with two lovely women, he kept seeing the dead man, still strapped to the pilot's seat where he'd left him so he didn't drift away. In the stark ray of his search light, amid the cold currents, he'd seen the man's hands rise and fall as if he were conducting a slow, silent dirge, his head nodding in time to eternal music. His face looked shocked, eyes still wide open, as if he were horrified to learn that he was dead. He was bearded with a short haircut, his cap with earflaps floating separately. His sunglasses had fallen into his lap and snagged there. But on the body, no wallet, no ID or papers, though those could well be behind the cockpit or in a lockbox he'd find later.

Without the required markings on the fuselage, and nothing specific inside, it was just plain weird. Could the guy have been smuggling something? Someone? Still, anyone doing that would know a plane with no markings looked suspicious—unless he only flew in the wilderness and landed strictly on lakes, ice and snow. But to hide or deliver what and to whom?

"Great cocoa," he complimented Meg as they sat at opposite ends of a leather couch, facing each other. "A nice change from late coffee. I drink too much of that to keep going sometimes."

"If I drink coffee after about three in the afternoon, I can't sleep that night. I guess the caffeine in cocoa's not that strong. I get this mix when I buy my chocolate for the various candy confections I make."

"I saw some of those at the desk when Suze officially checked me in."

She nodded. "There are some in your room too. And for sale at our gift shop out back and in several stores uptown. I call my brand Falls Lake Chocolates. The trick is to keep Chip from gobbling it."

"I'll definitely buy some, take it home when I go."

"So you said at dinner that Juneau is home?"

"After I took an early retirement from the navy, my father died. His will left me not only his house but his airplane. I was shocked and grateful. My brother had no interest in either, so he was left money and some family furniture. He's an architect—Greg."

"I'm sure your father was successful. I know how much your plane costs—or at least what it cost several years ago."

"He did make a success of his career. He had a dealership

selling small aircraft throughout Alaska and western Canada. I never could have afforded either the house or that plane on retirement navy pay, even though I'm also part owner of an algae farm."

"Really? I've heard about those. Where did you serve in the military?"

"I've dived some great places like Hawaii, Seattle, South Florida—and then Saudi Arabia, which was not so great—pretty dangerous."

"Your father was a pilot, then?"

"And my grandfather. My dad was in the navy but a diver, so I guess I'm a little of both of them. I'm a pilot not by career but by love."

She nodded and blinked back tears, looking down into her cup of rich, dark chocolate. "My husband was a bush pilot here. Dangerous too but in a different way from flying in the service or commercial."

"Definitely. I'm sorry for your—and Chip's—big loss. I can see your son loves planes and flying. He's young, but I understand that, even though my father died flying like Chip's dad did."

Her head jerked up. "Your father crashed?"

"Not exactly. He had a heart attack landing and managed to get the plane down before he died. You should see his—now my—house, though—on the edge of a cliff overlooking a stunning ravine with a view of the forests and mountains just outside of Juneau."

She nodded and took another sip of the cocoa. He'd said that as if she really should see his house. And every time their gazes met and held, she felt she was already on the edge of a cliff with a stunning view.

CHAPTER FIVE

"Glad you're back, Mr. Saylor!" Chip greeted Bryce when he came back to the lodge for lunch the next day after checking out his plane and the crash site on one of the lodge's snow-mobiles. "Sorry I couldn't go with you, but Mom said your friend will go with you when he gets here."

"I thought he might have arrived but didn't see his truck. It's a long drive from Juneau, lots farther than Anchorage. I don't text or phone friends when they're driving to ask their estimated time of arrival. Remember that, Chip, when you get a phone someday. Don't use it or answer it when you're driving."

"Driving?" he said, wide-eyed. "I just learned to use snowshoes."

The boy still had a brush in his hand from currying the two dogs he and Meg had evidently been bathing. The dogs ran out behind him. The cocker spaniel shook himself, though he looked pretty dry. Chip's clothes were splattered with water. His sweatshirt was stuck to him like a T-shirt. Bryce wondered if Meg was that wet.

"I like your special first name, Bryce," Chip said as Meg

came out of the back room behind him. She was holding two big soaked towels but managed to look dry.

"Oh, yeah, my father flew one time right down the middle of Bryce Canyon in Utah. He said it was awesome and beautiful. There were huge rocks, some balanced just right. It was about when I was born and he really liked that name."

"No, I mean the name *incident commander for deep dive discovery*," Chip said. "Mom looked you up online."

Meg put in quickly, "I just wanted him to understand what you do. That you are not a professional pilot."

"True," he said, fascinated that she was blushing. "Nonprofessional or not, I do a lot of flying, which is tied to my job. It gets me places far out in the wilds like Falls Lake," he added and ruffled Chip's damp hair as he went closer to Meg, extending the key to the snowmobile. "Please tell Suze to put the gas I used on my bill. My plane was there waiting for me at the lake and started right up despite the cold weather."

He looked at Meg over Chip's head as he put the key in the palm of her hand. Chip bounded off with the two bigger dogs and the little Scottie following close behind. "I may need that key again," he told her. "Or you might. If you don't want to come back to the lake while Steve and I are retrieving the body, I completely understand. Especially don't have Chip there then."

"Maybe I'll come over with Suze. She'd like to see where the plane crashed—that is, when our friend Mary comes to lodge-sit for us so we can get away for a little while."

"That's great. I thought you might not want to have anything to do with—with planes and crashes, unless you were on site and had no choice. Sorry, maybe I'm reading too much in. So, did you learn anything else about me online?"

"Nothing personal. I just like to know who I'm dealing with."

"Dealing with? I like that—it makes me sound a little dangerous."

"Mom, he does dangerous things," Chip insisted, running back into the room.

"But above all as incident commander," Bryce turned away to tell the boy, "I am helping people, sometimes rescuing people to keep them safe."

"I'd like to help you but I can't until I'm older," Chip said, his round, freckled face and voice so sincere.

"You have already helped me. We'll talk about how you helped and what you saw, if it's all right with your mother."

"Of course," she said, seeming to recover her poise.

Talk about being an incident commander of deep dive recovery, Bryce thought. What was it about this woman that made him want to stay in Falls Lake longer than anticipated? This woman lived out in the wilds, miles from his home, and pretty obviously didn't want to have anything to do with flying.

Hell, he had a job to do here as soon as Steve arrived, and it didn't have anything to do with a diversion like Megan Metzler. So why did he want to get off course in uncharted territory with her?

Meg saw Steve Ralston, another recovery diver from Bryce's team, arrive about an hour later. There would be a larger team assembled this spring to bring up the sunken plane, but it only took one extra team member to recover a body. Steve carried his gear, and Suze checked him in while Bryce was in his room. Steve was redheaded and stocky, somewhat shorter than Bryce. And unlike Bryce's short hair, this guy had a lot of hair scraped back into a ponytail. And a tattoo on the side of his neck that said *Semper Fi.*

Meg had started to walk him to his room when Bryce came out into the hall, so she stood between them.

"Sounds like a weird case," Steve greeted his friend as they shook hands, nearly pressing her between them. "Might be an alien."

"Yeah, right, but his craft doesn't look like a UFO. I'll take you to the site, and we can retrieve him tomorrow, get the emergency crew here from Anchorage so they can take the body for an autopsy. The ME has been advised and is waiting. You've met Meg?"

"And her sister," Steve said. He had a tiny gap between his two front teeth. "Meg was just starting to tell me that she saw the plane go down. You debrief her yet?"

"Only informally. Her six-year-old son was there too, so I'll also ask him what he recalls."

"A real stickler for the Big Man's tactics, huh? He always said let the dust settle before interviews but don't wait too long."

Meg felt she was in the middle of a meeting. One partly about her. Bryce had not mentioned a formal interview about the plane crash. Her stomach cramped a bit, not that she wasn't willing to help.

She said, "Steve, I'll just open your room door for you and let you two make your plans. Chip and I will be glad to help with any information we have, but we were so surprised, and it happened so fast..."

Her voice trailed off as she and Bryce exchanged looks. "So, should I write up what I recall?"

Bryce reached out to take her elbow. "I've found such information is more helpful if not taken right after a traumatic incident. The 'Big Man' Steve refers to is our superior. He's in Washington, DC," he added.

"Oh, not local NTSB then? He must be hanging out with all the politicians," she said.

"Something like that," Bryce said. "Our roles at the NTSB aren't typical by any means. We're part of a special task force—with a very particular agenda. We do work alongside regular agents on occasion, but most of the assignments we're given are a bit...broader in scope. Classified."

"Classified," Meg repeated, her interest piqued. "And your boss is 'the Big Man'?"

"That's right," Bryce said. "He prefers to keep his identity classified too."

Meg looked to Steve, who just nodded. "All right, well, I have to admit the incident really shook me up in more ways than one—to see the plane go down. You're right, I'm steadier about it now."

Steve said, "Not the first plane with a UFO—unidentified flying occupant—in the skies around here." He winked and punched Bryce lightly on the shoulder before going into his room.

"He's kidding about that, of course," Meg said as Bryce released her elbow. "The man under the ice—he's a normal human being, right? Wait—is that what you mean by classified?"

Bryce laughed. "The guy in the wrecked plane is unidentified but not an alien. Steve has a weird sense of humor. I'm sure we'll find some ID in the plane and learn if the pilot was just passing overhead, was lost—or meant to land at Falls Lake."

That night Meg was on kitchen duty while Bryce and Steve ate with the four skiers who were staying at the lodge. Later, after Chip talked at length to Bryce about what he remembered from the crash—Meg had asked to sit in on that but had agreed not to respond—she had told Bryce all she could recall while he took notes on his laptop.

After she tucked Chip in with the dogs sleeping on the floor, she went back out into the common room of the lodge. Suze was nowhere in sight, the skiers were watching a National Geographic program on coral reefs being stunted by global warming, and Bryce sat across the room in the only dark corner, away from the large TV and the glow and warmth of the fireplace. He seemed to be just staring out into the darkness.

She should just go to bed, she knew, because she was aching with exhaustion. But she'd say good-night to Bryce first if he was awake. In the morning, the ME's van should be here from Anchorage, so he and Steve were going to bring the body up.

When she got closer, she saw he was looking down into his laptop, but nothing bright was on the screen to light his face. Oh, he was watching a video or movie on a dark background with a darting single light on the screen.

It must be something he had filmed, something underwater, maybe the sunken plane. She stopped and watched the screen. A man illuminated by a light, a dead man with stiff, frozen arms being pushed in the black current and his face so white with eyes wide open. The dead pilot?

His screen went dark. Bryce didn't speak for a moment, then turned to look at her. "Sorry," he said. "I didn't hear you—then at the last minute saw you reflected in the window glass."

"The night outside acts like a dark mirror."

"Didn't mean for you or anyone but Steve to see that. Not very good bedtime video. I usually just shoot still photos but not this time. Join me, please. I want to ask you something."

She sat on the edge of the short leather couch, perched as if to flee, then forced herself to sit back.

"Let me explain," he said. "I keep thinking there's something I'm missing from what I filmed. I'll take more video tomorrow before we bring him up." He didn't smile but looked back out at the window. A single motion detector light that covered the patio went on, then off.

"When something large enough moves out there," she explained, "it does go on. I've seen deer, moose set it off before, even something as small as a beaver. Usually guests will rush to the expanse of glass to watch a bit of wildlife."

"I swear I saw something earlier that was tall move out there—along the tree line, probably too far out to make the light come on."

"Tall? The wind moves the spruce and fir branches, and sometimes snow cascades from them, and it looks like someone moved, though that doesn't make the light come on. What sort of idiot would be out in this cold with the snow so deep? If it was an animal, we'll see the tracks in the morning."

"I heard you have a security guy. Looking around, it seems everyone's accounted for but him."

"Yes, Josh Spruce. But he's not on duty most nights and works inside during the day this time of year. Besides, he has a girlfriend in town he was going to see tonight, so no way he's skulking around in the cold and dark out there."

"I'll go out in the morning. I know where I saw the movement."

A stubborn man, she thought. Things could not get stranger—or more exciting.

"I don't mean to freak you out," he told her and reached out to snag her hand in his. "I mean, more than I already have. You and Chip have been a tremendous help, and—like I said earlier—I appreciate it. The thing is, I don't think seeing someone out there was my imagination.

"And," he added in a lazy, slower tone of voice, "I don't think the fact we're getting along so well so fast is my imagination either. You're living pretty isolated here now."

Now, she thought, meant since Ryan had been gone. They had lived in town, but without his income she hadn't been able to afford the house and had been grateful to move here with Suze for support and work.

"And then," he went on, still holding her hand, turning toward her on the couch and ignoring his laptop when it slid off his lap to rest between them, "the plane crash happened, and I crashed in on your life."

"But you'll soon be gone."

"Maybe not. My boss said he wants me to oversee the resurrection and identification of that mystery plane. And, remember, I can fly and I know exactly where Falls Lake and the lodge are."

She hated to admit it even to herself, but that thrilled her. Of course, she didn't want him in her life, a pilot with a hazardous job. At least that's what she thought, what she should tell him right now in a polite, gentle way to end all this.

So why, when he put the laptop on the coffee table and slid closer, simply holding her hand, did she feel a lightning bolt jag to her heart—and lower? Being with this man, she could crash and burn, but she did not want to do anything to stop that.

CHAPTER SIX

Early the next morning, Meg was in the kitchen, ready to fix the lodge's six guests and her family pancakes, waffles or omelets on request. Josh Spruce was helping out, humming off tune and frying bacon and sausage on the other range. They always liked to give their guests a choice of hearty fare.

She did manage to sit down for a quick cup of coffee at six thirty with Bryce when he came to the table but said to hold his breakfast until Steve showed up. They were meeting at nine and heading out to retrieve the pilot's body at ten, when there was decent daylight. For one moment, sitting there with him seemed so normal, so lovely. Chip still asleep, the other guests not here yet, Suze and Josh busy, so just the two of them for a few precious moments.

"Even though it's still dark, I'm going outside to check where I saw that movement last night," Bryce told her.

"Our cousin Alex just married a professional tracker," she said. "Wish he was here to go with you."

"So I heard from the mayor. Quinn or Q-Man the tracker of cable TV fame. I've seen his reality show, tracking here in the Alaskan wilderness. I'll bet he's glad not to be here if he's on his honeymoon. As to your earlier question about what I want when I come back in—" He turned to look at her a bit too long while her heartbeat kicked up. "I'll take pancakes and sausage, please. Be right back."

She returned to the kitchen still feeling the impact of that. Of what? she scolded herself. That he looked at her intently over the rim of a coffee cup? That something unspoken always leaped between them and had since he'd used the word *kismet* when she'd walked him away from the hole in the ice and she'd actually thought he'd maybe said *kiss me?* She'd looked the word up. It meant *fate*, as if they were meant to meet. But he was everything she did not want—and everything she did.

After taking their cups into the kitchen, she still found an excuse to go back to the table—doing Josh's job of putting out Danish rolls and fruit—so she could watch out the window. The motion detector light was on. Bryce had also taken out a light that threw a stark streak of white ahead of him. He played it over the ground, again, again, in different directions. He must be up to his knees in snow out there but maybe he'd found something. It looked like he was heading toward the road, so perhaps coming in.

Back in the kitchen, she told Josh, "I'll be right back, okay?"

"Yeah, sure. No one else is here yet anyway, and I got things under control. Did I tell you Pam's a good cook?"

"No, but that's another point of many in her favor, right?"

"Like she needs more," he said with a grin.

If Josh could ever blush, he just did. He used to be so uptight, but he'd greatly mellowed since he'd started dating Pamela Cruise. He was absolutely their jack-of-all-trades around here as well as at Quinn's tracking school next door, where he worked part-time. Well, she could understand a love interest smoothing out someone's life.

That really showed Bryce wasn't for her: all he did was get her edgy and excited.

As she waited at the front door of the lodge, she heard Bryce outside, or someone, stomping snow off their boots. When he came in with a gush of cold air, she could tell he was startled to see her standing there.

"Don't tell Steve about all this, or he'll get on his alien invasion kick again," he told her.

"What do you mean?"

"I didn't see human footprints or animal tracks out there, but two narrow solid lines like small tires rolled along the ground." Frowning, he took off his gloves, earflap hat and down-filled coat and piled them on the bench by the door. He wiped his boots on the floor mat there.

"Like a bicycle, maybe? In this snow?" she asked.

"More like two huge, continuous scuff marks. It's one way to obscure distinctive tracks. From the street, I think whoever it was came back along the side of the lodge to look in your big windows, then doubled back to the street. There must have been a truck, snowmobile, something parked down from the lodge just a little way. The streets have enough ruts and truck wheel marks I bet nothing will show there."

"But you have a specific job here. You're not a detective. If someone's been trespassing, we can call in a state trooper or—"

"I wouldn't go that far yet. I just want you—all of us—to be safe. The anonymity of the plane, the pilot, now whoever's watching this place or even you and Chip, worries me."

"No one could be interested in us," she protested, but her pulse picked up. "Anyway, those tracks do sound really strange. It would be hard to scuff all that way. Most people would use snowshoes or just walk in the deep snow, not shove their legs and feet *through* the snow."

"And why park on the road when there is a perfectly clear, shoveled parking lot nearby? Then this," he added and picked up his coat, digging first into one pocket and then the other.

He produced a two-inch-square snag of white woven cloth, wool, probably. Their foreheads close together, they examined it. As small as it was, it gave off a faint smell—tobacco? Something stale.

She said in a shaky whisper, "So you were right that someone was peering through the lodge windows."

"And that it was not some kind of animal or someone in a space suit," he added, frowning at the frayed piece of cloth. "It has a slight smell that I don't think is smoke from a fireplace."

Her stomach cartwheeled at a thought. She had to tell him what she and Chip had left out of their statements, but they'd only answered questions asked about the plane crash itself.

"Bryce, I think I've seen that before but don't know who it's from," she told him as his blue eyes narrowed and riveted on her. "After the plane crash, when we were sitting in your plane, we saw a man watching your dive. Chip spotted him first, and I saw him too and couldn't identify him."

"That line is starting to sound too familiar."

"Of course, the noise from the crash could have brought someone hiking nearby. He disappeared either before or when the townspeople showed up. And he was wrapped in a white blanket, just standing there when we first saw him."

He drew in a swift breath through flared nostrils. "Some kind of crude camouflage in the snow? And who knows how long he'd been there? Maybe as long as you two were. Like you, maybe he heard the plane struggling. Or maybe he knew to be there to wait for a payload from a plane—or even a crash."

"I'm sorry I didn't think of it earlier. You only asked about the plane going into the lake and my head was still spinning."

He reached out to touch her shoulder just as they heard voices of guests coming in for breakfast. "I'll have a few more questions later—actually sooner, before Steve and I go out. When you and Chip are free, I need to know again exactly what you saw, any impressions or clues to identify the observer. Tell Suze I do appreciate her offer for you two to bring us out some hot food later."

Suze had volunteered that? She tried not to show him she was surprised. She nodded.

"If Chip comes out to breakfast, is it okay if I talk to him alone first?" he asked.

"Yes, all right. I trust you."

His lower lip set hard. "Don't know what I would have done without you in all this."

Before he could see her eyes were tearing up, she hurried back to the kitchen.

At nine thirty she took a break and joined Bryce where he was waiting for her on the couch where they'd sat last night.

"If it won't take long for you to ask your questions about the white blanket person, I can do it now," she told him.

"Great," he said and pulled his laptop up from the couch and opened it up. His taking notes made her a little more nervous, as if this was all so formal. Well, in a way, it was life-and-death.

"So Chip says, as you did earlier, that he saw the person first."

"Yes. I don't know how long he was there because that blanket did make him blend in."

"Any impressions of him—we'll call it a him for now? Short, tall, thin, heavy? Bearded? Did he have a hat?"

"Sorry. You know, I think he had the blanket pulled up over his head like a hood. For extra warmth, maybe."

"Or to keep his head and face hidden."

"But no one could know a plane was going to crash."

"No, but he could know one was due. Smuggling—drugs, for example—is one option for what the nameless pilot was doing in a plane with no markings."

"I don't mean to be nosy, but have there been other deaths the NTSB has investigated that were tied to smuggling? Of drugs? Money? Even people?"

"You know, the Big Man could use you on his staff—obviously you are working with me already." He smiled tautly and closed his laptop. "Got to go meet Steve and head out to the site. See you out there. I promise you we'll have the body covered if we have it up by then, so don't worry about that."

He gave her knee a quick squeeze and got up from the couch in one fluid motion. She rose too, partly so he wouldn't see her surprised expression that Suze had planned all this, and partly because they were going out there with food and coffee where a frozen body—under a tarp or not—was going to be brought up.

Just after they'd served lunch and the skiers had departed for the Talkeetna foothill slopes, Meg and Suze started out in Suze's snowmobile. Chip was hanging out with Josh, his brother Sam and Sam's wife, Mary. Mary worked the front desk at the lodge when they were away and sometimes the gift shop, and was six months pregnant, but that didn't stop her from staying active.

"I can't believe you set all this up," Meg told Suze through her woolen scarf she'd wrapped around her lower face under her knitted, pointed cap. "If I didn't know better, I'd think you are interested in Bryce Saylor."

"Hardly. Since I broke up with Mr. Pompous-Only-Lawyer-in-Town, I'm holding out for a fellow artist. I have Commander Saylor picked out for you."

Meg punched her shoulder, but the noise of the snowmobile kept them from talking further. Meg remembered Bryce's joke about working for the NTSB, since she was already working with him. Of course, he was kidding.

After all and above all, this was serious business. She had overheard a conference call Steve and Bryce took from their boss in DC, the guy they called Mr. Big. No, that was on *Sex and the City*. This guy was "the Big Man." The only thing she'd really heard on their conference call had shaken her: "Get that body up before someone else does or word gets out to the media. I can only sit on this so long. I embargoed it with the Anchorage paper, but they're easy to impress. Just pray the rabid mainstream media don't get hold of this. We don't need Russia in the news more than it is already—and not on this topic."

"Bryce's plane looks big out here," Suze was yelling back over her shoulder as they came to a stop and she killed the motor.

"It is big, especially compared to the one Ryan flew and the one under the ice. I don't see either Bryce or Steve. I thought he said they'd take turns diving because when he surfaced last time, the plane had shifted a bit."

"Bet it got frozen in place last night, so they decided to dive together. Let's just walk over to his plane. Maybe he left it open for us like you said he did for you and Chip. Darn cold weather."

Toting their insulated food bag, they walked past where Bryce and Steve had left a pile of gear. Some diving equipment was out on this ice too, near a DANGER STAY AWAY sign, orange barrels and rope Mayor Purvis had arranged to be left there. At least no one else was here, and they weren't going to stay long. Bryce had said that as soon as they got the body up and took it in a tarp out to the road to meet the medical examiner's van from Anchorage, they'd seal off the sunken plane until tomorrow, when they would search it more thoroughly.

"Look," Suze said, pointing at the trampled snow. "They spilled something."

Scarlet drops speckled the snow. Worse, there was a frozen blotch of crimson.

"Blood," Meg said. "I think it is. And surely not from a frozen dead body."

"Maybe one of them cut themselves."

Meg lifted her eyes from the ground and glanced around the area. At least she saw no one in a white blanket. And then she saw what Bryce must have seen outside the window of the lodge. Near this small snow bank, the tracks of someone dragging his feet. Those marks went out onto the ice where the trail just vanished. Nothing—she saw nothing out on the ice, blinding white in the sun.

"I'm scared," she told Suze. "I'm sure Bryce said one would go down, one would stay above for safety."

Her voice caught. Her insides twisted.

"Should I call for help?" Suze asked. "Like Josh or the mayor, to send someone out? How about the medical examiner in Anchorage so they can contact the van they have heading here?"

"That driver was told to stay on the road, and Bryce and Steve would bring the body out."

Meg stared at the drops of blood again. "Bryce and Steve are supposed to keep word about this low-key. Even though a lot of people knew about the plane crash itself, the lack of ID on it is so far still a secret. You know, the blood drops might lead to the hole in the ice. I'm going out."

Suze grabbed her arm. "Let's just wait here together. One or both of them will surely surface soon."

"No, I think—" Meg got out before a movement out on the ice snagged her eye. "Look, I think someone is coming up. Maybe they had to both go down to bring the body up, but what about the blood? Wait, don't call anyone yet in case it's animal blood, or one of them just cut himself."

She started out carefully on the ice as she had once before. Suze made a grab for her, then just shouted, "You be careful!"

She hadn't done one careful thing since she'd met Bryce Saylor, Meg thought as she half skidded, half walked toward the too-familiar hole in the lake ice.

CHAPTER SEVEN

A masked diver popped through the ice and motioned to her with one hand. Bryce? Steve? Why didn't he take off his mask?

He raised one hand as if to ask a question, then pulled out his mouthpiece.

"Even in the water, the body's heavy." Bryce's voice! He was gasping for air. "Where's Steve?"

"I don't know," she shouted. "We didn't see him but found blood in the snow."

"Can you give me a hand?" he asked through ragged breaths as she carefully went closer. "I can't lift him by myself. Don't bend over or you might go in headfirst. On your knees so we can get him up on the ice."

We, she thought. Yes, in a way, they were a team, at least right now.

"I can help," she promised, but the idea of handling a frozen corpse made her stomach cramp.

"But something's wrong if Steve's not here. The guide rope he was tending cut loose and disappeared. I don't see it.

I had to fight my way up with this body. The plane shifted since the last dive, but seems frozen in place now."

She could not believe she was doing this, grasping the frozen arms of a corpse. Rigor mortis was one thing—but this... Mostly, Bryce pushed him up, and she pulled, slipping closer to the hole, trying to maneuver the weight on the slick ice. The man was literally a stiff, nearly frozen solid, glazed face staring.

Bryce hoisted himself out and lay gasping for air while he ripped off his mask, air tank and other gear.

"I hope Steve didn't come in after me, if that rope broke. He can't be in the plane. I locked it. You sure about the blood? Got to trace it, find him. He may be cut or hurt."

She scrambled up to help him stand. He rose heavily to his knees, then to his feet. She steadied him as he ripped off his fins.

"It's not like Steve," Bryce said between big breaths. His teeth were chattering. "Show me where the blood is. We don't find him fast, we'll need help, but if he's just cut we can keep it quiet like we've been ordered to."

So this was some sort of secret retrieval. Some sort of government undercover work? At least Suze was just going to call the mayor. All of Steve's joking about UFOs and aliens aside, something really strange was going on. She wondered if even Bryce—and "the Big Man"—knew what it was yet.

Was Bryce to be trusted?

"See where Suze is standing?" she said, pointing. "Blood's on the snow there, and those scuffing steps you said you saw at the lodge, then nothing."

"You didn't tell me that! Did you see anyone around?"

"No. No one."

He gripped her shoulder hard. "Damn, this is going to blow sky-high," he whispered, as if the corpse could hear.

"Bryce, Suze can call the mayor. He may send local help, a doctor, someone."

"Tell her not to call anyone right now. We've got to find him. He can't be under the ice. Steve!" he yelled so loudly she jumped. "Steve!"

Bryce's blood drummed so hard in his head he thought normal sounds had gone silent. Suze was gesturing to him. He hated to leave Meg with the body, a strange, otherworldly looking one now that it was iced over in a grotesque position with eyes open and arms half-raised. And still no sign of ID in the cockpit. He had to find Steve fast, dive again, search the entire underwater plane.

He skidded to a stop before the deep-snow shore. "Where's the blood?" he asked Suze, sounding as if he'd run miles.

"It starts over here then comes this way," she said, pointing. "And back a ways there are bigger drops of it."

Bryce saw the red stains right away. Just as frightening, he saw the double-shuffle continuous tracks in the snow Meg had mentioned. But no drag marks of a body...

The thing was, Steve was careful. He'd even told him to be wary. He must have fallen on the ice, cut himself on his dive knife. But why had he left his position near the hole in the ice? And how to explain the missing guide rope? Steve had worn his dive suit in case he needed to get in to help lift the body out, so he must have cut or hit his hands or head for this much blood. Maybe then someone came along and helped him—or had caused Steve's injury in the first place.

"We'll find him," he told Suze. "Don't call anyone right now."

His head down, Bryce tracked the blood drops. Without goggles or sunglasses, the glare of sun on snow nearly blinded him. Pounding headache, pounding thoughts. Something so wrong in all this, and now there were two innocent women involved, one he was fast coming to care for. And the Big Man had stressed this needed to be kept as covert as possible until they got answers about what was going on. He'd told Bryce he'd already pulled some governmental strings to keep the crash quiet.

Bryce lost the trail, so he figured the stranger must have gone out onto the ice. He must be carrying Steve, which meant he was unconscious. But come ashore where? Maybe he should backtrack.

He pulled out his dive knife and gripped it in his cold hand.

There! Up the bank toward some spruce trees draped with snow that looked like they were shivering in the cold wind, he saw clearer tracks.

He glanced out at Meg. She was sitting near the corpse but not looking at it, only staring at him. Suze had started out on the ice to be with her.

He squinted to skim the area, concentrating on anything that moved. In the distance, a single deer. A couple of snowshoe rabbits in their white winter coats. Was a white-coated person watching?

He shoved a heavily laden branch of a fir tree aside. It cast most of its snow on him, obscuring more speckles of red. So he was going the right direction. Yes, here again were the too-familiar tracks that looked like two narrow tires had been rolled through here. But then, just beyond—the legs and feet of a man half-buried in the snow, a man whose legs were bound with the missing rope from the dive.

Meg's eyes burned from squinting to watch Bryce, even through her snow goggles. She had only looked at the frozen body once, but the wide eyes and mouth agape, all coated with a layer of ice, had been enough to imprint it in her mind. And the man's arms were raised as if he were being held up by a robber or as if he were begging, "Help me! Hold me!"

But now Bryce was windmilling his arm, gesturing, shouting, though she couldn't tell about what.

Suze reached her then. Meg told her, "Don't look at him, but guard him." She struggled to her feet, slipping, and nearly spread-eagled. "Bryce has found something—maybe Steve."

"So should I call for help now?"

"I'll let you know. He may be fine, just resting, or he fell."

"Okay, okay, but be careful! I'll call the mayor or 9-1-1 if Steve's hurt."

Meg made a straight line toward Bryce. He wasn't shouting now, but bending over something—someone. It had to be Steve. Injured? Surely not dead. Bryce was right. If there were two bodies, this was going to blow sky-high.

"He's not dead," Bryce said as she kneeled in the snow on Steve's other side. "Faint pulse. I think someone slammed him in the back of the head with something. He didn't get here himself—he's tied with the dive rope," he said as he continued to carefully untie his friend. "Go ahead and get Suze to call for whatever is the nearest ER squad. Maybe Wasilla, maybe clear to Anchorage. But don't bother the mayor yet."

"Should we do CPR?"

"No, he's breathing. I touched the top of his skull through his diving cap. It's wet with blood. Damaged skull, I think. See those tracks here too?"

She squinted at the snakelike long scuff marks that ran back to the edge of the ice. She cupped her hands around her mouth and yelled, "Suze, we found him hurt! Go ahead and call 9-1-1, even though they'll have to come a long ways."

She ran back to Bryce. "So that's medical help, but we can call the state troopers. They can follow those tracks to find who did this."

"No state troopers, at least not yet. I don't even want the mayor back here—too many questions from him. Once an investigation goes wide, jurisdiction and protocol can slow things down. Under these trees the snow's not as deep. I think his attacker dumped Steve here, then headed out on the ice."

"But he'll have to emerge on the snow shore somewhere—though it's a huge lake," she said, her voice fading.

"I can't leave him. Can one of you watch the pilot's body and one of you go out to the road to bring the coroner's driver in? Not for the corpse but to transport Steve. It's not really their job but I don't know how long the paramedics will take to arrive, and he needs help sooner than that corpse. A gurney won't work, but we need a tarp or something so we can get him out of here and to help fast."

She went to the edge of the ice, cupped her hands around her mouth and shouted to Suze that she'd watch the pilot while Suze went out to meet the coroner or any other help on the road.

Suze waved back, shouted something the wind ripped away as she trudged toward where they'd left the snowmobile. She started it and turned the machine away toward the road.

"Bryce, what if whoever did this and made those weird tracks is watching? Or trying to separate us—to hurt Suze."

She saw two tears track down his cheeks. He couldn't speak at first, and she kneeled beside him to put her hand on his back.

"He has a wife and a son," Bryce choked out, leaning down to listen to Steve's sporadic breathing again. Then, as if to apologize, he whispered to her, "Sorry to say that—with your own situation—you know…"

That hit her hard. A wife and son. If he died, she knew

how terrible it would be for them. Pain and grief she had
tried so hard to control nearly swamped her.

She reached out her mittened hand to grasp Bryce's
through his heavy diving gloves. Though they were layers
away from touching each other, it helped. She longed to hold
him, comfort him. Just like out on the lake, for her, the ice
was broken. Surely she could trust this man. Despite all this
secrecy, couldn't she?

An endless time later, they heard the increasing roar of
the snowmobile returning. At least they hoped that's what it
was. They were both chilled to the bone, huddled together
on each side of Steve to keep him warm. It was almost like
being in each other's arms. Meg had not gone back out on
this ice, but they kept an eye on the body from here.

She hadn't said so, but more than once she felt they were
being watched by someone they could not see.

"We could keep Steve warmer in my plane," Bryce said,
"but we can't risk moving him with that head injury. If we
only had a stretcher, something to stabilize his neck and
head. He'll get jostled when we get him to the ME's van.
Unfortunately, the guy with it's a driver, not a paramedic.
Who knows when he'll get here?"

"I can see why the coroner wouldn't send a medic for a
dead body."

"I'm just praying we don't have two of them."

They were both shaking, despite what body heat they
shared. Her teeth were chattering and bitterly cold air stung
way down into her lungs. As crazy and as horrible as this
was, even though she realized they might be watched, she
felt strangely safe with Bryce so near. He had insisted on
going to get his own coat from the plane to cover Steve, so
he now wore only layers of flannel shirts and a light jacket.

Steve had not made a move or sound, but his shallow

breathing and pulse assured them he was still alive. Maybe, Meg thought, the cold temperature would help to keep him stable until they could get him to a hospital.

When the snowmobile arrived, Suze's passenger came as fast as he could, stepping high through the snow. Out of breath, he gasped out, "We'll leave the dead pilot here if someone can guard him, and try to get this man to Anchorage instead. No sign of a squad yet. If I strap the injured man down, I won't have room for another body and my orders are not to move frozen limbs."

Suze came over to see how Steve was, then started out on the ice to stay with the pilot's body again.

"I can strap him down on the snowmobile too," the van driver went on. "You know, where I was gonna put the frozen body. It does seem his breathing is getting more shallow, and who knows how long it will take the squad to get here and hike in. We'll have to bounce him a bit to get him into the snowmobile, then the van. No medical help there either. I came alone and I'm not trained for that."

Bryce's gaze slammed into Meg's wide-eyed stare when she realized what he was going to say. What was logical. What might be life-and-death.

He said to the ME's driver, "How about you help me put this man on that folding stretcher you brought, and the two of us put him in the back of my plane right over there? I'll fly him to Anchorage, which will be faster, and you take the dead pilot to the ME as planned."

"Sure, we can do that. But can one of these women on your team go with you, watch his vitals?"

Meg sucked in a sharp breath. Fly in a small private plane over mountains after she'd vowed she never would again? She had broken that vow once, but still. To not go back to Chip today, but have Suze try to explain? Go off with another pilot into what Ryan always called the wild blue yonder? At least there wasn't a storm today, except inside of her.

She thought of Steve's wife and son.

Only a few seconds had passed, but both men were staring at her.

"It's all right, Meg. You don't have to—" Bryce started to say.

"We have to try to save him. Time matters. That's a good plan. I—I'll go with you to watch him, to help you. But Suze needs to head home on the road, away from here, as soon as she helps the pilot's body get loaded in the van. We can't take a chance on Steve's attacker still lurking here."

CHAPTER EIGHT

"I can't thank you enough, and Steve's family will be grateful," Bryce told Meg when they had the comatose man strapped in. He had helped the van driver strap down the dead pilot while she waited in the plane with Steve. "I called his wife, Jenny, to break the news to her. She and their boy—he's thirteen—will fly in to Anchorage from Juneau and meet us there as soon as they can."

Bryce's voice broke as they looked down at the unmoving man. He lay where two of the seats extended to make a bed. His body and head were taped down to stabilize them on the coroner's stretcher. The idea of where that stretcher came from bothered her, but everything did right now.

She strapped in just across the narrow aisle where she could watch Steve. The trouble was, each time she glanced over, she was also looking out a window. They'd left it uncovered so she had good light, since she'd pulled down the shutter on her own window.

"I'm glad to help him and you," she told Bryce, trying to steady her voice.

He leaned down to quickly kiss her cheek. "For luck. For strength. For us. Just yell if you need any help back here."

"I won't because you need to fly this plane. We'll make it."

He cupped her chin, brushed one thumb across her cheek and went into the cockpit. As she tightened her seat belt even more, she wished she were the one unconscious for this flight.

Her stomach flip-flopped when the engine started. They taxied over the ice, stopped, pivoted, and then he revved the engine. It seemed an endless path across the frozen lake, faster, faster, until they had enough speed for the gradual takeoff. More engine, then liftoff followed by a big loop to head toward Anchorage. She used to love to look out the windows at the passing scenes below, even at the mountains, but not now.

Glancing over at Steve again to see how he was taking the motion, she was tempted to close the blind by his window, but she didn't want to unbelt to do that.

As they came out of their large arc, she wondered if Suze or even Chip was watching the Falls Lake sky. She saw the frozen waterfall go by, the white-and-gray face of the mountain topped by a snow-laden cliff, then endless blue with puffy clouds. She sucked in a deep breath and looked over at Steve again.

She really didn't know this man, yet she knew he had a wife and son, so they mattered too. She had to help get Steve safely to Anchorage, then to a hospital for his family.

"Okay back there?" came over the speaker.

"We're fine," she told him. "You know what I mean."

Quite a plane, she thought. Not just Ryan shouting back at her when Chip took a short turn in the copilot's seat. She shook her head to banish the memory of flying with Ryan and Chip. Suze would surely tell Chip what had happened, that his mom would be back soon. But would they have to spend the night in the hospital waiting room—or some-where else? How long before Steve's wife or family would come in from Juneau?

And why were Bryce and his boss or even his boss's supe-riors getting even more secretive about everything? Just to avoid a crowd of gawkers and media swarming the lake and getting underfoot? She was involved now, part of Bryce's team in a strange way. He had to tell her more about what was going on. Was it a covert mission, or was he really not sure?

The steady hum of the plane and its vibration began to soothe her. She'd been foolish to refuse to go up again in a small plane. Commercial jets were one thing. Sure, she'd managed a round-trip flight to take Chip to Disneyland. Wait until Chip heard what she'd done without him.

Since she was feeling fairly steady and safe on this flight, maybe she'd find the courage to somewhat de-Ryan what Suze called her "shrine" in her bedroom. Although when she and Chip moved to the lodge, she'd been brave enough to sell most of their property, everything but her and Chip's bedroom furniture, she did have a lot of family photos and other marriage memorabilia in her room. Suze had kid-ded her she was turning into a hoarder. Yes, soon, she'd put some of the photos and mementos away, at least for a while, maybe rotate them.

"Entering the southwest Anchorage approach corridor," Bryce's voice jolted her from her thoughts, but she realized he must be talking to an air traffic controller. He was giv-ing the plane's registration number and explaining it was a medical emergency. The controller's voice started talking about runway numbers, wind direction, speed and timing.

She heard Bryce ask that an emergency vehicle meet them when they pulled onto the tarmac. She put her hand on Steve's arm as if to steady him, but she was actually steady-ing herself.

★ ★ ★

As the ER vehicle sliced through midafternoon Sunday Anchorage traffic, despite the steady sound of the somewhat muted siren overhead, Bryce was on his cell phone to his boss in DC. This vehicle had two medics in the back trying to stabilize Steve, so both Meg and Bryce were in the front seat with the driver, allowing her to hear Bryce's side of the conversation.

"I only had time to glance in there," Bryce spoke into his phone. "I'll dive again ASAP. I know you want to confirm if there's anything suspicious—contraband, surveillance equipment—on board. The pilot came first. By the way, I did look under the wings. No alphanumeric ID numbers there either. I'll call you back as soon as we know something. Steve's wife and son are flying in. We'll probably wait until they're here, then fly back to Falls Lake."

Bryce was silent for a moment as his boss responded. Meg couldn't help but notice his brow furrowed as he listened, then finally responded with, "Thank you. I appreciate any help you can send."

Bryce ended the call and turned to her. They were wedged in, both in the same seat belt with her almost sitting sideways in his lap. Definitely not allowed, but she wasn't sure what was anymore.

She gripped Bryce's hand as the ER van pulled into the entrance of the Anchorage Regional Hospital.

The emergency department admitted Steve as a Level 1 trauma patient with bleeding in the brain. Bryce heard words like *epidural hematoma* and *neuro-intensive care* before the small ER room where they first took Steve exploded with doctors and nurses. Bryce gave what information he could and told them Steve's wife and son were flying in from Juneau and would be here as soon as possible. No, he didn't have

Steve's medical information or ID with him because there had been an emergency, and they'd flown him directly here.

No ID on the dead pilot either, Bryce thought again. Sometimes, he just wasn't sure who was who in this busy, changing world. It was like trying to recognize someone through shifting water in a deep dive.

He took Meg's hand and they went where they were directed to wait for word of Steve's emergency surgery—an evacuation of the hematoma—and for his family to arrive. Eventually, they were told the surgery was complete, but, of course, the patient was still unconscious. At this early stage, they could predict neither when nor if he would awake nor if he would recover.

The waiting room on Steve's hospital floor emptied out of visitors after dark. Exhausted, the two of them sat side by side in the family waiting room after grabbing sandwiches and drinks from the Subway on the main floor. Steve had been admitted to the ER and then finally to this floor's intensive care, where they treated neuro-injuries.

They both kept falling asleep, propping each other up, holding hands, shoulders touching. She had used Bryce's cell phone, since only Suze had taken hers to the lake what seemed days ago. She'd called the lodge and talked to both Suze and Chip.

"You went in a small plane?" Chip had asked, his high-pitched voice incredulous. "Not a big one?"

"We thought Bryce's plane was pretty big, didn't we? Just do what Aunt Suze says, and I hope to be home tomorrow."

"I'll take care of the dogs. Aunt Alex called all the way from London, and she sounded pretty happy, I think 'cause she married Quinn."

"And because she's visiting her mom and dad, I bet," she'd said.

"Yeah, Mom. Remember, the queen lives in London, and she has all those cool soldiers in tall, bear fur hats."

She had reminded him to be good again, to mind Suze, and said good-night.

"Sorry," Bryce had said and opened one sleepy eye in the chair next to her, "but I heard that. Can't beat soldiers. Or former navy men. I didn't mean to eavesdrop."

"That's okay. I heard parts of your conversation earlier—from Washington, the land of the free and the home of clever politicians."

"And?"

She turned in her chair to face him before she realized he would seem so much closer. "Bryce, why all the secrecy surrounding the plane crash? I mean, I get it that the aircraft should have been marked with registration and the pilot would ordinarily have had ID. But what is this? Could he be a spy or something worse?"

"Or as Steve joked, an alien?"

"Never mind that. I know he was joking, but what's your theory?"

"Meg, spies these days use the internet. They don't send people in unmarked planes."

He fidgeted when he said that and didn't meet her eyes. But she ignored that and plunged on. "What about smuggling? I heard you refer to 'contraband.' A clever new threat of some sort to national security? Drugs? Or if you told me your secrets, would you have to kill me?"

He sat up straighter. He looked her right in the eyes again and dared to smile. "I wouldn't kill you—ever. I'd maybe fly you somewhere special. Fly you to see my place in Juneau, fly you to the moon… I mean that to be romantic—at least for this time of night in a hospital waiting room when we're both exhausted out of our minds."

"So you're not going to tell me what you think that plane—and pilot—might be doing?"

"I don't know yet. I hope it's just some eccentric idiot who didn't know how to fly very well and was in the process of repainting his plane so he could register it, and just went for a short test flight. You can't think of anybody like that in the Falls Lake area, can you? Mayor Purvis couldn't when I asked him."

"No. Not unless that recluse, Bill Getz, who lives on the far end of the lake, has taken up flying and come into money, and that would be the day. He's not even that old, really. Middle-aged. Maybe a bit older. Could've still made something of his life, but at some point, he must've run into some hardship or another. They say he's a hoarder and collects old posters and stuff, but hardly airplanes."

The look on his face told her he was filing that away anyhow.

"You—Chip and the lodge—are my one bright light in this mess," he said as he stretched and yawned, so she could see he was dismissing her curiosity, but then she decided to believe him. After all, if he knew what was going on, wouldn't he at least have told his boss?

"Bryce, look," she said as the elevator dinged and a woman and boy got off and looked around. "Is that them?"

"Yes, Jenny and Mark Ralston." He got up and went over to greet them.

Meg gave them a moment for hugs and talk, then went over to be introduced.

"I can't thank you enough for all your help," Jenny said and offered her hand, then hugged Meg, who hugged her back. She had long blond hair peeking out from earmuffs she finally took off, seeming so stunned she hardly knew where she was. But Meg certainly empathized with that.

Her son seemed tall for his age and wide-eyed. "So exactly what happened, Bryce?" Jenny asked.

"I honestly don't know who or what struck him, but I promise you I'll find out."

"You two weren't on something dangerous again, were you?"

That riveted Meg's attention. So he'd been assigned other missions that could be dangerous, maybe even deadly? No way was she going to let her feelings for him go further.

Bryce turned to Mark. "I'll take your mom first to see your dad, and then you can see him later. He's sleeping right now anyway and may be for a couple of days. Only one guest at a time in intensive care, so I'll wait out in the hall and bring her back."

"Oh, sure," the boy said, finally putting down the big duffel bag he held. "Glad he wasn't hurt underwater where he couldn't breathe. That will help when he recovers, I bet."

"He's tough," Bryce said, but his voice broke. He hugged Mark too, maybe so the boy wouldn't see him tearing up. Then he took Jenny's arm to lead her toward the double doors that accessed the hall with single rooms beyond.

"Here, Mark. We can sit over here," Meg told him.

"Bryce is a neighbor of ours at home—a nice guy," he said, as if to assure her as he dropped his bag at his feet and flopped in the chair. "But I think he's got secret stuff going on, I mean, like on some FBI TV show or something. Mom and Dad argued over that, but Dad likes to work with Commander Saylor."

She only nodded, but that rattled her even more. Surely, she wasn't trusting and getting too emotionally involved with a man she didn't—maybe couldn't—ever really know.

CHAPTER NINE

"Will you sit in the copilot seat on the way back?" Bryce asked Meg as they walked toward his plane to head to Falls Lake at 10 a.m. the next morning. The Monday morning rush hour traffic had been thick getting to the airport, but he wanted to get back, get a new crew together fast and dive again.

When she hesitated at the bottom of the short stairs, he added, "In a way, you've been my copilot through this whole mess so far." He had a feeling she'd gone as far in their early relationship as she was willing to right now, and that made him sad. Then again, she'd agreed to fly to help Steve and his family, so she'd done that for them, not really for him.

"I honestly don't know if I'm ready for that," she said, giving her blond, mussed hair a little toss. "The mountains seem to come so close out the cockpit window. But if you need me to keep you awake..."

"No, I'm still running on coffee and adrenaline. That's fine if you want to sit in the cabin. I understand you're still working through some memories. Tragedies usually have more than one victim, so I pray Steve's going to pull through."

As they climbed the stairs, he raised his hand to thank the guy who had just refueled the plane and now pulled the gas truck away on the tarmac. After they went in, Bryce secured the door. If only they could be refueled to get through this flight today—he and Meg were both running on fumes.

They had slept huddled together for a few hours after Jenny got permission for both her and Mark to stay in Steve's room, where they would definitely not get any rest as nurses bustled in and out. Bryce could only hope that his friend pulled through and was still himself. He was glad the Big Man was sending more than one diver this time. Keeping the crash site secure was essential, especially since they had yet to ID the pilot, his plane or mission. This could very well be exactly what his special task force had been searching for. At least the frozen lake acted as a barrier to anyone who was either curious or dangerous. But who had tried to sabotage his dive and hurt Steve as an extra warning?

"Did you manage some sleep?" Bryce asked Meg as he came back into the cabin after he landed the plane on Falls Lake.

"Actually no." Her eyes watered from a stifled yawn. "Too much to think about. I hope we don't have to hike back to the lodge through all that snow. And what if the mystery man shows up again?"

"Got that all covered. Mayor Purvis is sending two men in a snowmobile we can take back to the lodge. They will guard my plane and the crash site. State troopers are also on their way. Thankfully, looking into what happened to Steve should keep them busy long enough for me to finish my investigation of the crash site before I have too many eyes looking over my shoulder. My own men won't be here until tomorrow."

She nodded and unsnapped her seat belt, surprised to see she still had it on. She needed a shower. She needed to talk to Chip and Suze. She needed sleep and to get off the emotional roller coaster she'd been on since this man came into her life.

He helped her up. "Again," he said, "you have been a tremendous help. I should put you on salary."

"I would not be good at taking orders from your Big Man boss."

He grimaced, then grinned. Their gazes met and held. He said, "The assignment I had overseeing the pulling of thousands of pounds of old fishing nets from West Coast bays was worthwhile—green ops, the team called it, you know, eco-friendly. Same with the kelp-and-micro-algae farm I have a large share in. Sometimes assignments come along that are baffling but of key importance too."

"This beautiful area is worth protecting, especially if that unmarked plane and anonymous pilot were up to no good. I'm glad I could help. But I'm sure you understand, not just for my sake but Chip's, I can't become—well, further involved."

He nodded but he looked so sad she felt terrible. She sensed he understood she was saying she could not get further involved not only with a mysterious mission, but with him.

Sleep and showers back at the lodge were quickly put on hold, not only because Suze and Chip deserved to hear some of what had happened, but because the mayor, Rand Purvis, was there, pacing, waiting for an update of what had happened to Steve at the lake.

After she and Bryce filled him in, she went to wash up and spent some time with Chip. Even when she came back out, it seemed to her that the mayor's personality reigned in the common room of the lodge.

Mayor Randal Purvis, called Rand, was a large man with a loud voice who seemed to have his hands into everything around Falls Lake. His father had been a homesteader and hunter, but Rand was a man of the times and not a throwback to any of that local wilderness history. He owned the bank and had shares in the gas station and the largest grocery and dry goods store in town. Both of his sons were being educated at the University of Oregon. A man of many talents, Rand was a person to be reckoned with.

"Still nothing on that pilot or plane?" Meg heard him ask Bryce, nearly pinning him in his chair the moment Bryce appeared again from his room for the lunch Suze had laid out for them.

"Still ongoing. Thanks for lending me those two guards for a while. Can't afford to have anyone else hurt. Steve's injuries make this a criminal investigation already. I understand state troopers have started their sweep of the area, looking for any sign of his attacker. After another dive with my new team, I may have more news then—for you and my sponsors, not for media consumption."

"Hell, no. Don't want any of that. I'm not the kind of public servant that thinks any news is good news. My key concern is to protect the citizens of Falls Lake at any cost."

Meg had often thought that the mayor would fit the old stereotype of a glad-handing politician, but he did not physically look the part. He wore trendy, expensive sports clothes instead of the usual local lumberjack look. His hair had a conservative cut, and he was clean-shaven. He looked the part of a judge, or a big city mayor, not a rural one. He cared deeply about anyone in danger, she'd give him that. More than once she'd heard he'd donated to down-and-out individuals around here, and there were plenty of those on the fringes of Falls Lake. And he did keep the lid on drunks or lawbreakers in the area with no more than advice or coercion, which had always impressed her.

She sat across the table from Bryce, who was wolfing down a turkey sandwich. The mayor was now over at the reception desk, talking to Suze. The ski guests who had come for the long Thanksgiving weekend were gone, and Suze, despite being sad and angry about what had happened to Steve, had been glad to hear that three men were coming later today to join Bryce's dive team.

All Meg wanted to do was sleep, though she had to admit she'd miss having Bryce by her side, even though they'd spent last night half slumped, half sitting up stiffly in a strange place.

"You're going right to bed?" Bryce asked as he switched from his sandwich to a mound of coleslaw.

"I've got to get back in the saddle," she said, not looking at him. "I want to make it up to Suze for her doing all my work last night and today so far. I plan to get up early to make candy tomorrow so I can restock my outlets in town. So I guess I'll be retiring early, and also retiring from helping with secret diver business."

"Just the business part, I hope," he said as he reached out for a chocolate chip cookie. "Not the personal support to one diver, that is."

"Bryce, I just can't—"

"Let's talk about it in the morning when we're not exhausted," he said and simply gave her shoulder a little squeeze as he got up and headed down the hall toward his room.

She sat there, unmoving, feeling deflated, even empty. And she missed him already. He was right, though. She was just tired, she told herself. Just tired.

Then she saw something so strange that she had to get up and go over to the desk where Suze was checking someone else in. She could tell the mayor was surprised too. He hovered, pretending to watch the big TV on the wall but watching the scene out of the corner of his eye with his head cocked to overhear.

"Got me a little windfall," the guest was telling Suze as Meg joined her behind the check-in counter. "Sold a collection of old *Life* magazines, some stretching back to the 1890s. You believe that? Real valuable, so maybe I better start lookin' more at what I got squirreled away, know what I mean?"

"Sure do, Mr. Getz," Suze said. "So how long will you be staying with us here in civilization?"

He laughed at that. His guffaw was as gravelly as his voice, maybe since he was the town hermit, not usually talking much. Suze laughed too, and Meg forced a smile. People talked about the town recluse who was known to be a hoarder. She had never seen this man up close.

She'd hear that he would scavenge through trash cans and insisted on keeping Falls Lake "green," while collecting junk in his truck, then taking it to recycling places clear to Anchorage, where he got money back. But they said he just piled up stuff too. He was kind of a legend around here, like Johnny Appleseed or some Disney character. Chip would be enthralled when he heard Bill Getz was moving in for a while.

"Be staying just a few days. Put me down for four or five. Good hot showers, good food and not fixin' anything myself, like I done died and gone to heaven," he said, signing his name in the guest book Suze extended to him.

Meg was actually glad that the mayor had heard all that. Who knew how this loner would fit in here? Mayor Purvis didn't go over to talk to Bill Getz, but just lifted a hand to Suze and headed out the front door.

Meg heard his snowmobile start. She'd peek in on Chip

and the dogs, then take a shower and fall into bed. And hope she didn't dream about Bryce Saylor.

However sleepy she still was, Meg had set her alarm for 5 a.m. to give herself time to make some candy before she met Josh in the kitchen at six thirty to work on breakfast. At least they didn't have the voracious skiers to feed today.

Now she carefully melted the hunks of shaved dark chocolate in her cooking pot. She stirred it while she pressed the tinfoil paper wrappings into the tiny cups. She'd have to time them carefully to give each chocolaty peak a little loop on its top before it hardened, then cool them and close the wrapper with a twist. She loved the curly tops of her candy kisses.

At the last minute, she measured out the sea salt to stir into the dark, thick batch. It was just the right consistency, yielding but not too soft when she spooned a careful amount into each of the little cups.

While they were cooling, she popped one into her mouth. Delicious. She tried not to eat many of her wares but, after all, it was just like having a cup of hot morning cocoa. Well, maybe a bit richer. She set her timer to ding when the chocolate would be completely pliable for that last touch on top of the kisses.

"I thought I might find you here. You said you would be making candy early."

She spun around. Bryce, shaved, neatly dressed in jeans and a green-and-black-plaid wool shirt, was standing in the open doorway. He seemed to shrink the small room, to pull her closer without touching her.

"Yes, I'm working on a batch." She said the obvious as her cheeks heated, and not from the stove. And then she made it worse. "Kisses," she blurted.

His blue eyes burned into hers. "I like the sound of that.

I'm willing. Have been from the first time I climbed out of that icy water. I saw you and wasn't cold anymore."

"K-kisses, the kind of c-candy," she stammered.

He came around her worktable. "I know," he said, his voice comforting, mesmerizing. "It smells delicious in here, and I like what I see. I'll take the whole batch, but I'd like a little taste first."

She reached for one. "They're not quite ready yet," she said, but she blew on it and lifted it to his mouth. "A little hot," she whispered.

"I can tell. I like that."

He took the piece of dark chocolate from her fingers, licking them a bit too. Oh, no. This was going to happen. Not so early in the morning, after she'd definitely decided she could not let things—her feelings for him, her attraction to him—go further.

"You have some on your mouth too," she said.

He put his hands on her aproned waist to tug her closer.

She was going to melt in his arms. He pressed her lightly against him. He bent slightly, tipped his head, lifted her chin and took her lips. She felt his every touch down to her belly and beyond.

He kissed her carefully, then thoroughly, slanting his head, with his tongue skimming the inside of her lips, a sweet invasion. She kissed him back and neither came up for air.

Then she responded like a mad woman, throwing her arms around his neck and coming closer as their lips slanted, opened as if to devour each other's kisses. What had come over her? This man—who wasn't her husband—was making her feel things she hadn't felt since Ryan had died. She wasn't ready to process the implications of that. Not while she was wrapped in his arms and everything about the embrace felt surprisingly right. Maybe this was what it felt like to finally move forward? Bryce felt so good, so strong that she could have flown.

So what if the tips of her candy kisses were ready for a twist, just like her once quiet life?

CHAPTER TEN

"I can't believe you got that color on your cheeks from the sun's reflection off the ice yesterday," Suze told Meg that morning. "Are you feeling okay after all you've been through? I've heard hospitals aren't exactly the places to stay healthy." She peered closer at Meg, who turned away and kept clearing the table.

Her twin sister had eyes like a hawk. Meg knew she was still flushed from merely thinking about Bryce's kisses this morning—and the crazed way she'd kissed him back. He'd gone to his room after breakfast to confer again with his boss while he was waiting for the three-man dive team to arrive, so at least he wasn't around to see her blushes. She scolded herself for acting like a sixteen-year-old girl.

"I'm fine," she told Suze in the kitchen.

"Bryce thinks you are."

"No comment."

"Megan Metzler, just relax. As one who hasn't had that bell ring yet, like Alex did with Quinn and you did with Ryan, I'm just telling you, inhale and enjoy. Take advantage—smell the roses along the way, even in this cold weather."

"Get involved so he can fly off into the sunset the minute he's done here? Sorry. It's just I'm really torn."

"About falling for another pilot or falling in love period? He's good with Chip. He's doing important work. He lives in Juneau, not Miami or Morocco. He'll be here for at least a little while longer. What's that old saying—make hay while the sun shines?"

Suze was just too full of old sayings today, but Meg kept quiet about that. She kept rinsing plates and putting them in the dishwasher rack. "I need someone who's settled," she finally said. "I know he has a house in Juneau, but I mean someone who doesn't have a career with tinges of James Bond and those old TV reruns of *Sea Hunt* Chip likes to watch." She spun to face her sister. "Suze, his dive rope was severed. He's investigating a plane tied to criminals for all I know. Worse, his partner was almost killed by someone sneaking up and hitting him from behind!"

"I get all that. But I don't think the choice of men around here is the greatest. Who do we get staying here? Hikers, guys who attend Quinn's tracking camp and skiers. I think the ones who just left might have been smoking pot in their room. And now the town hoarder, Bill Getz. Sorry, hon, didn't mean to let my own longings creep in. Of course, you have to do what you have to do."

They both turned back to work as Josh came in to take waste baskets out to the dumpster. Meg knew Suze was giving advice because she loved her and Chip. Of course, she had to hold Bryce at arm's length. Yet no matter what her own mouth and brain were saying, why was she in such a battle with her heart?

It was midafternoon when an Uber from the Anchorage airport dropped off Bryce's newly assigned diving buddies.

Meg was at the front desk to give Suze her midafternoon break. The three men's gear alone gave away who they were.

She looked down at the note in Bryce's handwriting he'd left for them: Keith Okudah, Nate Young and Bob Morrow.

"Welcome to the Falls Lake Lodge," she told them with a smile. "We—and Bryce Saylor—are expecting you. I'll check you in, then ring his room."

"Hi, I'm Keith Okudah," a big-shouldered African American man introduced himself. "How much daylight is left? Want to see if we can dive today."

The oldest of the men, who introduced himself as Nate, answered his question for him. "Depends on how far Falls Lake is."

"How about signing in here?" she asked, pivoting the guestbook toward them. "Commander Bryce has all the answers you'll need."

The brown-haired, crew-cut Caucasian guy—he was signing as Robert Morrow—said, with a sideways glance at Keith, "He usually does, but maybe not on this gig."

She rang Bryce's room and told him his crew was here. "Thanks. Be right out," he said, all business. But she couldn't help remembering his mouth on hers, his hands...

"Here are your room keys, not the electronic kind," she said, handing their old-fashioned metal keys over. "Needless to say, this isn't our busy time of year, so it's pretty quiet."

"That can change fast, but we hope it doesn't," Keith said. "If it's calm and quiet around here, let's keep it that way."

But as Bryce came striding into the common room with a smile on his face and his hand outstretched to shake his new teammates' hands, Meg was certain things would never be calm and quiet for her again as long as he was here.

Despite the fact that light snow was falling about two hours later, Bryce took his new divers to the site of the crash.

The two guys from Mayor Purvis's staff were still on site and glad to get their snowmobile back since Bryce had rented the two the lodge owned. The open expense account and the fact the Big Man had sent three divers instead of one this time made him realize how important this assignment was, and he had to get things moving fast.

He made introductions all around, then thanked the two guys the mayor had loaned him and let them go. He had enough crew now and didn't want them to hang around to tell the mayor or anyone else what they might turn up today. It was bad enough having state troopers in the area, searching for evidence of Steve's attacker. It was only a matter of time before they'd ask Bryce to turn over his own findings regarding the crash site.

He had Bob Morrow handle the dive rope and watch the entrance hole—which they had to break through again— while he dove with Nate Young. He put Keith Okudah in charge of the overall mission and operation site while he and Nate were under water, so they had two surface guards again.

"We're looking for pilot and aircraft ID and possible contraband," he reminded Nate. "You watch and guard me, but keep your eyes open in case I miss something down there. At least we've got more underwater lights this time. You got the lift bags and my video camera?"

"Roger that, and a couple of evidence recovery containers. Been a forensic diver too long not to go prepared."

"Things are icing over down there, so we may have to break or pry something loose, but preserving information and evidence is everything. Let's go."

Their first-time guest Bill Getz was driving Meg and Suze up the wall. Not that he was a thief per se, but he did have sticky fingers, going through their trash, wanting to help

Josh at the dumpster, asking if he could have old magazines they had stacked on the shelves or side tables.

"Well," Suze whispered, "if he makes his money like this—cleaning up for others, in a way—I don't mind. If Josh ever quits, we could hire him part-time. Yes, that's a joke."

Meg just rolled her eyes and went into her bedroom for her afternoon break. She missed Chip since he was back in school after Thanksgiving vacation, but she didn't need him asking her *why, why?* He would probably really bug her since she was putting some of the many old pictures of Ryan away for a while. Her dear husband stared at her from numerous photo frames she should dust more often.

But then she came upon the plastic envelope of newspaper clippings she had saved. She stared at Ryan's obit through the shiny Ziploc bag. She'd kept cuttings from the Juneau and Anchorage newspapers: photos of Caribou Lake and the cliff above it, which Ryan had flown into in the mist and fog. She didn't read any of the articles again, but the headline FALLS LAKE BUSH PILOT LOSES LIFE IN CRASH INTO CARIBOU CLIFF shouted at her again.

She shoved the packet of articles on the top shelf of her closet and stacked the framed photos carefully in a snap-top plastic box to go under her bed. She'd save the articles for Chip when he was older and rotate the family photos, keep the ones out that had the three of them together. But for the first time since Ryan had been gone, she could let go just enough to store him away with many memories.

After all, she didn't want to be a hoarder like Mr. Getz, at least according to the rare few who had been to his cabin in the woods on the far side of the lake. She'd heard he had built a series of rooms out the back of the previously one-room place.

She sighed, wondering how Bryce and his team were doing at the now familiar dive site. Even Bill Getz seemed interested in what he'd heard about the crash. He probably wondered if something sunken could be added to his collection.

The huge underwater strobe lights illumined the darkness but made shifting shadows seem to lunge at Bryce. The silty lake water didn't help. Ordinary deep water dives, no problem. Dark depths, no sweat. But there was something too damn creepy about this wreck.

He and Nate used hand motions to position and move the two lights. Nate operated the video camera and Bryce his trusty still shot camera. Now that they could maneuver with the pilot's body gone, they took photos of the cockpit, then moved deeper down into the tilted plane. Repeatedly, Bryce touched the deep end of the dive rope he kept near to be sure it was taut. It was.

He visualized the accident—if it was that and not some sort of sabotage—as he had numerous times these last few days. According to Meg and Chip, the plane had hit through the ice at about a forty-five degree angle, but he could see it had twisted in the current, then settled more tail-down. For the first time, he noted that there was some serious structural damage—a jagged, four-foot-square hole—on the interior undercarriage near the tail. Could anything from the payload have fallen out or been washed away? Spills from this small cargo hold could have happened in the jolt when it hit the ice and then went underwater.

He noted a metal box with handles and motioned Nate to come closer. Strapped down with a canvas belt, it sat on top of an identical box. Finally, answers! He'd use the lift bags and help from above to get them to the surface intact. He'd promised the Big Man that any evidence they recovered would remain under wraps until it could be delivered to his team for analysis. The chain of custody of evidence was already at risk now that state troopers were involved. If some sort of espionage was going on here, the fewer who knew, the better.

While Nate was moving the lights and filming the boxes and loose cargo from every angle, Bryce swam closer to the break in the fuselage. The plane was at enough of an angle that it didn't sit exactly on the lake bed, which meant something could have fallen out onto the black bottom.

In the flickering, shifting lights Nate held, Bryce moved his fins firmly but slowly so as not to stir up the bottom more than it already was as he swam down headfirst through the opening. Like monstrous teeth, ice fringed the jagged mouth of the hole. He knew he should wait for Nate and his lights, but he'd let him finish his task. Bryce's handheld light and the more wan one on his head would do.

The depth, the cold down here, staying too long could screw up clear thinking, and he wanted this strange mission to be a success with no more casualties. He was doing this for Steve now too, praying he'd pull through.

He decided not to exit the fuselage but just shine his light out. Recon of the adjacent area would be for their next dive, maybe with three divers. He'd bring Keith down with them next time. He liked his self-confidence, whereas Bob Morrow seemed almost tentative. He'd always prided himself at being able to size people up fast. Which was why it had hurt so bad when his engagement had blown up. It was years ago. Maybe they were both too young. He'd thought she was solid and steady, but...

Damn, his mind was drifting as his light beam glinted on something shiny. Metal? Coins? He waited until the swirl of bottom silt settled. Could the pilot have been running laundered money? But for whom in the midst of this winter wilderness? If he had meant to land here rather than crash, why here? Could he have had a criminal record and be moving contraband or stolen goods? Fingerprints or DNA might have to provide the answers.

Bryce extended his gloved hand to pick up one of the pieces—of something. His gloves were iced and slippery, and the temps down here were getting to him in his fingers, toes, even his limbs. He dropped the small metal thing, and it spun back into the bottom sand and silt.

He noted there were several shiny objects besides that one. Not coins, but…gold jewelry. He fanned the silt away and picked it up again, bringing it close to his mask. He was trembling from staying down so long, but he steadied his hand and focused his light full on it. If the pilot had been carrying stolen jewelry, from where and why?

Definitely an old piece, so maybe the other half-buried items here were too. As he lifted this piece of jewelry higher, coils of attached gold links rose from the lake bed.

He squinted through his dive mask at it. A woman's locket, fairly large. In clumsy, two-handed motions, he popped it open and saw coils of something like woven thread under glass inside. He snapped it closed and brushed it off again. On enamel was the painting of a crying woman's face in the midst of filigree swirls of gold. And—damn—he must be losing it in these cold, dark depths, because the weeping woman looked like Meg.

CHAPTER ELEVEN

The next morning, Bryce and his dive team were ready to head out again. But, he told Meg, they had decided to wait for decent daylight.

"What about those big boxes you hauled in?" she asked.

"Locked in my room, which is why I told Suze I don't want it cleaned again. I won't open them. State troopers are coming to pick them up and guard them until they can be flown east—soon."

A bit later he stopped Meg as she bustled back and forth from the breakfast table to the kitchen. "Do you have a safe here?" he asked.

"Sure, and guests use it sometimes, but it's not big enough for those boxes."

"I just have an envelope with a couple of items I'd like to have stored there for today, maybe longer."

"I'll lock it up for you. Bring it into the office—the next door beyond the room where I was making the candy yesterday."

"I do know where that is," he told her, his voice warm. He produced a flimsy but bulging letter-sized envelope from the inside of his jacket pocket and followed her down the hall and into the office. Mostly, it was Suze's domain, but Meg knew where everything was and the safe's combination.

"No looking, now, while I dial the combination," she teased him.

"Can't help looking but won't touch—at least right now."

"Do you want a stronger envelope? We have larger, clasped ones in the supply cabinet," she said as she turned and reached for it.

The question couldn't have been better timed as he held out the envelope and the weight of its contents pulled apart the weak seal. A single item fell to the floor, one connected to a fancy neck chain.

"Oh, sorry," she said and bent to help him pick it up when he made a dive for it. "Old jewelry. It looks familiar."

"How so? It's kind of weird. This locket has sewing thread woven in a pattern inside it," he said, scooping it up. "And a painting of a woman—she reminded me of you—but she's crying."

"Can I see?" she asked.

"I haven't even let the team see it."

"It's from the wreck?"

He nodded as he opened his hand hiding the locket. She studied the woman crying with boughs of a weeping willow tree leaning over her. "It does kind of look like me," she admitted.

"Well, now that you've seen that much..." He pressed a little latch to pop the gold lid. "See, there's black thread woven inside."

"Bryce, I guess you don't know much about old Victorian-era mourning jewelry to commemorate a loved one's death, do you?"

"What? This woman's mourning someone?"

"No doubt she's grieving the death of the person whose

hair is woven inside. Suze and I have a couple of similar pieces in this safe our grandmother left us—from her grandmother, going clear back to the American Civil War. I'll show you ours. Not only tresses from the deceased person were often included but—if it was a mourning memento of a child or an unmarried woman—it might have teeth from the deceased that look like ivory. I know that sounds gross, but that was the custom for grieving the death of someone deeply loved and lost."

She studied his expression. Surprise, then a big frown. He leaned against the corner of the desk and raked his fingers across the back of his neck.

"You're like a gift in more ways than one," he said. "Yes, I'd like to hear more, see what jewelry you have, later, though. I'll show you what I retrieved from the sunken plane yesterday. But like we teased once before, you cannot let on you're helping with this mystery or—"

"Or you'd have to do away with me and then just put a snippet of my hair in a piece of memorial jewelry—ha. You could say, 'I knew her once—nice girl. Liked my kisses but had to look up the word *kismet* when I first said it to her.'"

"You're amazing," he said with a sigh.

Meg's heart beat faster. The feeling was mutual.

Bryce figured he had an hour before he and the dive team would set off for Falls Lake again. He'd overheard Meg tell Suze in the hall that she had some information that could help him.

"I'll finish the cleanup later. If you don't need the office right now, can he and I use it? I don't want to go to his room."

That got his attention. He scratched his neck again where his cold water dive suit had not had a good seal. He needed to put more protective silicone cream on it, but it was hard to reach the entire area just right. He'd look silly asking one of his new team to rub some on there.

"I'm out of breath just hearing that," he overheard Suze tell Meg. "Sure, go ahead. I'll knock and ask permission before I come in."

"It isn't anything you think."

"Aha," Suze said. "You don't know what I think."

"Yes, I do."

Bryce grimaced, then grinned over that. It made him miss his back-and-forth with his brother. He stepped away from the door to wait for Meg, already pulling out his pieces of jewelry from the brown clasped envelope she'd given him to replace the flimsy one.

"Coast clear?" he asked when she joined him and they went back in the office.

"She said fine. Believe me, she could tell you as much as I can. We weren't even aware Grandma had these pieces. Suze and I were shocked to find an old tortoiseshell jewelry box Grandma had left here with some beautiful but strange things in it. Leaving us the lodge was generous and amazing enough. Most of what I know about Victorian mourning jewelry I learned from a woman who owns an antique jewelry store in Anchorage when I went to get information on our pieces."

"You show me yours, and I'll show you mine."

"You had better stick to business and not teasing, Incident Commander Saylor, or I shall have to report you to the Big Man."

He sucked in a sharp breath. "Don't even kid about that. Okay, thanks for a verbal slap in the face. Please share anything else you know about your grandmother's legacy and the airplane jewelry. More pieces may be out there. I'm grateful for your help. Guess you're still on the team."

★ ★ ★

"I see now that this fine line painting doesn't really look like me," Meg observed, picking up the locket of the weeping woman again and studying it closely. "Just that she's blonde."

"And pretty. Oval face. Blue eyes," he said, scratching at his neck. She wondered if that's what he did when he was nervous.

"She's in mourning for someone she lost," she said, her voice quiet. "I would guess that this is her beloved's hair woven here for her to remember him. Of course, they did have photography then, so she no doubt had pictures of him too, but this sort of jewelry was traditional. I think my source—Melissa McKee—said the practice started back in the Georgian era."

But she was thinking of the photos of Ryan she'd been storing away. Times changed but maybe people didn't, caught in perpetual grief over the loss of someone they had loved. She realized she did not want to be that way, not forever, not anymore.

"Okay," she said, shaking off the icy pall coming over her, "let's see your other pieces."

He laid them out carefully on the corner of the desk. Then the two of them huddled close. "I did wash them off last night. I wasn't sure about that, but I wanted to study them before I talk with my boss next. He's not available again until late tonight. Other business."

"So he has to answer to someone too?" she asked. "His wife? Some politician? Someone even bigger than the Big Man, maybe at the FBI or Homeland Security or something like that?"

"Don't go on a fishing expedition because you never know what's under the surface. So, do you think these pieces are all antique mourning jewelry?"

"Yes, and here's one with what I'm sure are human teeth.

Ugh, can't stand to think of that. See here, this tiny one with the angel drooped over the tombstone etched right on the teeth. Like I said, some of this probably predates the Civil War era. Could it be that pilot was smuggling rare and expensive jewelry? Like maybe he robbed a home, jewelry store or museum? I'd be glad to look online for any such reports."

"If you have time, thanks. Any info like that would be valuable."

"It's a good thing we're going to lock all these pieces up, with Bill Getz loose around here. I won't mention a thing, not even to Suze for now. Oh, look, this other piece you found has words etched on the back."

She tilted it and raised it toward the window light. Heads close, they squinted at the scripted words—a name. Meg leaned away and opened the middle desk drawer to reach for a magnifying glass.

"Two words," she said, moving the glass over the piece. "Varina Howell. What a pretty and unusual first name. It's a long shot, but maybe I could trace that name too, like through a genealogy website."

"Meg, I can't expect you to spend a lot of time on this, but anything you can do will help. You have helped already, more than you know."

"Kismet that I recognized what these pieces were."

He nodded. Their faces were close. He scratched at his neck again.

"Do you have a rash from diving?"

"In a way. The seal at the neck of my suit rubs, and I need to put some protective silicone cream on as a barrier."

"And it's a bad angle to put it on yourself."

His intense gaze snagged hers. "I'm really going to owe you. A night on the town—not in Falls Lake but Anchorage, since I do want to go back to see how Steve and his family are doing. If I can get away from this assignment."

"Then we'd better get that rash taken care of, and another person could obviously do a better job than you're doing with that cream. Let me lock all this away, and I'll put some on you. By the way, I eat so much salmon and other fish here that I'd be an expensive date. I would order a filet mignon."

"I'm good for it. I just hope I can be good for you—like you are for me."

Like naughty kids, they jumped apart when a knock sounded on the door. Darn, she thought. He had been absolutely ready to kiss her again.

"Commander, you want us to gas up the snowmobiles?" a voice came through the door.

Bryce got up and opened it. "Right away. We leave in fifteen minutes. Meet out in front."

"Roger that," she heard the guy say. Were they all former navy men or pilots?

"But," Bryce said, turning back toward her at the door, "that gives me time to get a neck rub. I'll suit up and get the cream if you still have time. Then it's off to the frozen lake again when I was just starting to warm up."

She laughed as he ducked out. She was pretty sure she didn't even blush this time.

"I can get it on my wrists and ankles for a good seal and water barrier, but not my neck," he told her, sounding almost as nervous as she felt.

She rubbed the cream carefully but thoroughly onto the skin of Bryce's warm neck. He almost purred, moving his head up or down when she told him to.

"Forget making candy kisses," he whispered. "You could go into business with neck rubs—for me."

She was getting almost dizzy as she watched the circles of smooth white cream disappear into him. She felt the rhythmic motion of her hands on his warm, tanned skin.

This ritual he must do each time he dived made her remember sending a loved one off to work in the sky. How much she'd missed the little moments that were really so big, the daily rituals, the small talk, teasing and inside jokes—the closeness. But with that came risk and possible loss, so giving in, loving and wanting someone was a huge gamble, one she was still not sure she was willing to make.

He looked at his dive watch—he was late to meet his team out front. "More later," he whispered and kissed her quickly.

Still, it got to her, made her feel weak in the knees. She had the almost overpowering urge to hold him there.

But he headed out the door. Even though he was leaving, these moments had been so—so cozy and familiar and normal, as if they were more to each other than they were.

Even at the hint of the dangers he faced, at the terrible thought of possibly losing him, she felt ready for the risk, ready for him.

CHAPTER TWELVE

The online search Meg did for "stolen antique jewelry" and "thefts of Victorian mourning jewelry" yielded only sites selling such items. Sighing, she looked at some. A few similar pieces but nothing that would hint at a robbery, not in recent years, not even in Europe.

Because she would love to be able to help Bryce more than she had, she looked at a few of the big commercial websites offering pieces for sale. She was amazed at how the prices had inflated since she'd had Grandma's jewelry appraised. Not that she and Suze meant to sell those family heirlooms, but just so they knew what they were worth. She supposed they really should get them insured.

Then it hit her: despite Bryce's penchant for secrecy in all this, which Meg wished he could explain, maybe Melissa McKee, who had helped her before, could be of help now, at least to price or evaluate the pieces.

She went to Melissa's Olden Jewelry Store website, which she hadn't looked at for ages. It was tastefully done with an old-fashioned flavor. But unlike before, Melissa was now offering both Victorian and Alaskan Native jewelry, the latter mostly intricately beaded or carved from sea treasures like sperm whale bones or teeth. She admired ornate scrimshaw pieces carved by whalers and contemporary Native artists too.

On that same page, another surprise. The website was advertising and selling a beautiful coffee table–type book called *In Death Lamented: The Tradition of Anglo-American Mourning Jewelry.* It was expensive but looked intriguing. Maybe she should buy it, because it could take too long to get it through the Anchorage Library system, and it might help Bryce. But, undecided and always watching her money, she clicked on the FOR SALE page of jewelry items instead.

She concentrated on the mourning jewelry. Wait until she told Bryce even the few pieces he'd found tumbled onto the lakebed were worth a small fortune. And he'd gone to search for more today. Of course, without his permission she would not mention those pieces to anyone—especially Melissa—but maybe she could yet be of help if Bryce agreed.

She also wondered whether there would have been enough buyer interest in Anchorage so Melissa could keep her shop going with just old Victorian-era jewelry. Was that why she was now offering the beautiful and intricate tribal heritage pieces? No doubt the cruise ship trade could help because her shop was near the docks where tourists disembarked to explore Anchorage, and surely wealthy travelers would prefer a heritage memento from their Alaskan cruise.

She closed the laptop, sighed and wilted against it on her crossed wrists, putting her head down. She wasn't sleeping well, hadn't since the plane crash and Bryce came on the scene. But the excitement—and he—were worth it.

Bryce was tense about today's dive. He knew something about what they were searching for now. And he was dying to know what was in those two belted metal strongboxes to discover what answers lay inside. ID for the pilot and plane? Orders for dispersing the goods? Prices for the jewelry and lots more of it, or of some other valuable commodity? But the Big Man wanted the boxes shipped untouched, so that was that.

But he wasn't handing those few pieces of jewelry over until he got more answers. He was sticking his neck out here, more than he had on most recoveries and investigations.

The most he was going to let Meg get involved in all this was checking out things on her laptop, inside the safety of the lodge. When he could, he meant to keep a good eye on that Getz guy who'd suddenly showed up for a few days.

He hoped his and Meg's bantering about going to Anchorage together to have a real date would work out. It would be good, too, to check in to the regional NTSB office in Anchorage, where he had a supervisor, though since joining the special task force, he primarily answered to the Big Man in DC who was directly overseeing this case now. But could he let Meg know even that much?

He was worried about her, Chip too. Someone had watched the plane crash, maybe had seen them, then disappeared. Someone had also hurt Steve during their dive. Maybe the same person lurking around the lodge. Watching his moves? Or because the lurker had seen Meg and Chip and didn't want any witnesses talking?

"Let's dive," he said to Keith and Nate, then nodded to Bob, who would be guarding things topside. They double-checked the fit of their masks and mouthpieces. Then Bryce went in first.

Headfirst, he led Nate and Keith down the dive rope, shining his handheld light before him. He saw the fuselage of the plane had tilted a bit more, though it hadn't moved location. He illumined it, and the others followed. He should have brought an underwater slate with a glow-in-the-dark pencil.

His hand signals must have been clear enough, though. The new tilt of the plane meant it would be best not to go inside, but to swim around it near the tail and sift the sand and murky bottom for more jewelry. It was the NTSB's business to be thorough and careful. He had brought a sieve in his gear, so he and Keith lifted careful handfuls of silt and sand onto it from the site of his original finds. Nate searched the outer perimeter.

The silty glacial melt water had been stirred up recently—strangely, more than he had seen before or expected. Maybe that was just from the slight repositioning of the plane between his last dive and now.

Their routine, boring practice soon turned exciting. Keith, then Nate, turned up more pieces of jewelry. It all looked old to his still unpracticed eye, but none of it had the elements of mourning jewelry, at least he didn't think so. Perhaps this really was from a major jewelry theft somewhere, and the pieces were to be hidden in this sparsely settled area of Alaska and sold later, after any investigation had died down. He'd just stumbled on the mourning jewelry first and thought the entire cache would be that.

They then found some coins and a single gold bar, not big, not like the ingots he'd seen at Fort Knox. But this was a treasure hunt! As soon as they ID'd the pilot's body, they could trace who stole what and where. And where it was going, here in wild, wooded Alaska.

After helping serve lunch and clean up, Meg delayed making peanut-cream-filled chocolate candy to return again to her laptop. Before she gave up on finding something to help Bryce and his crew, she had another lead to check out.

She googled the name from the piece of jewelry—Varina

Howell. This was probably a long shot, despite the woman's lovely and unique first name. If she ever had a daughter, she'd consider using it. Ryan had named Chip, a nickname for Charles, after Chip's grandfather he had never known.

She stared at the screen and gasped. It was the woman's maiden name. It came right up with numerous links, even old photographs—tintypes, some were called. She checked out a Wikipedia entry, drinking in the information. She studied a black-and-white picture of a woman with dark hair parted in the middle and pulled back in a tight bun, a woman in a full-skirted, floor-length dress standing next to—the picture was labeled *American Civil War Confederate President Jefferson Davis and his wife Varina Howell Davis.*

Wide-eyed, she read on. Second marriage. Four children. Their young son died. When the Confederacy collapsed, she sold many of her household goods and fled Richmond with her family to avoid capture by the victorious Union forces. The escapees had been captured five days later by a Michigan regiment of Union forces and imprisoned. She had long outlived the husband she had dearly loved and supported.

And when the family fled Richmond, they had a fortune in currency and jewelry with them. When they were arrested they had nearly nothing! It was a long debated mystery where that fortune had gone.

The hair stood up on the Meg's arms as if she were suddenly chilled.

How amazing that one of the pieces of mourning jewelry Bryce had found had belonged to the First Lady of the Confederacy. Meg recalled the name of the book on mourning jewelry—*In Death Lamented*—as she skimmed the rest of Varina's biography. Evidently she had never been able to move on from the loss of her husband. With that, Meg could empathize.

A quick knock on her door jolted her.

Suze popped her head in. "Meg, someone here to see you, to buy some candy and say hi." She lowered her voice. "It's Melissa McKee, that store owner from Anchorage who told you about Grandma's jewelry. Maybe she's going to make another pitch to buy it. The mayor evidently told her about you seeing the plane crash, and she just wondered if you're all right. She also mentioned wanting to stock your candy in her store, which would be a big boost for your sales with her shop being down by the cruise ship docks."

That thought excited Meg, but what a crazy coincidence. Still, the world was filled with those. But the woman was suddenly inspired to have Falls Lake Chocolates in her jewelry store? Maybe the cruise ship business and online sales were not so good. No, this could not be a coincidence. Melissa must be up to something.

Meg turned off her laptop and went out to meet their guest.

It took Bryce a moment to tamp down his excitement of this turning into a treasure hunt. The other night he'd seen Chip watching reruns of an old TV show called *Sea Hunt*, one he used to watch in reruns too. It starred Lloyd Bridges, the father of more current stars Jeff and Beau Bridges. That show had turned him on to scuba diving, and there had always been some mystery to solve, some bad guy in it. Now, he and his team were living that.

He shook his head to clear it. His mind was wandering again. He'd been down here in the cold for too long, but he wanted to complete the search. This site was not only vulnerable but valuable now. In this climate and isolated area, there was no way to leave a guard on the lake surface for hours, especially at night.

While Keith and Nate kept digging deeper and wider, Bryce circled back toward the plane to be sure no other spillage holes had opened up either in the initial crash or when the plane evidently settled more. He swam along the length of the fuselage, playing his light up, down. When his beam hit the plane's dark windows, they seemed to follow him like huge blank eyes.

He saw something that shouldn't be there, that hadn't been there during his initial study of the exterior: a six-inch-square, white plastic box almost the same color as the plane. It was the kind of device he'd seen before on another assignment, one for underwater demolition to fragment rock so it could be dredged and removed from blocking a narrow harbor entrance in the waters off Saudi Arabia. For underwater blasting…a naval mine…one operated by a nonelectrical acoustical transmission signal from above the surface… long-distance…

He jerked around and swam for Keith and Nate. He hit Keith on the shoulder, shined his own light at himself and signaled STOP! SURFACE NOW! Then he used a slash of his hand across his throat motion, because didn't know how to signal *explosive*.

If there was one explosive mine, there could be more.

Both men grabbed the evidence bags they'd been filling and followed Bryce to the dive rope. Thank God, no one had cut it this time, but why bother if the plane and the divers were all going to be blown to bits?

CHAPTER THIRTEEN

Just as Meg went out into the common room to greet Melissa McKee, two Alaska State Troopers came in the front door. Bryce had told her and Suze that they were to give the troopers the two boxes he had secured. They were in the lodge's office near the safe. He had also made Meg promise not to mention the jewelry until he had more time with it to get some answers.

Suze took care of the troopers while Melissa got up from her chair and walked to greet Meg. Quickly, Meg took her over by the windows so her guest wouldn't see what the troopers were doing. What was that line Bryce had mentioned that the Big Man had told him over the phone? *Trust no one, my friend.*

That reminded her that she'd seen Bill Getz hovering recently, but when she looked, she didn't see him now, thank heavens.

Melissa glanced at the troopers as she and Meg sat on the couch facing the back windows. The fiftysomething woman was striking—red-haired, green-eyed, toned and looked to be in her thirties. As Meg had noted several years ago when she'd consulted her on their grandmother's heirloom jewelry, not many Anchorage women had facial tucks and used Botox, but Melissa must have. She seemed to be always dressed in a beautiful jacket and matching slacks. Today she also wore red boots and a silver coat she draped over the arm of the couch. Meg made sure they had their backs to the main desk, though her guest craned around more than once to glance behind them.

"Is there some sort of problem here?" Melissa asked.

"The troopers drop in now and then, especially since the plane crash out on the lake, doing general area security, I guess."

Meg hated that she'd lied so easily. It reminded her she was getting in over her head since she'd met Bryce.

Melissa twisted around in her seat again. "That whole plane crash and an unknown pilot was very weird, your mayor says."

"True, but in Alaska, what's new about weird? So, how is your shop doing? I appreciated all your helpful information about our jewelry, but we still don't want to sell it."

"You should make a display case for it here," she said, craning her neck to look around again. "I'll bet the store— literally—that you two never wear those lovely old pieces."

"True. You were in town to see the mayor?"

Meg realized she'd been asking this woman a spate of questions but she didn't want to be answering many herself. So, was this visit at this time just because Melissa wondered how Meg was doing? Why was she even here in little Falls Lake? And why had she seen or talked to the mayor about the plane crash everyone—including him—had said they would try to keep under wraps? Bryce was suspicious of Bill Getz's appearance—infiltration, he'd called it. Should she wonder about this visit?

"Oh, yes, the mayor," Melissa went on, turning forward

to look at her again. "He mentioned you and your son had witnessed the plane crash, and I was hoping you were doing all right. Amazing the media hasn't picked up on that story, but I guess nothing is very interesting in Falls Lake except to Falls Lake. Hope the whole thing is settled and doesn't blow up soon. That murder you had here last summer was bad enough.

"But about Mayor Purvis," she went on, though Meg wished she wouldn't. She'd been hoping to talk to the troopers, to watch them carefully stow the boxes in their cruiser so she could report back to Bryce. She tried to concentrate on Melissa's words so as not to appear too interested in the troopers as she heard them thank Suze and their voices fade.

"The mayor and his wife have been married for almost thirty years," Melissa continued, "and he ordered a fabulous art-deco-inspired 1920s necklace and earrings for her as a surprise, so please don't tell her or anyone else to ruin the surprise. Lucky lady! He's bought her some beautiful pieces over the years. Here Jordan and I have been married longer than that, and his Anchorage Real Estate business is doing well, but I'm lucky to get a yearly trip to Vancouver or Seattle." She laughed, a forced laugh, Meg thought.

"But, of course, he wouldn't think to buy you jewelry with all you have and do at your jewelry shop."

"I suppose," she said and heaved a sigh. "My problem is I always want the best for my clients and for myself so—"

A big boom shook the lodge, rattling things on shelves.

Melissa gave a little shriek, and Meg jumped to her feet.

"What was that?" Suze shouted. "Not another plane crash! A car accident?"

"I don't know," Meg cried, "but I'll see if the troopers are still outside. Maybe they know and can help. Wait here," she ordered Melissa and ran outside.

Bill Getz was hovering around the troopers' car. The

troopers had just secured the two heavy boxes in the trunk of their cruiser and were looking around. Crouched back to back as if they would be attacked, they both had their hands on their guns. No other sounds followed.

"Is there mining going on around here?" one officer asked Meg as she ran toward them. "Maybe someone blasting stone or even big trees? Lumber mills still do that from time to time."

"No, but there is a dive team back by the site of that plane crash. Before you leave, could you drive down the road to see if that boom came from there? I could show you where."

"Ma'am, we're under strict orders to get this evidence to the airport. I'd have to call for permission, then—"

The radio voice in the cruiser crackled, then in the one strapped to his coat. He turned away to answer it, but holding her breath with her teeth chattering in the cold air, Meg heard every word coming in. Of course, so did Bill Getz.

"Secure your evidence boxes and guard them. But drive past the tracking camp on the road to the lake to where the road dead-ends. Wait there for a police chopper and reinforcements, but do not leave your vehicle. We are sending med and rescue responders from Wasilla to a disturbance at Falls Lake. 9-1-1 call came in. Do not hike in but stay with your cruiser in case needed," the voice repeated.

Meg almost fell to her knees in fear. An emergency call from the lake? What had happened?

"I can drive you there," Bill said, coming closer, very close. "Got my truck parked here."

She nearly took him up on that, but something told her not to. "Thanks, but I can get there another way," she said. She didn't even excuse herself or talk to Melissa, who was standing in the door with Suze as she ran back in past them. "I'm going to the lake," she told Suze.

Bryce's team had both snowmobiles, and snowshoes would

take an eternity to hike in. No, she'd put on those skis one of their guests had left behind and use two hiking sticks for poles to take a shortcut through the woods. It had been years since she'd skied, but then it had been years since she began to fall in love.

The impact of the blast threw all three divers out of their exit hole on a plume of water like a giant fist. Ice cracked, then shattered into sharp missiles all around them. Bryce slammed down onto a piece of broken ice, then had to fight to stay afloat. He had cut his hand right through his torn gloves and was smearing a crimson stain. Had he cut it on a piece of the plane? On shattered ice?

His mask had smacked into the ice, but it probably saved his face. He tore the mask off to see, but the lake was shaking with aftershocks of waves, tossing him up and down like he was riding a surfboard. He saw Nate had been thrown clear, almost to the shore, sprawled flat on his stomach but moving his limbs. Keith. Where was Keith? He'd been just ahead of him with Nate trying to surface first.

He kicked hard to get to a bigger piece of ice. Tried to scramble up on it, scraping his stomach and thighs. Kicked hard, harder.

What about Bob, who had been on the surface? Bob knew Steve had been attacked there, so surely he had been more careful. Hopefully, he'd seen something, someone—that device had been somehow controlled and set off while they were diving. By whom? Had the evidence bags survived?

Suddenly, someone helped to pull him up. Keith. Keith and Bob too, both on their bellies, reaching for him. Keith was bleeding from the mouth, spitting blood.

"We didn't see you at first there. I called 9-1-1," Bob said, sucking in air, breathless. "Help's coming."

Kicking off their flippers, the three of them made it to the shore to check on Nate. They flopped next to the evidence bags. Thank God, his plane was intact, sitting a bit tilted, though it would have floated anyway. Bryce hoped another charge had not been set there but he had no time to check on that right now.

Dizzy, his ears ringing, he pointed toward Nate and choked out, "Help him!"

As Bob and Keith got up and scrambled through the snow, Bryce looked around the snowy shore hemmed by crouching trees. He drew his diving knife. Big help that would be when they were dealing with a sophisticated enemy who was now using underwater detonation. But if someone was watching again, the mastermind of all this, Bryce would die protecting these men and this evidence. He had no doubt the crashed plane was now destroyed—and someone had tried to take him and his crew with it.

Dazed, he tried to get to his feet but kept sucking air as if his lungs had been smashed. Headache. Vertigo. That damned ringing in his ears.

He had to see to his men, take care of the evidence. He had to call the Big Man. Tell him that they were into deeper water than he'd ever thought with someone clever and evil who played for keeps.

Meg skied the back forest paths, taking every shortcut she knew, pulling herself along by poles made to help hikers or by grabbing spruce branches, despite getting showered with their snow. She tried to concentrate, to remember things Ryan had taught her when she was learning to ski.

She knew she had to be careful she didn't get hurt, not so much for Bryce as for Chip. He was her first priority. He could not lose a second parent, even if Suze would raise him and love him like her own. No, she couldn't think that way.

One anonymous dead pilot did not mean anyone else would die. Steve had survived. Bryce and his men must too.

Out of breath, aching in every muscle, she spotted the frozen lake ahead through the silhouette of trees.

She gasped. Not one hole in the ice but several—big broken pieces. Another plane crash? A bomb dropped from a plane?

She heard the whap-whap of helicopter blades, the shouts of men. Surely Bryce and his crew had not been diving when—when whatever hit.

Her tears steamed her goggles, so she yanked them off and let them dangle around her neck, though she then had to squint in the sharp light. The sound of the hovering chopper was loud. Did it even have a place to land with all that broken ice?

She forced herself to speed up, faster, faster. She had to see Bryce, to know he was safe.

Bryce was pretty sure he was hallucinating. Maybe dreaming. Meg was bending over him but she kept turning upside down, then around. He wished they were in bed together and she was teasing him. The noise in his ears prevented any sound coming from her sweet mouth as it moved so he shook his head to clear his hearing. That hurt even more.

"The helicopter landed farther down the lake where the ice is still solid." That's what she said. He could hear her now, but she sounded like she was in a barrel. "You might have a concussion, Bryce, so just lie still. The others are all alive. They said a bomb went off underwater."

No kidding, he thought, and drifted away, but he was so glad to have her hands on his shoulder, her face so close. Her voice came again, a little clearer this time.

"Bryce, I said, please lie still. The guys from the chopper

are walking down the side of the lake toward us with their medical gear. And your plane is okay."

"Saw it. Good. Good—you're here."

He had to get up and be sure his crew were really all right, but she was holding him down with both hands. She was shaking with cold since she'd put both her gloves over his hand where he'd been cut.

"Hell of a way to find out we're onto something big here," he whispered. "Can't believe I'm bleeding. Got cut by ice, I think."

"If ice can bring down the *Titanic,* it can cut Bryce Saylor," she said. She was like a stern nurse. Probably like she'd treat Chip if he were hurt, but he liked it, just having her here, close.

He tried to remember exactly what had happened. He saw the remote control firing device attached to the plane. Got the team to head up. It went off. Underwater shock waves. Almost made it to the surface, ears screaming, pain, fight for the surface, but everyone alive...

And Meg with him here.

CHAPTER FOURTEEN

Meg tried to concentrate on what Bryce said. She kneeled next to him in the snow where the medic had covered him with a thermal blanket. His sentences were sometimes broken, yet he spoke with authority and passion. He frowned and moved his head from time to time, as if he could clear his ears from the buzzing he'd mentioned.

But she had to tell him something else she'd learned online about Varina that could tie into his discoveries yesterday and today. She quickly brought him up to speed on her internet search. "Bryce, the fortune Jefferson Davis escaped with included a massive amount of heirloom jewelry that Confederate women had donated in support of the Confederate cause."

"Then that's it," he said. "We've stumbled on the cache of Confederate money and jewelry that must have been missing for years. The treasury and riches of the South." He took a deep breath. "The fortune that Jefferson and Varina Davis tried to escape with—but it disappeared before Northern troops captured them. But who had it and why did at least some of it show up in the wilds of Alaska in an unmarked plane? Where did it come from and where was it going?"

"I'll help you try to find out. But, yes—why here? And *who* here?"

"Listen to me," he whispered, seizing her hand with his uninjured one. "We only have a few minutes until they put me on that chopper, and I get to go visit poor Steve. Someone's picking us off like ducks in a row. I need you to go into my room at the lodge and pack my things for the hospital. Will you?"

"Yes. Of course."

"I'll bet they test me for concussion, maybe try to keep me there for a while. But I can't let that happen. I don't have my phone, or I'd handle this another way. It's in my room in a shoe under the bed. Laptop's under there too. Can you bring both to me in Anchorage as well as my clothes?" He gave her the code to his phone. "You can call the Big Man— that's what it says on my phone list—Big Man. Ask him for someone at the regional NTSB office in Anchorage to escort you, guard you once you're there."

"You're making sense. Your head has to be okay. Maybe you won't have to stay there long."

"No matter what they say, I'm not staying there long. Nate and I will probably have guards on our room doors but you'll be allowed in."

He frowned and slowly moved his head, so he must be in pain. Either that or he was getting the buzzing in his ears again. Or had he thought something terrible could happen to her in all this and regretted asking for her help?

"All right. I can do all that. I can drive to Anchorage."

"Not drive. On my phone's another name and number— Carter Jones. Retired pilot in Wasilla. Tell him I'm asking him to come here, fly my plane out so it won't be blasted apart next. The keys to start it are in my room at the lodge.

Tell him to check its exterior and landing floats for IEDs and underwater explosive devices. He'll know what to do. Will you be brave enough to fly with him in my plane to Anchorage?"

"Not in the copilot's seat, not looking out a window, but otherwise—piece of cake." She burst into tears, wiping them away fast with her coat sleeve. She did not tell him that Carter had been a friend of Ryan's. And that the old gentleman had been with her when she faced her worst fears to honor her dead husband.

How had it ever come to this? Was she dreaming? More like a nightmare. But Bryce knew this was something big and he trusted her enough to call the Big Man, maybe find out who he was.

She heard the crunch of footsteps and looked up. The chopper pilot and medic were coming to help him get into the chopper after they'd carried Nate in.

"One more thing," he whispered. "Get the envelope with the jewelry out of the safe and bring it with you. I'll contact someone to take it, secure it. Meg—if you have second thoughts about this, it's okay. It won't change my mind about you."

"I can do it. I know it's important."

"I won't say 'that's my girl,'" he whispered, "because you're not mine—yet. And you're not a girl but one hell of a woman. I promise I'll get someone to protect the lodge, maybe come in as a guest. I'll set that up as soon as you bring my phone—so don't worry about Suze and Chip, because I've seen she locks up tight at night anyway. I'll tip the guard off to keep an eye on Bill Getz too. But I swear to you, I'll get released soon, be back at the lodge until this is solved. Someone local has to be involved. Hey, I'm feeling better already—tell the Big Man that," he said, but he frowned and grimaced.

"They're hours ahead of us in the East. Office hours are long over."

"He answers day and night."

That stunned and scared her too. But she wasn't taking her promise back.

Keith and Bob also came over to help Bryce up. With the pilot and medic hovering, they walked him toward the chopper. He looked dizzy when he turned to glance at her before he mounted the steps. He was unsteady on his feet. So was she. How had all this happened so fast and with such high stakes—a secret worth killing people for?

Meg knew she was running on pure adrenaline. She backed off to avoid the heavy air wash from the rotors and watched with tears in her eyes as the rescue chopper lifted away. She was going to go back to the lodge on the snowmobiles with Keith and Bob, who had been examined and were patched up but didn't need hospitalization. At the lodge the two men were going to be picked up by yet another state trooper and taken somewhere to be debriefed by someone.

"Let's get going," Bob Morrow told her. "Change of plans. Keith's going to stay here with the other snowmobile until that pilot friend of Bryce's shows up to fly the pontoon plane. He'll stay hidden and he's armed. Let's go. I need to pack up for the team at the lodge, but I hear you're doing that for Bryce."

"Yes, for Bryce." But was she risking herself for a man and a cause she still knew too little about?

Meg only told Suze she was flying to Anchorage with a pilot friend of Bryce's to take his belongings to him for a short hospital stay—and she'd take his envelope out of the safe. Suze was shocked to hear she was going to fly again and to hear what had caused the blast. As much as Suze and Meg had shared over the years, Meg had never told her about that secret flight with Carter. At the time, it had felt too overwhelming to talk about. She'd gone expecting the trip would somehow bring her closure, and when it didn't, she hadn't wanted to put herself in a position where she might have to admit it. What had started as an effort to say good-bye to Ryan had ended up feeling too personal to share with anyone—not even her twin.

"At least they won't be diving in that strange wreck any-more," she said, shaking off the memory.

"Hate to lose paying customers, but it made me nervous to have that dive team around. I'll bet the fact Bryce is re-lying on you means he intends to keep seeing you, even if his work is done here. Want me to go help you pick up his things so Bob can get you back to that plane in time?"

"No, I'll be fine. I got the impression Bryce will be back here to continue the investigation since someone local must be involved. Right now, I have to grab a few things to take myself since I'll be there at least one night. I'll rent a car and drive back or Uber like some of the visitors around here do. Right now, I've got to explain to Chip without really ex-plaining too much."

"Listen to your big sis, now," Suze said, putting her arm around Meg's shoulders. "You just be sure Bryce is not re-ally working for the CIA or FBI or something like that. I mean, the NTSB is one thing, but it's obvious something really dangerous is going on."

"I trust him. I'll be careful. And be back tomorrow one way or the other."

"You're going flying again without me?" Chip protested when she told him she had to fly back to Anchorage. He bounced down hard on his bed, almost tossing her to the floor from her perch on the edge.

"This is just to take Commander Saylor his things, Chip. I said I'll be back soon, tomorrow for sure."

"But the weekend's almost here, so I wouldn't miss much school or anything if I went too. I mean, I want you to help him, but I could too."

"I promise you I will ask him to take you up in his plane when he can."

"Yeah, but what if his hit on the head means he can't fly?" He sighed and seemed to deflate to half his size as he put his feet back on the floor and crossed his arms over his chest. All three dogs at their feet looked intent on his every word.

"When he talked to me he seemed better," she explained, "and the hospital might even help him more. I need you to do what Aunt Suze says while I'm gone, and not to tell anyone, even if they ask, where I am. I'm totally trusting you or I would have told you some story about where I'm going."

He heaved a huge sigh. "He's trusting you, and you're trusting me," he whispered, finally losing his frown. "So that kind of means we are all working together."

"It sure does. I depend on you, and he does too."

"You know what he told me—Commander Saylor?"

"No, what?"

"That he could get me a soccer net for out back and show me how to be a goalie—like defend the net. See, here's the thing, Mom. The goalie is a kind of leader. That means he gets blamed for things if the soccer ball gets past him, but he also gets famous for saving the game. Like in life, there are good things and some bad, but you and me knew that already, right?"

"Right," she whispered as she hugged Chip to her and kissed the top of his head. "That was really nice of him to say he'd bring the net and work with you. I think he likes you."

"Yeah, but he likes you more, which is okay with me, really."

She hugged him again. She loved Chip so much—really.

★ ★ ★

As familiar as Meg was with the rooms at the lodge, as many times as she'd been in them—even cleaning them before they felt they could hire help to do that—it was so strange to be in Bryce's bedroom. She had not known what to expect. It was quite tidy. He had smoothly pulled up the sheet, covers and quilt on the bed. He'd hung the DO NOT CLEAN sign on his door, but he'd asked for fresh sheets and towels.

Clutching the flashlight she'd brought since she knew she'd be peering under the bed, she noted his duffel bag and a few hanging items of clothing in the closet. Nothing just thrown around. The rest of his things were probably in the drawers. She kneeled on the braided rug beside the bed, lifted the quilt coverlet and aimed the light beam under it.

She found his laptop, pulled out the old pair of running shoes and saw the phone pushed down into the toe of one. The recharging cord was in the other.

She pulled everything out. She'd been nervous even unlocking the door to his room, but she was even more shaky now. *Call the pilot first*, she thought. He'd need time to get here from Wasilla—if he was able. If not, she supposed she'd have to drive to Anchorage. She had an instinctive, automatic aversion to the Big Man but had to call him next. People seemed afraid of him, and she didn't like that. She thought it was a bad way for a leader to lead.

She felt reassured when she found Carter's name in the call list. When she touched the number, it rang only twice before someone answered.

"Bryce, you old dive dog! How the hell are you? I heard you're not too far away. Want to come see scenic Wasilla?" The man obviously had caller ID.

"Actually," she said, "I'm a friend of Bryce's too, and he wants you to come to the Falls Lake Lodge to fly his plane to Anchorage. He's in the hospital there. It's Meg Metzler, Carter. Let me explain."

★ ★ ★

That, Meg thought when she got off the phone and had a promise Carter would be here ASAP, was the easy part. She'd trusted Carter with her life before and she wasn't afraid to now.

But she actually felt sick to her stomach when she touched the link that said simply, BIG MAN. Only one ring. A man's voice. He sounded young. "Incident Commander Saylor, hello, sir."

"No, this isn't him. He asked me to make an important call to this number. This is his friend Megan Metzler in Falls Lake, Alaska. He might have a concussion and is being flown to the hospital in Anchorage, the same one where Steve Ralston is. He was conscious, though, and asked me to—"

"Just one moment, ma'am. Please do not say more or disconnect."

So this wasn't direct to the Big Man? She heard murmuring but couldn't catch the words.

"Ms. Metzler, this is Bryce Saylor's administrator." An older voice, calm at least. The man went on, "Since you are calling on Bryce's private line, I'm sure he gave you permission. Tell me what I should know, all of it."

To her surprise, the voice was kind. Deliberate. Steady. Absolutely in control. She might be crazy, but she thought that she recognized it, though she certainly wasn't going to ask or let on. No, she was probably wrong to associate a face—from a newspaper, TV, online—with this voice.

But she was probably crazy to be jumping in with both feet and a trusting heart into what must be some sort of big-time, powers-that-be, deadly danger.

CHAPTER FIFTEEN

Winter darkness enveloped Bryce's plane as it flew into the night toward Anchorage. Bryce had trusted it—and her—to Carter Jones, so she did too, at least that's what she kept telling herself. Besides, Carter, a close friend and mentor of her beloved Ryan, had been with her through a grueling tough time before. She'd trusted his flying abilities before too. A flight and destination she had told no one about and perhaps never would. Well, maybe Chip when he was old enough to understand.

She knew Carter was totally competent. He wore his years well with his silver hair and somehow, in the dead of winter in Alaska, was still very tanned. Who knew that so many men in this area had worked together, and evidently for the government one way or the other, for he'd known not only Ryan, but Bryce.

When he'd asked if she was ready for the copilot's seat yet, she said she'd still like to sit in back. He said he understood.

Of course, he really didn't, but she refused to go into detail again. Because of where he'd taken her before, he no doubt thought she was braver than she was. Besides, they were in a hurry. She was right on the edge of a crying jag, and talking about losing Ryan in a crash would set her off. Carter said the gas gauge showed enough fuel to get them there, and he'd trusted Bryce to have taken care of that. He'd spent a good half hour checking the plane for what he called "blast devices," which didn't seem to faze him. Carter was of that same breed of men as Bryce and his team.

They were in such a hurry that she didn't even have time to ask him about his past work with Bryce, whom he'd called "you old dive dog." She realized that Keith was glad to see them go since he'd spent hours hiding in the trees here, guarding the plane, and had seen nothing. The last thing she had recalled when she'd boarded the plane was that the lake ice had refrozen in rough, broken pieces.

To get through the flight, she sat in the same seat as when they'd transported Steve. Again, she kept her window shade pulled down.

As exhausted as she was, she couldn't sleep. Her mind drifted... How strange it had felt to gather Bryce's clothes from his room at the lodge. He wore plaid boxers, not briefs... His T-shirts smelled outdoorsy, like his hair. It had all seemed such a domestic, intimate thing to open the dresser drawers and pack his clothes.

Into his duffel bag, she'd put his toothbrush—an electric one, same brand as hers—his razor and other masculine items she hadn't seen for almost three years. He'd even hung up the damp towel he must have used in the shower that morning, and his...

She jolted alert. Where was she? Whose voice? Oh, she wasn't in Bryce's room at the lodge...she knew where she was. In an airplane heading for Anchorage again. She'd seldom been there before she met Bryce, and now twice in a few days.

"Hope I didn't startle you," came Carter's voice over the speaker. "Almost there, Meg. Going to begin approach. This is a great plane. Love flying it."

She had slept, had dreamed...that her bath towels and clothes were next to Bryce's. It had been a nice dream—and a good sign. For all her anxiety about flying, she'd managed to fall asleep. That was something. That was progress. And she had a feeling it had something to do with a certain incident commander.

From the airport, they took an Uber to the hospital. She and Carter found a state trooper guarding Bryce's door on the top floor. She had been cleared to enter, but Carter had not.

"That's gratitude for you," Carter muttered with a grin. "But I know the drill. Protocol, privacy, protection. Knowing Bryce from way back, I'm sure you're in good hands now. Gonna get something to eat and rent a car to get home. Tell him he owes me big-time. And," he said, shaking her hand, "take care of him, but yourself too. Things can get sticky in this game, especially for a noncom." He nodded a goodbye and walked down the hall without looking back.

A noncom? She thought that meant a noncommissioned officer in the service. He must be teasing or kidding, for she was not even that. But had he meant it as a warning?

She turned to the trooper who sat outside Bryce's door way down at the end of the hall, far past the nurses' station.

"He was asleep but not now," he told her when she approached. "You can go on in."

He opened the door for her. Clutching Bryce's duffel bag, suddenly trembling, she entered his room, uncertain what she would see. She felt she was walking through a door to a whole new life, not only growing closer to him but becoming part of a team on a key quest she knew next to nothing about.

★ ★ ★

Meg looked nervous and tired to Bryce, but so damn good. He'd been scolding himself for getting her even more involved, but he needed her in more ways than one. This enigma of a once simple dive-and-recover assignment was getting darker and more demanding by the hour. Steve and Nate injured. He and his team targeted for death in an underwater explosion. By who and over what?

He reached out his hand that didn't have stitches and bandages. She took it, and he tugged her closer for a quick kiss, then down so she sat on the edge of his bed.

"We can do better than that—and we will," he whispered. "In a better setting too."

She nodded and blinked back tears. "I'm glad to hear that—that you're still yourself, I mean. Yes, we must stop meeting like this in such a private, romantic setting."

"Darn right. Meg, it means a lot to me that you came, that you're helping me when you could have said I should take a flying leap. I've still got that buzzing in my ears that you didn't set off this time. I promise you, payback will be extensive once I get the heck out of here one way or the other and soon. Now, you obviously talked to Carter. Great guy, but sadly, he doesn't have clearance anymore."

"Neither do I, though. He called me a noncom."

"Just think of that as noncombat instead of noncommissioned. But necessity—and desperation—is the mother of invention, and that's where I'm at. At least they've told me Nate is going to recover well, but I'm still worried about Steve. How did it go with the Big Man?"

"I told him about a possible missing treasure. He said that could be used for good or bad, and that he—and you—were trying to find and stop the bad. Also, he mentioned he'd send a guard to stay at the lodge ASAP because he knew you'd ask for that. He said to tell you the man would pose as a photographer-writer working on a book called *Wild Winter Alaska*."

"Great title for my life in general lately. Okay, yeah, I know the guy he's sending us. Rafe Coffman. He's a good guy. I'll fill you in on him later."

"When I told him you had suggested a security guard for me, he said I should stay in your hospital room all night and the guard on the door would do because he wanted to keep the lid on things until the dead pilot is ID'd and traced. He is going to have a sketch of the man released to the media, because he felt he couldn't keep it secret much longer—and he is desperate to know who and why. The Big Man figures someone will turn up who knows the man, maybe throw light on who he was supposed to meet, et cetera."

"He says 'et cetera' a lot, and it's usually because he doesn't want to actually say more. I'll call him to let him know you're here and tell him I'm not staying in this place long, I don't care what they say. I owe him for asking you to stay here. I owe you too, Meg. Seriously. I can't thank you enough for all you've done. I know you already have plenty on your plate with the lodge and Chip. Being a single mother can't be easy, even if you and Suze make such a great team. So, thank you. I truly couldn't do this without you."

Meg could feel her cheeks warm as she smiled at him. "I wouldn't be helping if I didn't think it was important—if I didn't think you were important."

Bryce met her smile with a grin of his own. "I appreciate that and I hate to ask another favor of you, Meg, but Steve is now in a medically induced coma, and they won't let Jenny or Mark in to see me, so I was hoping, if you could call his room and meet her out there in the hall, maybe you could help her. I know you understand some of what she's going through."

She realized they had been holding hands all this time.

Nodding, she squeezed his. "Yes, I'll try to comfort her—if anyone can right now."

She tugged her hand back and pulled up the only chair in the room to sit close to his bed. "Do you want me to unpack your duffel bag?" she asked, dipping in it to retrieve his cell phone.

"Just my razor because I would feel guilty if I scratched up your face with this stubble." He winked at her. "Then I'll order us something to eat. First, got to call the Big Man, give him my own update." He reached for his phone. Their fingers touched as she handed it to him.

"Bryce, his voice sounded familiar."

He quirked a brow. "Familiar how?"

Meg shrugged. "Just the sound of his voice. The way he spoke. The expressions he used, you know, 'et cetera.'"

"I'm currently in no position to confirm nor deny," Bryce said with a sly smile that made her even more certain she had recognized the voice. In fact, she could think of a certain political figure whose speeches on TV sounded an awful lot like the Big Man Bryce reported to.

Her stomach cartwheeled and not only because she was in this so deep. Surely this assignment of Bryce's was not just about recovering a body or even now about lost Civil War treasure. Something else must be going on, something big.

Meg ate a late supper with Bryce in his room—a far cry from the steak dinner date he'd promised her in Anchorage, she teased him. Yet she ate a lot. Physical exertion? Nerves? Bryce was allowed to check off anything on the menu list. He'd doubled up on things and they'd even split some dishes. He said he'd take a nap until she got back, and she was to send his best wishes to Steve's family.

She went to the guest area on Steve's floor to meet with

Jenny. Mark, she'd said on the phone, was insisting on staying with his dad though he had not woken up yet.

Meg hardly knew Jenny, but they hugged and sat facing each other in a corner of the waiting room like old friends. Meg realized she must look bad with no makeup and messy hair, but the poor woman looked as if she'd aged ten years since she'd seen her a few days ago.

After Meg told Jenny that Bryce was fighting having to rest for several days under "concussion protocol," Jenny blurted, "Someone's desperate to try to hurt—kill—all of them. Out to stop anyone who goes near that sunken plane. It's like a curse!"

"A curse that's been obliterated now," she told Jenny and explained about the explosives and that another team member, Nate Young, was recovering in this same hospital.

"His poor family. But since you're visiting Bryce, thanks for taking time to see me. I'm scared to death I'll lose Steve—or he won't be the same when he—when he wakes up. He's in a drug-induced coma now for who knows how long?"

"I understand your anxiety and anguish, really. I've been through something terrible like this, only my son and I didn't have even a chance to see my husband, Ryan, fight for his life. I'm a widow. A fatal plane crash, on our boy's birthday. Sorry to spill all that on you, and I'm sure your story will not be the same—and will have a happy ending—but just wanted you to know why I do understand."

She nodded and sniffed back tears. No doubt, she'd already cried herself dry. She reached for Meg's hands, and they held on to each other.

Jenny whispered, "There's something dark and awful about this assignment—about that plane. Steve and Bryce have worked together before, some secret stuff, but nothing like this. I hate to think of it this way, but at least Steve—and that other injured man, Nate—are out of evil's path now.

I just hope you can convince Bryce not to get back into it. You know, as much as I love Steve, as much as Mark looks up to him and needs him, I wish I'd married a car dealer— a banker, a baker—you know what I mean."

"Yes, I do," Meg told her. "More and more I really do. Love's a risk, but you can't help loving a man who helps and protects others."

"Scary but true," Jenny whispered. "So you and Bryce— what about you?"

"Too early to tell. As you can imagine, nothing has been normal or calm around him yet. I'm hoping."

"You'd think I'd be good at that by now—waiting and hoping he comes back, that he's okay, that he's not heading off to someplace he can't tell me about, though I knew about the Falls Lake assignment and figured that would be like a walk in the park. Stupid me."

Meg could only hope, if she kept close to Bryce—which maybe for her and Chip's sake, she should not—that would not be her story too.

CHAPTER SIXTEEN

After Meg returned from seeing Jenny, and Bryce had woken up from his nap, she ducked into the bathroom attached to his room while he called the Big Man. She had closed the door, but when she wasn't running the water, she could hear what Bryce was saying, especially when he raised his voice.

"What do you mean, don't go off script? There is no script on this case, so I can't read it even between the lines!" A pause. His voice level dropped. "Yeah, I know. Actually, I'd like her clear of this, but she's valuable to me. Yes, it's partly personal, but you understand that. Your wife is a great support to you, even in official business, on foreign trips… Right, right. No, I realize that's completely different from a woman I met recently, but I feel I know and trust her. Come on, the soft side of you—if it's still there—understands that."

Though she was ashamed of herself for eavesdropping, she held her breath and pressed her ear to the door.

After a pause, Bryce went on, "I'm telling you, the best thing you can do for me and this case is get me out of here. I don't have a concussion—had that twice before, and this isn't it. The ringing in my ears comes and goes, and the doctor thinks it will lessen in the near future. Out of here tomorrow morning at least, sir. For me. For this mess. Acoustically detonated bomb in little Falls Lake, Alaska? Somebody skilled, with money and bad plans, is in this, and I need to find out who."

More silence. Should she stay here or go back out?

"Okay, here's my advice on that," came Bryce's voice again. "I agree the pilot's face—in a sketch—should be released. But if that brings an onslaught of media to the sight of the crash, one look and they won't believe that a single plane went down. The explosion shattered the ice for the width of a football field. Then the questions would be, what happened here? Why? What divers barely escaped? They'd say they need to talk to them. Sir, the detective work on this needs to be done there, quietly if possible, to ferret out who was waiting for an unmarked plane to land with that historic treasure haul."

More silence. What he'd just said was right, but it scared her. Another horde of reporters. The lodge besieged. She couldn't stand that.

"Good idea, let's have the state troopers cordon off the entrance to the site. The more security around there, the better. Rafe and I can field questions at the lodge if the media invasion hits there. Glad the article won't mention that Meg Metzler and her son saw the crash."

Meg sucked in a deep breath and wilted in relief against the bathroom door. All she needed was Chip giving interviews and both of them being hounded. At least this partial release to the media would save poor Jenny from having to answer questions about what happened to Steve. Bryce was right: just release a drawing of the dead pilot and mention a crash in Alaska in the hope someone would come forward with an identification and explanation.

"Rafe's doing the sketch of the corpse?" Bryce was saying. "Yeah, I knew he draws as well as photographs, and the fewer people in on this now the better. His pictures always look like art shots anyway. Thanks for sending him to the lodge. Is Rafe Coffman the name he'll be using? Oh, yeah, sure, his publishing name. Okay. Got all that. Sir, I repeat, please pull strings to get me out of here. And has anyone opened those two boxes from the plane yet? They were big and heavy."

Another pause. "Yeah, I can understand why it takes time. Forensic experts want the contents hermetically sealed? Like what contents? Gold coins and papers with donors' names? More jewelry?" A moment of quiet, then, "That much? Depending on who it all legally belongs to, that could help solve the national debt. And I'd sure like to see those photographs."

So her initial research about jewelry for the cause had been right, Meg realized. She dared not ask, at least right now, or Bryce might suspect she'd overheard, but later, maybe she could just work it into a conversation.

Not certain if he was done talking, she used and flushed the toilet, then ran water a long time to wash her hands at the sink. When she went out, Bryce was out of bed, readjusting his printed cotton gown, which tied in back. His legs from his knees down protruded. She had to stifle a smile at the sight.

"My turn in there," he said. He walked past her at a good clip, holding the gown together in back. "Here we are," he said over his shoulder, "sharing the same lovely room, same bathroom. Again, I promise you better someday. Tell you some of what the Big Man said in a couple of minutes."

He went in and closed the door.

While Bryce was in the bathroom—she could hear he was taking a shower—Meg called Suze and talked to her, then to Chip. The trooper on the door, a different one from earlier, knocked and asked if everything was okay, said that he'd be there all night in case Commander Saylor needed anything.

His hair still wet, Bryce emerged in jeans and a T-shirt she recognized as ones she'd brought him. Hospital scuffs barely covered his big bare feet. He sat on the plastic-looking couch next to where she'd parked herself and her bag earlier.

"There's a new trooper on the door," she told him. "Just ask for anything you want."

He grinned. "The trooper said anything I want, or are you adding that?"

She punched his arm. Surely he wasn't thinking of making a move in here? But she saw him immediately shift to all-business mode. She hoped he was going to tell her what was in the two big boxes from the plane.

"Let me tell you a little about the photographer-author who will be at the lodge when we get back late tomorrow."

"Oh, you're definitely getting released?"

"Bet on it. Otherwise, I'll have to make a break for it. So anyway, Rafe Coffman has worked for the NTSB as a consultant, not full-time. The photographer-author career is not a cover. He really is all that, very talented. Travels a lot but is supposedly coming to stay at the lodge while he works on his new book on Alaska. But don't let his arty pursuits fool you. I've only worked with him once before, and he's tough. Tough and smart."

"It takes one to know one."

"Sweetheart, I'm not sorry we met and got thrown together, but I'm sorry it had to be like this." He took her hand in his unbandaged one. She saw he'd covered his injured hand with a plastic sack for his shower and had forgotten to take it off. Shaking his head, he pulled it off and tossed it aside.

He went on, "At times I think I should stay as far away from you as I can for safety's sake, but Rafe and I can watch the lodge for trouble, including that weird Bill Getz and maybe even the mayor and his antique jewelry store contact, Melissa, you told me about over our elegant dinner tonight. It's obvious someone local must have been waiting for the cargo on that plane. I think the crash was probably not some sort of sabotage but a malfunction or pilot error—but that's only a guess at this point."

"I thought about Melissa being the recipient or at least the keeper of the jewelry part of the cargo, but that's a long shot," she admitted. "And the mayor? I can't think how or why. In Falls Lake, he's a big man—pardon that description—but surely not in the East or the South of the US, wherever that jewelry has been for decades, even centuries."

"Since the engine and mechanics of the plane may not have been damaged in the crash landing, we could have checked things when the plane was hauled up in the spring. Maybe the engine acted up and the poor guy couldn't handle a decent skid landing on the ice, but now we may never know. But we may know the pilot's identity soon since they have his DNA and are going to finally publicize the crash in the media with Rafe's sketch of his face. We're trying to keep swarms of media from the lodge until we can investigate locally more, so there won't be a lot of info like that in the article. I'd love to know who, besides White Blanket John Doe, was waiting for that plane."

"That murder we had near the lodge last summer—we've been there, done that with being swarmed by media."

He tightened his hand on hers. "So here's hoping for some quiet, sane, personal, safe time for you and me that's not in a hospital room."

"Sounds good."

"Before we head back tomorrow, let's do two things. I need to check in at the regional office of the NTSB here. Then let's catch dinner at a decent place. Filet mignon for the lady. And some time where I can watch you in softer lights, and we can talk about the real us."

She nodded, amazed her voice came out so softly. "All right, Commander."

He smiled, then tugged her close. She thought he meant for it to be a quick good-night kiss, but it went on, deeper, his tongue dancing with hers. So intimate, so stunning. The way she felt with him, even here, they could have been at a café table in Paris or in the heat of the Caribbean, for she was flying high.

The intensity of her reaction scared her as they slowly broke the kiss.

"And to all a good night," he whispered. "Right now, 'Thus do all things conspire against us.' But I swear to you, I—maybe we—are going to change all that."

"Promises, promises," she said, trying to lighten his mood. "Did you get that quote from the Big Man?"

"No, the Big Man isn't nearly as wise as I am." He winked, then got up with a quick caress of her cheek. "And speaking of wise things, I need to get some sleep and you do too. The nurses will be popping in soon to read my vitals and give me a couple of meds. I have their entries—their intrusions—timed."

He headed for his bed, stripped off his shirt and got in with his jeans on. "They'll probably have a fit that I'm dressed in civic clothes. But I'm taking my shirt off so they can get to my chest and arms for all their diabolical deeds. You know, the doctor was hopefully right, because the buzz in my ears isn't as constant or as loud."

"Maybe I'm your good luck charm."

"Good medicine, that's what you are. Try to sleep. A lot lies ahead professionally—and personally."

As she flapped open the blanket she was going to sleep

under on the couch, she realized that was one of the most
hopeful and romantic things he had ever said.

Meg sat in the reception room at the National Transportation Safety Board regional offices while Bryce had a meeting. While waiting, she picked up an informational pamphlet
evidently meant for the media or employment seekers. A
fierce-looking eagle was the emblem on the NTSB logo.
If requested, the agency could assist the American military
and foreign governments. She read that the NTSB was an
independent US government investigative agency, empha-
sis on *independent*, existing outside the Executive Office of
the President.

Or it was supposed to, she thought, shaking her head but
reading on. Career paths in the NTSB included disaster as-
sistance specialists and aviation accident investigators. She
wondered if Incident Commander Bryce Saylor was technically either of those.

She tried to mentally sift through all she knew about
this case. Proud she had helped him with it, she considered
what he'd said about suspecting someone local, namely Bill
Getz but also Melissa McKee and even Falls Lake's illustrious mayor Rand Purvis. Obviously, Bryce had been trained
to look at everyone as a possible perp. But if those last two
were suspect, he might as well be looking at Steve's pretend
extraterrestrials, even Chip or her.

She watched the clock on the wall and wished she had
gotten more sleep. Bryce had slept as if he had not a care
in the world. She had listened to his steady breathing—at
least he didn't snore, even sleeping on his back—and wished
her mind would let her body sleep. As he'd said, the nurses
kept coming in. Finally, she had slept but plodded through
dreams. Not nightmares, at least, for she'd had enough of

those lately while awake. Was Bryce her dream man, her second time around love?

She jolted when she heard his voice close. "Megan Metzler, may I have the honor of this dance?" he asked, looking so intense, standing over her in the reception room, where she must have dozed off. "Or if not, let's just grab a good steak dinner on the way home."

Home. He'd said *home*—only a figure of speech, of course.

"I'd be honored. And I'm hungry," she told him, rising and taking his proffered arm as they went out.

But that fierce eagle armed with weapons in both talons frowned down on them as they left.

Bryce knew a good restaurant nearby. She wondered if he'd been there with other women. At least he'd had such a busy life that he'd not been married, or so she assumed. Had she assumed too much?

He let her do the driving of the rental car because it hurt him to steer with his cut hand, and he didn't want to drive one-handed in ice and snow. She was glad to help again, but he was an exacting navigator. She wished she'd packed a dress or better shoes for the restaurant, but people dressed very casual these days. What mattered was who she was with.

"We'd better skip wine and drinks 'til next time," he told her as they looked over their menus. "You're driving, and I'd better stay on the wagon until this headache and ear buzz is really a thing of the past."

"You didn't tell them you still had a headache. I heard you imply that you were fine."

"I am fine. Please don't turn me in. At least I feel fine eating here with you, but when we get back I won't be fine. I'm going to be a hell-bent maniac to solve this plane wreck and explosions that could have been multiple murders, not to mention grand theft on a historic scale. Now, I promised myself we wouldn't talk business for an hour except for one thing."

He stopped talking each time their server appeared. Meg stuck with coffee too and tried not to fill up on the delicious hot bread that came right away.

"So before business is completely off the table," he went on as they attacked their Caesar salads, "let me fill you in a bit more about Rafe. His real first name is Raphael. He's half Italian, lived all over the world for his NTSB and creative work. Those great oil paintings your sister did for the lodge walls—he'll appreciate those."

"Does he have a family with all that moving around?"

"Is he married, do you mean?"

"No, that's not what I mean—well, maybe a little."

"No, he's not married, and I plead guilty to the same."

Meg had to laugh, nearly choking on a crouton.

"Hey, careful," he said.

"Oh, I've given up on being careful." She took a drink of water. "I'm with you."

"I deserve that. I was almost married once to the supposed girl of my dreams, but it didn't work out. The dream could have turned to a nightmare. I see now it was for the best."

"Because she would not have been happy you were gone so much—and on dangerous duty?"

"Because then the two of us—you and me—wouldn't have been a possibility. I want you to know, since you've seen up close and personal how damned dangerous my line of work can be, that you can opt out of it, and of me, if you want, at any time, though I'd fight hard not to let that happen."

"Hard to opt out now. I feel—involved."

"I've weighed decamping to somewhere else nearby the lodge but I think it will be better guarded if I'm there— Rafe now too."

"No, I mean hard to do now since I've come to—to care

for you. I'm grateful you've been so good to Chip—promising soccer lessons and all that."

"There is a net, metal frame and two soccer balls en route to the lodge, via Amazon. I just hope we can clear enough snow off that back patio and lawn—and that Rafe can watch those woods while I teach Chip a few things. In better weather, better times..."

He put his fork down and reached across the table to gently clasp her wrist. "Meg, my feelings for you—I think some mutual—complicate things, but we can find time to be together. You've seen the stakes are high, but anything worth having and keeping and treasuring is obviously worth fighting for. I just don't want anyone at the lodge to get hurt, so forgive me if I get pushy."

"I can be that way—push back too."

"I see our food's coming," he told her, loosing her wrist and sitting back. "And, I hope, a lot more is coming than that for us, sweetheart."

He'd called her that at least three times, and it touched her, thrilled her.

"No problem with who gets what," their server said, "since you both want the same. I'm sure you will love it."

"I'm sure we will," Bryce said and winked at Meg.

Once again, she could have flown.

CHAPTER SEVENTEEN

It was like old home week at the lodge for Bryce, when they got in around nine that Friday evening. Since Chip had no school tomorrow, he was still up to greet them. He hugged not only Meg but Bryce, which really touched him. Suze was beaming to have them all back. Or maybe that smile was on her face partly because she'd just checked Rafe into the lodge and had seen all his art and photo equipment coming in the door—another artist.

Rafe high-fived Bryce, and he introduced him all around as a friend who was here to work on his book. Bryce had kidded Rafe more than once that he looked like Superman in disguise: Clark Kent with dark-rimmed glasses but one hell of a physique, a man living an arty life on the outside who could also explode in physical confrontations if needed.

"Bryce recommended this place as great—scenic," Rafe said with a big smile Suze's way. "I may even do some ice or snow sculptures outside to include in my photos if that's all right. The working title for the book is *Wild Winter Alaska.*"

"It's been that way around here for sure," Suze said.

"Hopefully, things will calm down between now and Christmas."

Don't bet on it, Bryce thought. Despite his worries about this case, he wouldn't mind staying here over the holidays. Or maybe he could talk Meg—Chip too, of course—into visiting his home in Juneau.

But he knew to kiss such dreams goodbye unless he could find who was behind this—in more ways than one—historic heist. As soon as the morning news hit tomorrow, he was hoping Rafe's sketch of the dead pilot would pay off with new information to get this case jolted to life again.

He noted Bill Getz, with a stack of magazines in his hands, was leaning against the wall, just watching and listening.

Bryce sat in Rafe's room later that evening while his friend unpacked. He filled Rafe in about his plans to investigate several local individuals, like Bill Getz for one, since he had no idea how else to proceed unless Rafe's sketch of the dead pilot helped identify him.

"The Big Man didn't want me to keep the original drawing," Rafe told Bryce. "He wanted it, so I faxed it to him and destroyed my copy as ordered. However, I still have the prelim sketch I did first," he added with a tight grin. "Got to keep some souvenir from spending a half hour drawing a corpse in the morgue."

"We all break the Big Man's rules, don't we?"

"That's the name of the game. That's the way of it in DC anyway."

"If the Big Man was FBI, he could put the pilot's face on a post office Wanted poster. Not exactly wanted but wanted to be ID'd."

Rafe finally quit rummaging around in the canvas case that held his work supplies. He fished out a folded piece of paper he handed to Bryce.

"Suzanne said I could use her studio area to store things, that there's an extra table there too," Rafe said. "She's shy about letting me see what she's been working on, but I can tell from her oil paintings on the walls in the common room that she's talented. So Meg's her younger sister and a widow?"

"They're actually twins, but you're right," Bryce said, opening the folded paper. "And the first woman in a long time I've felt serious about, despite all that's going on."

Bryce glanced down at the sketch. "Yeah, that's him. Him without that death stare and not coated with ice. Rafe, he was frozen down there with both hands raised as if—as if..."

"Praying or asking a question? Like how did this happen to me?"

"I was thinking," Bryce said, still staring at the very good sketch, "it was like he was conducting an orchestra. Or like he was the victim in a robbery with his hands up."

"Yeah, a robbery of his plane and life. But it's doubtful he's a thief of that treasure. As for looking like he was asking questions—more like he was the one who we wish could answer them."

Saturday morning, Bryce drove a snowmobile into town to get an Anchorage newspaper at the lone coffee shop, though Josh always brought several papers to the lodge later when he came to work. He just couldn't wait to get going on what he hoped was a new phase of this case.

And he hoped that included somehow casing Bill Getz's place, because the guy was really getting on his nerves, though he'd be a too-blatant, obvious spy. Maybe the eccentric loner was just curious, living his life through other people's things and events. Bryce knew he couldn't just slam him into the wall and demand answers like he wanted to next time he saw him lurking and staring. He might learn something but also give too much away. No, he had to see what the guy had in his own house, even if he had to break and enter. He'd had permission to do that before in a dangerous case and probably needed it now again.

The coffee shop turned out to be a restaurant too. It was warm inside with the buzz of conversation and mingled aromas of coffee and bacon. But then he'd had both this morning, served by the woman he wanted.

When he saw some locals sitting in a row at the counter, he realized he'd missed a good place to get information earlier. But then it would probably have looked suspicious if he'd started leaving the lodge to hang out here. Besides, he'd been busy diving.

Mayor Purvis sat at the stool dead center, which might as well have had his name on it. He was taller than the other customers and better dressed.

"Our favorite winter scuba diver!" Purvis called out, swinging around on his stool but not getting up. "Bet you're checking the newspaper. The med examiner in Anchorage finally got a picture of the dead pilot, or at least a likeness. And, hell, we all know who he is—was. I was gonna come out to the lodge and tell you in person after breakfast."

Bryce came to attention almost as if he was waiting for orders. "The pilot's a Falls Lake local? One nobody noticed was missing all this time?"

"He lives—lived—out in the boondocks of the boondocks," the mayor said, seeming to love being the center of attention and importance even here. Everyone had quieted and hung on his every word, but then, Bryce did too.

"Yeah," he went on, "lived partway between here and Wasilla, on a back road not too well marked, name of Spruce Road, I think. It twists around a big foothill where the big lumber trucks go in and out and flatten the snow."

Several guys around him nodded or verbally backed him

up. He paused, which annoyed Bryce. It was as if the man wanted applause.

He finally said, "The dead pilot is Lloyd Witlow, owns the LL Lumber and Sawmill Company on that same road. Older fella. Didn't know him all that well. Had no idea he had or could fly a plane. Did you, boys?"

Shakes of heads and murmured agreements all around.

Damn, Bryce thought. A whole new path was opening up already. But a guy who owned a backwoods lumber mill was flying historical treasures around? Items so precious they were now being studied and preserved by Washington, DC, forensic experts who were keeping them hermetically sealed so they wouldn't be damaged?

"Thanks for the information, Mayor Purvis," Bryce managed to get out without clenching his teeth. He did not like or trust this guy, now more than ever. He'd probably been planning to tell Bryce later or to go around him in general, maybe let the troopers know, but this bunch of townies had already been discussing it over coffee, eggs and doughnuts.

Trying to calm himself, he paid for the paper and went back outside. He had to call the Big Man. And he had to ask Suze if he could rent her old truck that had tire chains to make it through the snow. For someone to say a place where a suspect had lived was out in the boondocks when Falls Lake was out in the boondocks really sobered him. It didn't sound easy to find, but he needed to head for LL Lumber, wherever it was in this snowy wilderness. And Witlow's house was on the same road. Why hadn't someone reported him missing?

"Bryce," Meg said when she'd heard his plans and knew Suze had said he could borrow her truck, "I've never noticed Spruce Road, and I've been back and forth to Wasilla many times. It must not be marked, though I think I've seen a lumber mill sign along there somewhere, so I know approximately where the turnoff would be. Wasilla used to have visitors when its most famous resident, Sarah Palin, was running for vice president, but not many outsiders go there anymore, I bet. How about I just ride along with you?"

"Whoa," he told her. He'd already filled Rafe in and asked him to stay there to guard the lodge. "Not a good idea."

"I think I know something about this guy's background. I mean, not about flying planes, but I'm pretty sure he had a daughter who ran away more than once and then left the area. I think she's the one Grandma told us hitchhiked to Falls Lake rather than running away to Wasilla where her dad would easily find her. Grandma took her in for a night until she got someone to come pick her up. If I recall right, the girl—she must have been only in high school then and I can't think of her name—claimed she was fleeing an abusive family situation."

"You know any more about the family?"

"No, but that lumber mill is where we got the paneling to update the entryway here. Suze might know more. I'm pretty sure Grandma said the girl's mother was deceased."

"If the daughter was and maybe still is estranged from her father, that might be why she didn't report him missing. But why didn't his workers at the mill?"

"I think Grandma said she left the state. To where I don't know—it was all hearsay. Bryce, I should go with you. I do pass for an Alaskan around here now, and that might get you better answers at the mill than some 'outsider' they wouldn't trust. I'll go ask Suze if she remembers more of what Grandma said and tell her I'm going to ride along with you. Be right back."

As she darted off before Bryce could stop her, he realized he'd just been bulldozed—*handled*, as the Big Man would say. But he saw now how important this case had become to her too. She'd looked in the dead man's face, she'd dragged his body to the surface. And, he'd like to think, she just wanted to help him too.

★ ★ ★

Bryce, who almost always felt in control, was still amazed at how in control Meg seemed as the two of them set off in Suze's truck in a light snow. For sure he could use her help. He supposed he could have just phoned the lumberyard and asked to speak to the supervisor. Why in hell hadn't someone reported Lloyd Witlow missing? He had to find out, and it was better to be there in person, and—he had to admit—to have a local person with him.

He had taken time to tell Rafe to keep an eye on Bill Getz and explained why. "A hoarder?" Rafe had asked. "I spotted that guy as a possible kleptomaniac the minute he asked me if I had any sketches I didn't want and kept watching me. Any sketches? There's no way he could have known I'm the one who drew the pic of the dead pilot. But who knows what he knows, right? You're thinking he's a plant—a spy?"

"Remains to be seen, like too damn much in this investigation."

CHAPTER EIGHTEEN

Meg and Bryce heard the sharp whine of the lumber mill before they saw it. He drove while Meg sat forward, straining her seat belt, to watch the snow-covered road ahead.

"At least the turnoff was where I thought it would be," she said. Snow, already jammed down by heavy trucks, crunched under the tires and rattling chains on the rutted road. "I just hope we don't meet a loaded truck coming out and have to back up. Thankfully, there's room to pull to the side in places, if we do need to get out of someone's way."

"I wish everything would get out of my way right now. Even with my sunglasses, the glare's hurting my eyes. Good, there it is. Crazy to have it so far off the main road."

"Somebody probably owned this land way back when, surrounded by heavy forests. Maybe Lloyd Witlow or his family."

They pulled into a small plowed parking lot at the near end of the building. Although it had evidently been bulldozed, it was being slowly covered by snow again. Piles of it hunkered around the edges, making Meg feel closed in. The long, rambling sawmill seemed to go on forever, but they could see a sign that read OFFICE on this end of the building. The buzzing sound of saws increased as they got out. The smell of sawdust was in the air, and she felt tension hovering too.

Bryce took her arm, and they walked carefully toward the office. LL LUMBER was painted on an old sign, then under that in slightly smaller letters, L WITLOCK, Owner.

Meg said, "Actually, this place is not that far from Falls Lake, as the crow flies."

"Or as an unmarked plane flies. But, the eternal question—why?"

The whole place seemed so rough, and—well, masculine—that Meg was surprised to see a woman at the desk inside. On the wall were lists of men's names with boxes to check off their in-and-out times. The sign over that said SWAMPERS. Strange.

Some old black-and-white photographs were framed on the wall, scenes of the old days cutting trees, of floating logs down a river, even one of rock being blasted away to bring down the trees with them, so they could be harvested.

"Can't believe we have visitors way out here this time of year," the woman said, getting up to stand on the other side of the wooden counter and introducing herself as Margot Lane. She was probably in her late fifties or sixties with streaked gray hair pulled back in a ponytail and large, dark-rimmed glasses. She wore a ski vest over a plaid shirt. Her desk had piles of papers pierced by spikes to keep them in place. Meg saw no laptop or computers anywhere.

"Need to place an order?" Ms. Lane asked. "Gotta admit we don't have a website yet, but we're getting one. Hard to teach an old dog new tricks—well, mostly. We got the best Sitka spruce and cedar around."

"I'm Bryce Saylor, and I work for the National Transportation Safety Board." He extended his hand, which the woman shook. "This is my associate, Megan Metzler."

"We do something wrong with our delivery trucks? Our drivers know the ropes, been with us for years." The phone rang. "Let me just answer this," she said, "get their number, call them back. If it's an order, we could use it."

She answered the phone, listened, then sank into her chair with her forehead in her other hand. Even while listening to the speaker, she looked up at them and frowned. "Are they sure?" she asked. "I got folks here right now from a transportation board. I told him not to take that up at his age."

Meg shot a look at Bryce, who frowned but didn't so much as blink. Could it be these people really didn't know their boss had been missing for days? And had only now learned that he was dead?

"Yes, thanks for the news, Louise, tragic as it is. I'll spread the word. It'll be a shock. Can't believe it."

She punched off the phone and stared at a calendar on the wall. "He died Thanksgiving Day," she said in a monotone. Bryce didn't move, but Meg wondered if she should try to console the woman. "Is it true? He crashed?"

Meg touched Bryce's elbow to keep him there, but went around the counter. "Yes, we're so sorry. He crashed through the ice, and his body had to be retrieved from the bottom of the lake. He didn't have identification on him, nor was the plane marked. Once he was finally identified, we were amazed no one had reported him missing." Meg squatted beside her chair, putting her hand on the woman's arm.

"He—he just took up flying last year. In a big hurry too. Always wanted to, he said. I seem to recall he said he had a customer—didn't say who—bought him a plane and helped pay for his lessons. Seemed strange to me. I don't know, maybe helped pay for his little airstrip too."

"Do you know who gave him the flying lessons?" Bryce asked, leaning on the counter.

The woman shook her head, still looking more dazed than grieved. She went on, almost as if talking to herself. "I bet the donor spent a fortune, getting a small runway laid out back of his house—down thataway, not far," she added with a nod toward the mill itself. "He took two weeks off, like a long Thanksgiving holiday, instead of at Christmastime, he said. Our foreman, Rencie, knows the ropes, so he didn't worry when Lloyd put him in charge and didn't call in. He musta been taking a joy ride, then something went wrong. Bet that wayward daughter of his who lives somewhere in the Midwest doesn't know. And bet she won't want this place or his house."

She was crying now. Meg snatched a tissue from the box on the desk and handed it to her. She blew her nose.

Bryce said, "Sorry for your loss, and we hate to ask a favor right now, but we need Lloyd's daughter's address so that she can be properly notified. Do you know how we can contact her?"

She shook her head but reached for a small console on the desk and pushed a button. "Clarence might—he goes by Rencie. Foreman here for years, keeping an eye on all the swampers. I'll get him in here, see if he knows that ungrateful woman's name. Hated her father, hated Alaska."

A man's voice on the console: "Got a problem or a customer?"

"Need you to come in here, Rencie. Need you to come in here now."

Rencie was over six feet tall and looked like a real bruiser, Bryce thought. He wore old-fashioned overalls and had a set of serious-looking earplugs hanging around his neck. He took the news about his long-time boss's death really hard, punching the wall.

"Damn stupid idea to learn flying! Too many mountains round here, and he liked to fly low to see the trees."

Bryce saw Meg nod, maybe thinking again of her husband. She'd done so well so far today, strong, compassionate. He really would like her as an associate—and more.

"I'm sure the news would have come to you soon, but the pilot and the plane had no identification," Bryce explained. "How long has he been flying that he didn't have his plane marked?"

"Don't exactly know 'cause he didn't tell me 'til he was pretty into it. Only saw the thing close up once, then always at a distance, and he flew when I was watching things here. Kept it in a big old equipment shed out back at night."

"We really need to notify his daughter, however estranged they were. Would you know how to find her contact information for us or at least know her name?"

The big guy swiped tears from under his eyes, leaving gray streaks. "Sure do. Yeah, name's Rina. She's married now, that's all I know. Well, that and they live in Michigan or Ohio, I think. You know, that's one good thing," he with a sniff. "Lloyd was a real private man, but I got the idea he was softening toward her lately—or maybe the other way round. Not sure they buried the hatchet, though. Nothing in his office about her, I think, but I got the key to his house and maybe can find something there."

"We'd really appreciate it," Bryce said. "His place is on this same road, right? Can we drive there?"

"You don't mind a little hike in the snow, we can walk," Rencie said, wiping under his nose with his index finger. "Just on the far end of this property, never bothered him to be this close, noise and all. Don't want to tell the swampers yet, but we'll walk through the mill. Man, I hope him and his girl made up some before he died. 'Specially if she inherits this place now, probably would want to modern it all up—or just sell it."

Bryce wanted to ask why lumber mill workers were called swampers, but that could wait. He felt they were about to get some answers at last. This mess had to unravel, and he was going to pull any string of information he found.

Rencie let Meg wear his earplugs that looked like headphones as they walked through the mill. Still, she could hear the scream of the saws as tree trunks were debarked, then went down conveyor belts to be cut to size. Sawdust made her sneeze. It almost made her dizzy that entire trunks kept moving past, moving past. The various workers didn't even look their way. Rencie said they were called swampers for the logging camp men who used to wade through streams and standing water to transport tree trunks by floating them toward their destination, the more rudimentary mills of the time. She smelled cedar, but Rencie shouted to them it was mostly Sitka spruce being cut today.

She'd have to tell Chip about this, maybe bring him here in warm weather, or it could be part of his class's field trip. Someday he'd go to high school in Wasilla. On her walks with him, they'd seen deer, elk, bear and hares eat the cones that fell from spruce trees, and bald eagles roosted in their branches. Yet here they were cut down and cut apart. And, Rencie had said, sometimes blasted free from rocky soil with detonated charges.

She breathed easier outside when they emerged from the end of the mill under the open sky with the light snow still falling. Rencie pointed ahead at a wooden bungalow. As they walked through a lot with huge parked machinery, she was tempted to take Bryce's hand, but thought better of it.

When they passed under huge, crane-like machines that

dangled what looked like giant claws, her heartbeat kicked up. Silly, but she recalled her childhood nightmares of monsters with massive jaws chasing her. She'd wake up screaming until Suze, in the next bed, comforted her. She didn't believe in omens or signs, but that bothered her as they neared the dead man's gray-and-white house, where the eaves hung heavy with snow.

This particular trip to help Bryce and learn about the dead man was safe, of course, but her stomach cramped in foreboding. However much she was coming to care for Bryce, should she have stayed home?

"This was his place from the get-go," Rencie said as he fumbled with the key and unlocked the front door while they all stomped snow off their feet on the porch. Rencie even took his boots off before he went farther into the house. Despite the bright day, the closed curtains made the house seem gray and ghostly.

Just behind the door was a photograph of a small cabin in a vast, grassy wilderness with mountains in the background. Not only was the front of the little place decorated with two caribou antlers, but a herd of the same animals grazed all around it.

Rencie led them in, looked around, then said, "Can see, I guess, why a single child, a girl, didn't like it here. But sure hope they made up. Can't remember what he said made me think they did. Now I'm gonna ask you two to wait here in the living room while I check the bedroom he used for a second office. Well, lookie here!" He pointed at a framed photo on a corner table in the dim room. "Bet I'm right. Pretty sure that's his daughter, and it's a recent pic, 'cause she's definitely an adult here, and that must be her husband in it."

He picked up the picture and looked at it closely, tilting it toward the window. He snapped on a lamp, handed the photograph to Bryce, then went down a hall, where they heard him open a door.

Meg looked around Bryce's shoulder at an amazingly beautiful blonde woman with a not as good-looking man. They were both dressed formally, maybe for a special occasion. It was a posed photo, her back to his chest, both smiling. Meg could see no resemblance to the sketch of the dead man, but Rina could look like her mother. She didn't necessarily have to look like either of them.

Besides, the window light made a bright square on the glass so she couldn't quite see all of it, so she reached out to tip it a bit.

"Oh, there's an inscription in the bottom right corner," she said.

"Yeah, hard to read. 'Daddy, glad we're working together again,'" Bryce said. He quickly flipped it over and lifted the guards that held the photo in the frame. Turning away, perhaps in case Rencie came back into the room, he lifted the eight-by-ten-inch photo away from the glass and looked at the back of it.

Meg gasped as he swore under his breath. There was more writing there which read, *I'm not in mourning but rejoicing. Love, from your modern-day Varina.*

CHAPTER NINETEEN

Rencie shuffled back into the living room, his head down as he read an address aloud from a piece of paper. Bryce had quickly reassembled the photo in its frame and set it back on the side table.

"Found it in a top drawer," Rencie said, still sounding hoarse as if he would cry. "Right by a necklace I used to see his wife wear."

Meg saw Bryce's head jerk up. "Maybe some antique jewelry?" he asked.

"Naw. I'm no expert, but pink plastic stuff. She liked all things bright-colored. Round here, I can guess why. Darn long winters." He extended the paper to Bryce, who frowned down at it.

"Rencie, did Rina ever go by any other name?" Meg asked, unable to stop thinking about the note on the back of the photo.

"I believe Rina was short for Varina," Rencie replied. "Didn't much suit her though. Probably why she went by Rina. Her mother had been a bit of a history buff. She liked older names, stuff like that."

Meg and Bryce exchanged a look. A history buff in the family? Maybe one who passed down an interest in Confederate treasure?

Studying the paper again, Bryce asked, "Do you know where Sylvania, Ohio, is, Rencie?"

"Nope. Bet you'll find out."

"You've been a big help," Bryce told him and shook his hand. "We'll see that Rina Galsworth—Mrs. Todd Galsworth, it says here—is informed of her father's death."

"If she inherits the mill and this place, hope she sells it to someone who wants it. No way me and my Mrs. could afford it."

"I understand. I'll put in a good word for you and how well the mill seems to be run."

They all went out, and Rencie locked the door behind them. Meg wondered if the next people inside would be Rina Galsworth and her husband, Todd, or state troopers and Bryce with a search warrant.

When Bryce and Meg had driven almost to the main road, they had to back up to allow an empty logging truck to pass them as it came in. The snow had finally stopped. Instead of driving on, to her surprise, Bryce turned off the engine.

"What?" she asked, clutching the paper Rencie had given them.

"I've got to call the Big Man with the update. I don't know if he'll want me to go to Ohio in person or send someone else."

"And order a search warrant for Witlow's house and maybe his office at the mill?"

Bryce turned toward her and cupped her chin in his hand. "Exactly. If you're reading my thoughts now, I'm in trouble. But yes, Rina has to be told. Hopefully, she'll come here even if she still hates the area—at the very least for a funeral and especially if she's inherited Lloyd's properties." He stroked her cheek with one finger, then dropped his hand to pull his phone from his jacket pocket.

"If you want to make a call," she said, "I wonder if the cell tower will work way out here. That office looked like one from the last century, but that may just have been because they never changed."

He tapped his phone on. "Yep," he said. "It's going to work. Close enough to Wasilla, I guess, because it says that's where we are." But instead of making a call, he asked the phone, "Where is Sylvania, Ohio?"

The crisp female voice answered, "Sylvania, Ohio, is a suburb of Toledo, Ohio, and is situated almost on the Michigan-Ohio state line."

"See if Todd Galsworth has a website," she prompted, "because it's scribbled here that he owns an independent insurance company."

"You're way ahead of me, boss," he teased, putting his free hand on her knee. Despite her wool pants, it felt like a caress on her skin.

A website came up with not only the photo of a smiling Todd—the same guy in the photo they had seen—but with a picture of the front facade of his office. It was a small storefront with prominent letters, TODD GALSWORTH—WORTH YOUR TRUST FOR ALL INSURANCE NEEDS. Bryce scrolled down to read text off the screen. *Serving citizens of both Michigan and Ohio with trust and distinction.*

"Rina's a looker, and he isn't," Bryce went on. "Maybe he's charming or wealthy or both."

"Or he's everything her father was not—though I feel bad for saying that since I didn't know the man. But you know, Rencie said her mother loved bright colors...it makes me think about what she might have loved, or not loved.

Maybe she just wasn't happy here. You have to love and ac-
cept Alaska to be happy here—or have someone you love
so much that there's just no place else."

Their gazes met and held. "Very astute," he said, his voice
a husky whisper. "I would not have had that kind of intu-
ition. I don't know what I'd do without you."

"Then trust me enough to tell me what was in those two
boxes that were sent to the Big Man. More jewelry or coins?
Bryce, I want to help, but it is a risk. I suppose that's classified information, but—"

"Okay, but I'll have to tell you-know-who that I've told
you. Inside the boxes were some priceless historic letters
and papers that will have to be restored, but mostly it was
what was left of the Confederate States of America treasury
at the end of the Civil War—bullion bars, coins, bills and
a lot more jewelry Southern women had donated. Most of
it wasn't mourning jewelry but gold and gems. All that is
worth a fortune and will make one hell of an exhibition in
DC someday."

"And make someone's already lofty career even bigger—
like maybe running for a higher office, though I'll bet there's
only one higher."

"I told you, don't go there. Everything about the task force
is classified, including the Big Man's identity. I've promised
never to reveal that. Meg, I want you to know—"

Her phone music sounded. She could have thrown it
through the car window. Because it could be something
about Chip. "Hold that thought. It's Suze," she said, looking down at the number before she accepted the call. "Suze,
we haven't headed back yet. Is everything okay?"

"There's a woman who went to Mayor Purvis because he
was quoted online about the plane crash. She's insisting she
see you. Meg," she went on, lowering her voice, "the mayor's
with her, and Melissa McKee is back, wanting to make us a

huge bid for Grandma's old jewelry. Things are going nuts around here. Can you two come back right away?"

"What's the woman's name?"

"Rina Galsworth, from the Midwest, flew into Anchorage today. She insists she'll only talk to you—first, at least—because the mayor said you saw the crash. She's not a reporter, but the pilot's daughter. And there's a lawyer here with her—it's Mason Nowles."

"We'll be back as soon as we can. Keep her away from Chip. Hold the fort—with Rafe's help."

"Rafe's already corralled Chip. I feel a lot safer with him here, and he's managed to turn a couple of reporters away. The mayor stepped outside to give them some sort of statement. When he's inside, I swear he and Melissa are thick as thieves."

"As thieves—that's a good one. See you soon."

Bryce let Meg drive them back to the lodge while he quickly conferred with the Big Man. He soon had permission for a search-and-seal order on Lloyd Witlow's home, though he figured it was going to tick off his daughter, who had chosen to investigate the circumstances and site of her dad's death instead of going straight to his house. Meg had told him the mayor had even provided Rina with a local lawyer.

He got permission for Meg as well to wear a wire while talking to the woman, and he'd stay in the background at first so as not to inhibit or panic her. They had to find out what backwoods contacts Witlow was delivering priceless historical goods to—and where those treasures had been all these years.

When he finally ended the call, they were close to Falls Lake. "I feel like I'm losing control of this whole thing," he admitted. "I try to take the next logical step—when I figure out what it is—and then find out I'm one step behind.

We're standing there at the mill to announce the pilot's death when they get a call announcing he's dead. I'm headed to psych out the pilot's daughter, and she comes demanding to see us—you, at least."

"But notice the common denominators," she said as they turned onto the road toward the lodge. "The mayor has bought jewelry from Melissa McKee, who shows up again, wanting to see and buy our antique jewelry when we told her no before. Bill Getz is always lurking, though I can't see someone like him being involved, unless the mayor's hired him to spy on us. I think someone local like Melissa or the mayor could be involved. She'd be the perfect one to sell stolen jewelry, mixed in with non-stolen stuff like Suze's and mine. Just call me Sherlock, but if I'm going to wear a wire, we have to sneak in the back door to your room first to get it, right?"

"Just call me Dr. Watson if you want to go by Sherlock. I packed one wire in my duffel since I didn't know if I'd need it at the mill. Stop the truck while I reach behind and dig it out. It's gonna have to go in your bra. I'll be in my room at the lodge listening, so stall a little when you go in so I can get set up."

"All right. As long as you're there close."

"As close as I can be," he said, unfastening his seat belt and reaching in the narrow back seat of the truck to unzip his duffel bag while she pulled over on the side of the road.

"Bryce, Rina has her lawyer with her. The lawyer's name is Mason Nowles, and Suze used to date him. He's a lot like his friend the mayor, pompous and pushy."

"Sorry about Suze. And just what we need, another blowhard barrier to getting all this solved." He produced the wire for her to wear and held it up.

"Oh. It really is a wire attached to a small receiver or microphone."

"We can change plans. Despite the Big Man, despite how desperate I am to get answers, I can't ask you to do this. I've involved you too much in this. I can wear it. I'm sure, after she talks to you, she'll want to talk to the man who dove the wreck and retrieved her father's body."

"It sounds as if she's doing her own detective work."

"Smart call by her—or her insurance-minded husband, or that lawyer. They probably didn't want to fly their own lawyer here from Ohio so had the mayor suggest one."

"I wonder if she's already been to view the body. But should I not mention that someone tried to hurt you and your crew—twice?"

"I'd let her talk first, let her ask questions."

"Okay, I'll do the same—first. I want to continue to help with this, and the lodge is a safe place. The bad stuff has all happened outside, where there are places to hide, including detonators being hidden under the ice. Let me try first, then if you can tell from listening in that things are going nowhere, or you think it's time to step in to talk to her yourself…"

"Meg, I don't want you to think I'm using you. I care for you."

Bryce saw tears gild her eyes. "I want you in my life," she said. "I want to help not only for you but because someone—more than one, maybe—is hurting people, maybe stealing a historic fortune. If someone planted a remote-controlled bomb on the sunken plane, they're not amateurs or dummies. Maybe they rigged Lloyd Witlow's plane so it would crash, and they could get their hands on the treasure. The plane could have gone down and crashed into the lodge. I'm in this for more reasons than 'just' you, Incident Commander Bryce Saylor!"

He nodded. What a hell of a woman, and how far she'd come in so short a time. "Then open your jacket and your shirt, Assistant Incident Commander Metzler, and I promise I will only attach this wire right now," he said, his voice husky.

She loosened her seat belt and turned toward him, unzipping her jacket and unbuttoning her flannel shirt. She held the shirt apart. A black lace bra appeared, almost making him want to toss the wire and his restraint. Soon, he told himself. Soon, somewhere private and safe.

He perched the tiny receiver between her firm breasts, running the wire down and along the lower edge of the bra. His fingers tingled. Burned.

"Feel okay?" he asked, slightly adjusting its fit again.

"Feels fine," she said, then blushed from her cheeks down her throat.

He thought of several things to say, teasing, sexy, but he forced himself to just nod. And to get his hands off of her so she could refasten her clothes.

"It's a bad time to say this the first time," he rasped out, almost a whisper, "but I love you. Your courage, your sweetness, your—just you."

Love. Meg hadn't been expecting it, but now that the word was out there, floating in the space between them, she couldn't deny she felt it too. She was falling in love with this man, but she wasn't sure she was ready to say it out loud. Not yet anyway. She nodded and threw her arms around him.

"Careful! Don't displace that. I promise I'll find a good way to take it off you later."

She caressed his face with one hand, then turned away to refasten her seat belt. "Right back at you."

CHAPTER TWENTY

"Bryce, I swear that's a TV station truck behind us. See that satellite dish on its roof?"

He looked in the rearview mirror on his side, then craned around. "Damn. Glad they didn't pass and then stop us when they saw the Falls Lake Lodge on the side of this truck. Keep going. Park at the far end of the building, and we'll both go in that way. If they pull in too, I'll bet the mayor can detain them while you get Rina Galsworth off somewhere private to talk. Just say you only want to talk to her first—try to stash her husband and that lawyer with Rafe or Suze."

"Not with Suze. She fell hard for Mason at first, then learned not trust him. I found out he was seeing someone else while he was stringing her along as his one-and-only."

"Bastard," he muttered. "As if we need another suspect like a dishonest lawyer hanging around the lodge and this case. But then, if the mayor or Melissa are suspect, maybe he is too and we should keep an eye on him."

Hoping no one inside saw them, Meg pulled the truck into the last parking space at the far end of the building. They got out and hurried around the back, Bryce lugging his duffel bag. The far door was locked, though they used to keep it open in case their guests went in or out that way. But that was in the old days when people could be trusted.

"Don't ring the bell," Bryce ordered. "I'm calling Rafe to let us in."

He pressed twice on his phone. When Rafe answered, Bryce said, "Meg and I are at the north door. Don't let on, but come let us in."

"I don't want to talk to the media," she said, stomping snow off her boots again.

"Except to say, 'No comment.'"

Rafe swung the door open. "Chaos in here," he told them. "At least the mayor's gone out to talk to the media since Suze says they can't come in. Man, that lawyer thinks he can order her around."

They both rushed in. "Thanks. If you can handle him, keep him away from her," Meg told Rafe over her shoulder. "He's not a trustworthy person, but then, who is lately?"

She heard Rafe relock the door behind them. Bryce sprinted for his room. Stripping off her coat, hat and gloves, she forced herself to slow down and breathe, just breathe, as she walked the hall toward the common room. She tossed her things on the closest chair.

"Mom!" Chip barreled at her with three barking dogs behind him. He hugged her hard around the waist while she clamped him to her, until she felt the wire against her chest and set him back a bit. All she needed was to get that disconnected.

"Mom, there's a lot of new people here from really far away," he told her, at least now in a quiet voice.

"It's all right, hon. This is a welcoming place, and I'm glad to meet them. Take the dogs into your room for a while, okay?"

"Yeah, but where's Command—"

She put two fingers over his mouth. "He had to rest for a little bit. I'm sure you'll see him soon."

As Chip corralled the dogs, she steadied herself and went over to Suze, who was perched on her stool behind the desk. In the seating area by the fireplace, she saw Melissa McKee in intense conversation with Rina Galsworth. The two women bookended Rina's husband, Todd, who wasn't talking but seemed to be taking in their every word. About what?

Suze said, "Glad you're back. The mayor and our favorite lawyer are outside talking to some TV people. I'd hoped never to see Mason again. I only told Rafe I didn't like the man, and it's like he's been guarding me."

Meg was tempted to encourage her to enjoy Rafe's attentions, but she just nodded, steeled herself and walked over to the trio on the leather couch. She hoped Bryce had had enough time to get his equipment ready in his room.

"Hello, I'm Suze's sister, Megan. I'm the one who happened to be out for a walk and saw the plane crash. As you may hear later, once we found out Lloyd Witlow's name and address, I and a friend went to notify those he knew at the sawmill, since they had not reported him missing. It turns out he'd taken some vacation days, so they weren't alarmed they hadn't seen him. They got word just as we were about to tell them."

Rina stood, blocking out her husband and Melissa. She not only extended her hand, but covered Meg's hand with her other one.

"I heard you were the one who saw the plane crash," Rina said. To Meg's surprise, her tone was comforting, solicitous, but she also seemed very nervous. "As you may have heard, I'm Rina, the pilot's daughter and only child. Please—I'd like to talk to you about the accident. Sadly, my father and I were estranged for years—my fault—and only recently connected again. Too little, too late."

Tears shimmered in the woman's eyes, and her voice trembled. Meg scolded herself for thinking she would not like this woman, who seemed sincere and so sad. Meg and Suze greatly missed their parents, who had died in a boating accident on a rare vacation in the Bahamas years ago, but at least they'd had each other and their grandmother. This woman was an only child who evidently now blamed herself for the lost years she'd shunned her father. But at least she had a husband who had come all this way with her at such a difficult time.

"Let's go into the office," Meg said, "just the two of us right now."

"Yes. Yes, that's fine. But let me introduce my husband, Todd, born and bred in Michigan, though we live in northern Ohio now. I see Mayor Purvis has gone outside with his friend he's offered us as legal counsel if we need it, though Todd's pretty sharp about—I hate to say it this way—business arrangements. We want to have Dad buried next to my mother in Wasilla, see to selling the house, sell the mill..."

Not mentioning the search warrant, Meg exchanged a few words with Todd Galsworth, who seemed extremely nervous. Then Meg escorted Rina into the office and closed the door. As they passed Suze, she gave Meg a what's-going-on look. Meg realized she'd filled Suze in on very little of this, even before the trip to the mill. That reminded her that family members kept secrets from one another, so Rina might know nothing about her father's having no ID in an unmarked plane flying historic national treasures around backwoods Alaska. Besides, Bryce had said just to let her talk and he'd take care of the questioning.

Bryce was pleased and surprised the audio reception was so good for the wire Meg wore. She must have been sitting close to Rina because both voices came through great. Meg described the Thanksgiving Day walk in the snow, the crash—though she didn't say she'd been walking with Chip. Smart move not to involve him. He wasn't sure she'd tell Rina about the man in the white blanket, but she did.

Rina: "Well, I suppose it could be someone else just out for a walk after a big Thanksgiving dinner. But you're certain you don't know who that was? You couldn't see their face?"

Meg: "No. Then in the chaos of the crash, the person disappeared. However, there were some tracks in the snow outside the lodge that matched ones he or she may have left, because we found a snag of white blanket there."

Rina: "So—spying on the lodge? Or just maybe passing through?"

Meg: "We have no idea. However, I'm sure the mayor told you that National Transportation Safety Board divers came to recover your father's body. Someone attacked them and, during another dive, blew up the airplane underwater—a sophisticated job. I'm sure you'll want to talk to the incident commander too, since he's still here."

Rina: "Yes, of course I want to talk to him. With my husband and our new lawyer present. Terrible—the attacks on them, and I can't imagine why someone would want to kill people trying to help. When the divers were looking for my father's body at first—I have no clue why he didn't have some ID on him—did they recover anything from the plane I could have for a—a final keepsake from him? I want to ask the divers what they found. Things in the plane might legally be my property through inheritance or even his will. He was so thrilled about learning to fly and had always wanted to."

Bryce sat up straighter. The woman was jumping top-ics now. Since Rina had been estranged from her father for years, would she know he'd wanted to fly? He could have told her after they were reconciled. But asking for a keep-sake or even legal property from the plane? She probably thought at this point she could have access to his entire house of "keepsakes."

Meg: "Would you like to spend tonight at the lodge before you go on to the mill and his house? It's getting late. Darkness falls early here, you know."

Rina: "Don't I remember my early dark days here! That's kind of you, but the mayor offered for us to stay at his home tonight until we get some answers tomorrow at the mill. He said he's having people in for his wife's birthday party tomorrow, but they have room for us."

Wait until Rina and Todd hear her father's home is off-limits from a search warrant, Bryce thought. As least Meg must be saving that for him to tell her. Then, the obvious question would be why. And that would open up Pandora's box about what was in the plane.

The two women kept talking, now about why Lloyd Witlow might have taken an early holiday break from the mill where he'd always been so hands-on. "He never wanted to leave the area, even if Mother went stir-crazy and I hated it—used to, I mean," Rina said, sounding calmer now.

"It's great he could change his mind about traveling a bit later in life," Meg said. "And that he could afford that plane and flying lessons."

As he strained to listen, silence screamed at Bryce. He hoped Meg hadn't somehow screwed up her wire. But then, Rina's voice again, with an icy tone now. "We have no idea where he got the funds, of course. Some client at the mill, we assumed. We certainly could not have afforded it—the plane—or the concrete runway."

Why did Rina's tone change when Meg asked that question? It was time to go knock on the office door and explain that the NTSB had the right to investigate all plane crashes, especially ones with strange circumstances. And this crash had been fatal not only for the pilot but potentially for the investigators too.

★ ★ ★

The moment Bryce took over talking to Rina—and her husband and lawyer—Meg returned to the common room. She had mixed feelings about Rina and wished she'd had the courage to see if she had any explanation for her father flying a plane without markings while he carried no ID. But she'd let Bryce handle that.

She wished she had insisted Bryce wear a wire and she could listen in. But at the explosion of voices from behind the office door, she realized she didn't need one.

"NTSB involvement? Why? Absolutely no right! Looking for what at his house? You want this kept under wraps, but we'll go to the media!"

Todd's voice? Meg wasn't familiar with it. Maybe that was Mason's. Yes, because Suze looked panicked. Rafe, who was sitting at the front desk with her, stood and headed for the hall.

Then Bryce's steady voice, but she couldn't hear his words. Official incident commander tones. Calm. Controlled. In charge of the situation, and even at a distance, increasingly in charge of her heart.

CHAPTER TWENTY-ONE

Meg headed for Suze at the main desk to bring her up to date on what had happened at the mill when Melissa jumped up from her seat and blocked her way.

"Meg, I've talked to Suzanne about this, but I really need to speak to you too about buying your antique jewelry. I'd like to make you an offer."

Meg stepped back rather than yanking away. She crossed her arms over her chest and felt the wire in her bra move again, but no one, not Bryce or even Suze, was listening right now. Only, maybe Bill Getz, standing by the front door, looking out—or pretending to.

"This is something you absolutely should not turn down," Melissa went on, "especially not with your son growing up so fast. Despite how lovely this isolated lodge is, surely it's hard to make ends meet, and more so to save your profit. I'm sure you'll want money to invest for your son, college, maybe some travel."

Meg was tempted to just walk away, but if Melissa could be at all involved in the stolen Confederate treasure, especially its antique jewelry, it would be best to hear her out.

"Let's sit over here," Melissa coaxed and gestured toward the corner rather than taking her arm again. "I'm sure you and Suze have your own opinions on things, and, like I said, you have a son to think about."

Meg hated it that this woman kept mentioning Chip. Was that a bargaining tool, even a veiled threat?

They sat in chairs facing each other in the corner of the common room near the window. With the shortened daylight, it was dark outside. Meg's stomach rumbled as if in foreboding, but it was because she hadn't eaten in a long time.

"Look," Melissa said, leaning forward, "I'm going to level with you. It's the dead of winter, and my business won't pick up until the cruise ships come back to Anchorage. But I need to build up stock, and you'd be surprised how well antique jewelry, even Victorian-era mourning jewelry, is doing right now."

"I'd be surprised by a lot of things," Meg said, staring the woman down.

"Yes, well—a lot has happened lately. But my point is, to increase my store's publicity and my stock of precious items, I'm willing to pay you three times what I offered before for your grandmother's jewelry. If Suzanne says no, I'll take your half. After all, she doesn't have a son to worry about."

It was true that stashing money away for Chip from her candy sales was slow going considering the cost of college today, even with the University of Alaska and its branches not far away. But Meg was also agonizing over Melissa's desperate need for sales items. Weren't those beautiful Native Alaskan pieces going well? Were her ties to the mayor only that he bought his wife expensive jewelry at her store? Maybe some of that airplane cargo was meant for Melissa. But would she risk selling traceable antiques—or, since they hadn't "existed" for years—were they traceable? The entire

Confederate stash must have been a well-kept secret for over a century. In a way, it was still a secret now—so far.

Although Meg had no intention of selling her share of her grandmother's jewelry, she needed to keep tabs on Melissa to help Bryce's case—and hers.

"You make a good point," she told Melissa. "I'll think it over and let you know."

Meg and Suze fixed a huge plate of sandwiches and put out chips and a vegetable tray with dip in lieu of a larger supper. Chip had fallen asleep on his bed with the little Scottie curled up beside him and the other two dogs in their baskets on the floor. He didn't budge as Meg took off his shoes and carefully covered him up.

She saw the metal frame of the unassembled soccer net Bryce had bought him. It leaned against his bedroom wall near the two brightly colored soccer balls on his desk where the dogs couldn't play with them. Chip had said it had come in a big truck with a curved arrow on its side all the way from Anchorage. He'd shown it to Bryce before he and the dogs went to bed. Bryce had told him they'd assemble everything and clear the patio of snow for soccer practice as soon as possible.

Later, after Rafe ate, Meg saw him go back to a chair by the largest table lamp with his sketch pad on his lap again. Suze said he'd been drawing all five of their new guests in a "wanted poster" format as he'd once done courtroom sketches. Meg couldn't help but wonder if the huge Confederate treasure heist would end up in a courtroom, or if the Big Man would keep all this under wraps. He had more or less spirited away the gold bar, jewelry and the boxes Bryce had salvaged from the wrecked plane.

Meanwhile, the mayor kept pacing, and Getz was hovering while Meg whispered a short version to Suze about their trip to the mill—as best she was allowed to share.

Finally Bryce, the Galsworths and Mason Nowles emerged from the office. Meg had heard voices raised inside but had caught none of the conversation after the initial protests. Without any explanation, the mayor immediately escorted Rina, Todd and Melissa out to his truck while a frowning Mason strode past the desk and exited without another word. Meanwhile, Getz went down the hall to his room.

Bryce walked over to the front door to watch them go. "Let's lock up for the night," he called to Suze. "Wish we could lock some people out for good."

"Me too," she said. "I thought I had."

Rafe stood and laid his sketch pad aside, having pulled from it several drawings he laid on the big ottoman nearby. "I'll check the doors, all of them," he said. "Just stay put, Suze. I know the drill. Since your security person and all-around handyman, Josh, asked for the weekend off, just let me know if there's anything else."

Coming out from behind the front desk, Suze asked him, "Are you drawing what I think?"

"All the possible perps—and one of you," he said, turning back to hold that one up for her to see.

The three of them crowded close to look at it. Meg was totally impressed: he had captured her twin, even her personality.

"Oh, it's very flattering," Suze said, her hands fluttering to her chest.

"Nope. Realistic," Rafe insisted. "From the pen and from the heart."

Wide-eyed, Suze stared at the drawing as he went off to check the doors. Meg and Bryce kept quiet as she finally propped it against the lamp on a table. She sighed and started away, calling back over her shoulder, "I've got to check the office to make sure our visitors didn't leave it like a battleground in there."

Bryce bent down to look at the hastily made line drawings on the ottoman. "Our possible rogue's gallery," he told Meg. "You and I have to confer about today—and plan for tomorrow."

"I do have a plan, if it suits you, other than conferring, I mean."

"Tell me," he whispered.

She turned to Bryce and said nothing for a moment. At least for now, Bill Getz had gone to his room. Perhaps he was upset that they might be on to him, or that the mayor had ignored him, but she'd discuss that with Bryce later, because she had something more important in mind.

"I don't think Suze or I have mentioned to you something about the bungalow our cousin, Alex, and her new husband, Quinn, own—you know, the tracker."

"Wish he wasn't on their honeymoon. We could use his talents to nail whoever's spied on the lodge—and that plane crash. Sorry to interrupt, but I guess I've done that since I first met you, and you ain't seen nothing yet. Tell me your idea," he said, cupping his hands under her elbows and pulling her a step closer.

She looked up into his face and almost forgot what she meant to say. The man absolutely vibrated with intensity.

"Okay, so the house they'll move into when they get back is on the edge of town, on the other side of a ravine which more or less divides the lower value area from the houses farther up the hill—the few expensive ones, including the mayor's. His home has huge floor-to-ceiling windows and, with binoculars from the rear windows of Alex's new home, you can see in—as well as who is driving up their twisting driveway. Suze and I have been helping Alex and Quinn fix up their place, so we have a key, and I'm sure they wouldn't mind if..."

"If you and I camped out there to watch the big birthday bash? See who's there, though we know some of the guest list already?"

"Right."

"I swear, once again, I'm putting you on salary if the Big Man doesn't. I pay well, but it may not be in money."

They stared into each other's eyes. She whispered, "I hate to stoop to spying the way someone has done to us from outside—not to mention Bill Getz inside—but at least it's a next step. I think the mayor's involved, Melissa too. Maybe with attorney Mason Nowles's help they plan to 'handle' Lloyd Witlow's family. Buy Rina off, help to sell the Witlow property here fast—to get them out of here, something like that so Rina doesn't pursue what was in the plane or even why it crashed."

"So they don't figure out the mayor was using Witlow to run stolen goods? The mayor could be the one who bought that airplane and lessons. Maybe he had Lloyd pick up the Confederate contraband from someone else, maybe out of state, and fly it in here to be hidden, some of it sold through someone like Melissa. Falls Lake's illustrious Mayor Purvis talks to everyone. He has to have connections. For all we know, he also hired Getz to keep an eye on us. That's the other place I want a good look at—Getz's hoarding hideaway. What better place to stash historic government treasure than among other people's trash?"

He loosed his hold on her elbows but took both of her hands in his and went on, "I have never said this to another woman, but—in more ways than one—I don't know what I'd do without you."

"I'm starting to feel the same. But in case Getz comes out again and starts spying, let's go into my workroom."

"I do need to finally take that wire off of you."

"I can do that," she said, realizing she'd set up a private tryst with this man who rattled her poise and seduced her senses. "Just think, we're going to take up spying."

"As they used to say in the old days, I want to take up in general with you, Megan Metzler. I'll grab a couple of those sandwiches, and then let's continue this huddle in your workroom."

She smiled at the mere thought of time together, maybe someday not to be hatching schemes and fearing someone was watching or hostile. He'd be gone with the wind once this case was settled. So why was she trying to help him to solve it?

Bryce knocked twice and came into the cluttered room she used as a pantry and kitchen adjunct and to make her candies. "There's something homey about this," he observed, looking around. "I'd better take the wire back. You've worn it a long time."

"I can do it."

"Darn, but I do like a woman with a 'can do' attitude. Kismet that we met, right? But not enough kisses."

She had turned slightly away to open her blouse and take the wire and its little control box out of her bra, but his hands came around her to help. That *didn't* help because that mere move robbed her of what strength and self-control she had left around him. She was exhausted and yet energy shot through her at his merest touch.

He helped her lift the wire out of her bra and put it down on her worktable. His hands were back on her immediately, sliding under the bra where the wire had been, then lifting the black material away to cup one breast.

Her entire body leaped alert. Heat, but goose bumps.

Desire weakened her knees as she turned in his arms for a mutual kiss.

At least he held them both up, because the room was spinning. He slanted his mouth over hers, taking, but giving too. She loved it, loved him, she realized, and wanted him too. They grappled at each other, both breathing hard, keeping the kiss going.

One hard hand dropped to her back, then lower to cup her bottom, pulling her even tighter to him. She caressed and gripped his shoulders, his neck. He nearly lifted her off her feet. If there had been anything but a worktable and a chair, she was certain he would have laid her down on it and she would have welcomed each touch and thrust. Anywhere with him would be wonderful, would be so right. She stunned herself that she was so needy, so ready for him in here and in her life.

Dizzy, crazy. But footsteps in the hall, maybe Suze. Surely not Getz or even Chip.

Breathing hard, looking as frenzied as he did the night she'd seen him almost drown, he set her back a bit.

"Kissing you is like that underwater bomb going off," he whispered. "But I don't want to get away—just closer. But that sounded like Rafe in the hall. Got to go out before he comes looking for me. We have a date tomorrow—at the newlyweds' house."

He steadied her, looking her up and down. She realized her blouse was still open and her bra askew. He looked there, then up to her face. Her lips tingled, and her stomach cartwheeled. She felt she was blushing but he seemed reddish too.

"Get some sleep, sweetheart," he whispered. "More ways than one, we're both going to need it."

CHAPTER TWENTY-TWO

The next day, after conferring privately with Rafe about sur-
veilling the mayor's house and then his plans to check out
Bill Getz's place as soon as he could manage, Bryce invited
Rafe to his room, where they called the Big Man.

"Those ideas may be shots in the dark," their boss said,
"but go ahead with the surveillance today. As for that local
eccentric character just happening to show up at the lodge
in time to watch everything, why would he be so obvious
in his lurking?"

"Unless he's such an eccentric that everyone has just
learned to ignore him. But if he's hoarding—collecting, as
he says—odd things at his house, who knows what could
be there?"

"Yeah. His lair is worth a look. But another search warrant
is not forthcoming, and you cannot get caught for breaking and entering, so figure that one out. And I want you to
steer clear of our men going through the dead pilot's place.
Your civilian informant will need to get you there—to the
lookout building to watch the mayor and his pals, then to
the hoarder's cache."

"Right. If I thought she was in danger, I'd leave her here, but she's been invaluable. I kid her that she's going to be put on salary."

Rafe rolled his eyes.

His boss replied, "More like if she can help to solve this mess, I'll ask the Bigger Man to give her the Medal of Honor. Just kidding, but we could use more women in our line of work. We just cannot have civilians talking too much, filing lawsuits or showing up as collateral damage."

"That's for sure. I won't let anything happen to her."

"Including getting too involved with you? I'm picking up vibes here that go beyond business."

That was enough of that trending topic, Bryce thought as he shortly after ended the call.

Rafe asked, "He's letting you use Meg?"

Bryce nodded. "But I don't like to think of it that way—using her."

"I hear you. I'm trying to keep my thoughts off Suzanne, trying to just keep things friendly. I want to encourage her artistic talent but she's really shy about it."

"This stakeout of the mayor's house is a long shot, but what else do we have right now? And the antique jewelry connection to Melissa McKee is another maybe-too-obvious link."

"You check into her husband's activities? You said he's a real estate broker, something like that. If so, he could have a lot of safe places to stash stolen treasure."

"Never met him, never saw him, but he may show up at the birthday bash tonight. I suppose the mayor's wife and McKee's husband are worth looking at for their possible connections. I'll ask Meg what she knows. She's packing a picnic basket as if this is some fun little day trip."

"Yeah, well, good luck, and I'll keep an eye on things—and people."

"Especially Suzanne," Bryce teased, jabbing his arm lightly as Rafe headed for the door. "You can't kid me."

"Takes one to know one. And be damn careful you don't get spotted. This isn't underwater surveillance."

"Then why do I feel I'm swimming against a deep water current with sharks lurking?"

Later that day, Bryce let Meg drive again since he had no idea where Alex and Quinn's place was. No one had shoveled the driveway, which meant leaving tire tracks. But Meg had a garage door opener as well as a key so they could go right into the single-car garage. He didn't worry about the fact they were entering in the last hour of daylight since it was evidently fairly common for Suze's and Meg's trucks to be in and out while helping Alex to set things up. The gray-and-white bungalow had been newly repainted, and he bet the interior looked redone too.

He was right. The faint smell of fresh paint greeted them. The kitchen appliances looked new, and a perfectly clean and non-sagging sofa unit was grouped around the fireplace. No way they could light a fire tonight, and it was chilly in here, but the whole place looked inviting. Meg had told him about how Alex and Quinn had ended up together—with a wistful expression, he thought.

"Until it gets dark, let's lie low, not step in front of a window," he told her when they put their gear down. They took off their coats but kept their heavy sweaters on. "We can't use anything but our flashlights after dark either, but I bet that big place across the way throws a lot of light over here through its windows."

He fished his binoculars out of his duffel bag, then moved a floor lamp back a bit from beside the windows so he could wedge himself in to look across the ravine without stepping into view. "Glad it's winter so the leaves are down, and there aren't too many spruces here." He whistled low. "That's quite a spread—modern, multileveled—and already decked out for Christmas with swags of pine tree ropes and wreaths."

"You're thinking a small town mayor's getting a lot of money from somewhere. He does own a few businesses in town, you know."

"What can you tell me about his wife, Gloria, or about Melissa McKee's husband?"

"I'm pretty sure Gloria Purvis had money from her family. Her father's deceased, so probably left her a nice-sized inheritance. She has a brother who runs the family business in Anchorage, so her share was supposedly bought out."

"No wonder the mayor buys her gifts. Got to keep a wealthy lady happy in this little burg—excuse that description, but you know what I mean."

"She has red hair so she'll be easy to pick out. She wears clothes a notch up from everyone else—hardly shops around here."

"And Melissa McKee's other half?"

"I don't know much about him. He's in real estate, but doesn't do a lot of business around here. He owns the company—doesn't just show and sell, doesn't pound the pavement, as she put it once."

He nodded and resisted the urge to put his arm around her as she hugged the wall to peer out the window past him. Frost had etched the glass but not enough to obscure their view as daylight faded fast.

He said, "Maybe what we see here will help something break loose in all this, or else the search of Lloyd Witlow's house and office at the sawmill will, but that'll have to be in the hands of the state troopers to keep it on the up-and-up."

He squeezed behind her and went to the other side of the living room window overlooking the mayor's property and house from a different angle. "Bingo," he said. "Car just came up their driveway, and speak of the devil, Melissa's getting out of it."

"I wonder if she's staying there like the Galsworths did last night. But then, it's a big house, four bedrooms, I hear."

"No husband—no one else—in sight."

"That's odd. Maybe he'll be here later. Who would want to miss this bash? See, a caterer's truck from Wasilla is parked by the third garage door." She pointed and then snatched her hand back as if someone might see it.

He smiled at her across the window. "This is kind of like watching a movie unfold. You don't know what's coming next, but it will up the ante somehow."

They both gasped as the mayor hurried out to greet Melissa and put his arm around her waist. There was something strangely intimate about the way he then guided her inside. With his wife and a houseful of guests around?

Bryce said, "Did that greeting look to you like a welcome-to-my-wife's-party?"

"Hardly. His hand was practically brushing over her bottom! They are brazen!"

As early darkness descended outside and twelve other guests arrived, those greeted by the birthday girl herself, Meg was able to identify most of them for Bryce.

"I guess Suze and I are now in competition with this new lodge in town," she said.

She and Bryce used their flashlights, being careful not to let the beams off the floor or reflect in the windows. Not that anyone at the crowded party inside would probably have noticed. Everyone had wine or champagne glasses. People chatted, sat and stood with plates of food and then what looked like chocolate cake with white icing. Some were even dancing, but Meg and Bryce had to go into the guest bedroom to

see that. Since the house they were in sat lower on this side
of the ravine, they could only see partway into the room.

"Birthday girl Gloria is showing off her jewelry—see?"
Meg said. "I hope it's new jewelry and not something from
those long-dead Southern women who gave to the cause."

"You know," Bryce said, still staring through his binoculars, "sometimes I think I've become your cause and I'm
grateful."

"I want to help you. Oh, look! They've turned out all the
lights in that room. Do you think they spotted us?"

"Look at that flickering light. I swear they're watching
a movie."

"Or showing home movies? I wish the ravine wasn't in
our way. Then we could sneak up to a window and see what
they're doing. But the party's over for us until they turn the
lights back on."

"So let's break out some of the snacks you brought. I can
hum and we can do our own dancing, have our own party."

She smiled in the dark. "I brought sliders and cookies
and soda."

Training her flashlight toward the floor, she started back
into the living room, where she'd left her pack. But he put
his binoculars down on the dresser and snagged her arm as
she passed.

He started to hum something slow and mellow she didn't
recognize as he gently pulled her into his arms for a dance
hold and spun her around once. "I think this song's called
'Dancing in the Dark,'" he whispered in her ear. "My father
used to sing it and a lot of other oldies."

She relaxed from her surprise of being tugged into his
arms. Dancing…in…the dark. Here, just the two of them,
alone. Watching others, looking for answers, spotting for-
bidden emotions between two suspects, but now…

He moved them back and forth, then stood still. "The

minute their lights go back on, we're back to the windows," he told her. "Maybe dereliction of duty is just what I need right now."

His lips moved in her hair. His voice seemed to vibrate clear through her. He dipped his head to kiss her, and she kissed him back, as ever swamped by her senses around this man.

"You think Alex and Quinn would mind?" he asked and tugged her down on the double bed with him.

She didn't answer as he kissed her deeper, harder. His hands caressed her waist and slid beneath her heavy sweater and shirt to ride up under her bra. "Great place for a listening device," he whispered. "Great place for kissing," he added, as he opened her sweater and skillfully unhooked her bra.

And then it began, mad and mindless touching, stroking, kissing—her mouth, down her throat and beyond. His hands were everywhere, including inside her pants, while she held on to him, dizzy, crazy.

Finally, he lifted his head, out of breath. It was dark in here but she was certain she could see his face, his eyes.

"I told myself this would be all business," he said, sounding breathless. "I didn't mean for this to happen, but I have real trouble keeping my thoughts and hands off you."

"Well—well, good," Meg said, surprised by the confidence in her voice. She hadn't felt ready to be with another man after Ryan—until she met Bryce. He'd caught her off guard and something about being with him just felt so... right.

"I'm wondering if we can find some time together like this—not on a stakeout, not when I'm not prepared with protection—you know what I mean," he almost stammered. He seemed to radiate heat, but she did too. And to think it had been cold in here.

"I'm hoping you and Chip too, if you want, would come

with me to see my home in Juneau over the holidays or even before," he continued. "I know you need to be with your family at the lodge for Christmas Day itself, maybe just a day or two with me. We'll take Chip's new soccer stuff because I have a basement we can play in—and two guest bedrooms, one of which you can have so you and I can play. Think about it, because I know it's a big step for you, but—"

They both gasped as a sharp light flooded the room. From the outside. And then a roar split the air.

"Sounds like a train, but there are no tracks around here!" she cried as they scrambled up. "You think they found us?"

Keeping back from the window, they squinted out into the light. "A helicopter!" Bryce shouted over the noise. "But it can't land in the ravine. And there's no way it can be NTSB."

Its lights were still almost blinding, but Meg squinted into it while tugging down her bra and shirt. "Oh," she said, "it's letting down a big, long banner. I think there's writing on it."

In the glare of landing lights—though the chopper continued to hover—they read the words on the unfurled banner backward as the letters showed through the wide white piece of cloth. MORE YEARS, MORE LOVE, MORE JEWELRY! —RAND it read from top to bottom.

"And he was just so cozy with Melissa!" Meg said, almost hissing the woman's name.

"Maybe," Bryce said. "Hard to tell exactly what's going on from this distance." The chopper hovered a while longer, then lifted away, trailing the banner. The lights went on across the ravine. Meg felt they'd proved nothing but that she and Bryce wanted each other and he was serious enough to ask her and Chip to visit. She was still shaking either from his touch and kisses or from the shock of that darn helicopter.

"That banner as good as shouted 'MORE JEWELRY TO COME!'" she told Bryce. "More shipments of stolen treasure to add to previous deliveries? Ones that aren't on a doomed plane next time?"

"More jewelry for Melissa, maybe? From Confederate treasure some other local has hidden away?" he said, echoing her suspicions.

They continued to watch, but as the evening wore on, the party died down and people started to leave. It wasn't long before they spotted the mayor leading Melissa outside, just as he had when she arrived—then said good-night with not only a hug but a passionate kiss, one hand clearly rubbing or squeezing her bottom.

"The plot certainly thickens," Meg said. "I suppose that confirms it, and explains why the good mayor seems like he's been hiding something. He has been—an affair!"

"That definitely helps explain it, but it doesn't rule him out, especially if this illicit affair has links to precious cargo and a bomb blast at the bottom of Falls Lake."

After Melissa was gone, they watched as Mason Nowles came clearly into view for the first time that evening. So he was keeping close contact with the mayor too. A close friendship or a conspiracy to cover up a massive jewelry heist? Instinctively, because of Suze, Meg didn't like Mason—but who did she like or trust in the glare of light across that deep ditch filled with darkness?

CHAPTER TWENTY-THREE

Late on a cold Monday morning, after Meg's tasks at the lodge were done, she and Bryce told Suze they were going into town. Chip was playing checkers with Rafe, a game Bryce had taught him last night. At least that kept Chip from wanting to go along. Their cover story for taking a look at Bill Getz's house was that they were delivering some of Meg's new candy to stores in town—which she intended to do, so that wasn't a lie.

However, the truth was that she was going to do that after she dropped Bryce off. What she was keeping from Bryce was that she intended to be back to help him in a hurry, whether he wanted her there or not. She'd given Suze one hint about the fact this trip wasn't just a jaunt to town, though: she made her promise to phone her if Getz left the lodge in his truck.

"And why would that be?" Suze, ever savvy, asked with her knowing, narrow-eyed look.

"He just makes me nervous. I don't want to run into him or have him trailing me."

"Okay—right."

Rather than discuss that further, Meg gave her a one-armed hug and went out to climb in the driver's seat next to Bryce.

"You're not going to be part of breaking and entering, even if I am," he told her.

She could see his breath even in the truck, so she quickly started the engine and the heater.

"After all we've been through together?"

"You've really changed from wanting nothing to do with this—and with me."

"Call me crazy."

"Call me in love and overly protective of a very strong woman."

She almost stopped the truck right there to hug him, but he was obviously in a hurry. Suze had said Getz had talked about going home tomorrow. Were they really off base to think he might be some sort of spy? And who would have hired him?

"Boy, Getz's place is way out in the boondocks too. Guess it's common out here," she told him. "It's far back in the forest off a one-lane road on the other side of a salmon stream. He actually hikes in over big stones in the stream or walks the ice. His dad was an early settler, and I hear he still lives in the same house where he grew up."

"So, no other family? How did his father die?"

"A natural death, I heard, maybe of a broken heart after Bill's mother died young. Not everyone is cut out to live here."

"You and Suze seem to thrive here. Would she be okay running the lodge if you ever moved away?"

The truck hit a bump, and she nearly drove off the road. Not only because the steering wheel jerked, but at that apparently innocent question and what he might be thinking.

"I—I never considered that—before. It depends—would depend on so much."

Relieved they were there so she wouldn't stammer around more, she parked in a pull-off spot across the frozen stream from Getz's house.

"I forget the name of this waterway," she told him as he pulled on his gloves and earflap hat over his snow goggles. "But it has a small salmon run every year. No electricity lines out here, but I heard he recently bought a generator."

He turned to her. "Take your time delivering your candy, and I'll meet you here in an hour. What a place. All the piecemeal additions out the back—some sections are clapboard and some huge slabs of tree bark."

"It reminds me of some kind of monstrous snake. I'll be back, or you'll have to walk too far."

She hoped he wouldn't be angry when she returned in less than half that time and came across the stream to see how he was doing, see if she could help. Four eyes were better than two.

He hesitated a bit before he got out. "Like I said, I'm going to drag my feet so my prints can't be identified, like the marks we found near the lodge. I'm still wondering if that's giving Getz some of his own medicine or the person watching the lodge was someone else."

"Be careful!" she insisted, as he leaned over to quickly kiss her cheek.

"My motto, always—and evidently never," he said with a low laugh as he got out, closed the door and moved slowly away, dragging his feet.

She used to emotionally do that after Ryan's death, she thought, dragging her feet about facing life, living only for Chip. But no more.

When Bryce crossed the barrier of the frozen stream and turned to wave, she backed the truck away and headed for town.

★ ★ ★

Although Bryce had never really been an undercover agent—only an underwater one—he'd had some schooling by an NTSB official who was former CIA. The lessons had not included B and E—that is, not exactly. But he knew a few tricks of that trade.

As he scuffed along through the snow and studied the patched-together house ahead of him, he fingered the small paint-scraping tool in his pocket. He knew his best bet was not to break anything, but rather to find an entry or window that was not locked. And out here, with that long, patched-together building with so many windows, there must be a way in. If not, this tool would be step two—slide it along a door lock to see if he could spring it.

He didn't even try the front door, but shuffled right past it around the building to partway back. He even skipped an old-looking second entry door and started lifting windows. When the dogs at the lodge had gotten underfoot, Bryce had heard Getz tell Suze that he collected anything but animals. Besides, a watchdog would be starved to death by now unless Getz had left food in every one of the damned add-on rooms—seven additions, it looked like to him.

He shook his head in amazement. It seemed Getz hoarded pieces of other buildings too.

The fourth window he tried stuck a bit but lifted. He left tracks far beyond it, then came back and climbed in. The dusty, stale odor of stacks and piles of whatever hit him hard and reminded him of the smell of that scrap of white blanket he found outside the lodge. Maybe not proof the lake and lodge stalker was Getz but a vote in his favor. What if he stumbled on that blanket in here?

"Whew!" he said and sneezed as he moved quickly away from the now closed window into canyons of—of whatever. As he walked through the crooked canyon path past small rooms and cubbyholes, he noted that things seemed to be somewhat sorted by area. Stacked old chairs. Magazines. Plastic containers like frozen food came in. Calendars of all sorts studded the walls. One room was a jumble of Christmas decorations, ornaments, strings of lights. On and on. He felt oppressed and overwhelmed. In a way it was like diving underwater and finding an alien landscape with things that didn't quite come into focus.

Damn. Where to look in this utter chaos? And look for what? He didn't want to endanger Meg more than he already had, but he wished he had her with him.

Meg quickly hit the four stores she had candy for and was pleased with the tidy sum she'd made in return. With a son to support, every little bit counted and as she hurried back to her truck, she realized that Melissa McKee had been right. Even though she saved money here and there, it would help to have a chunk of it from selling her grandmother's jewelry, yet she just couldn't. Not now at least. She felt great sympathy for those poor women who had donated or sold their keepsakes and heirlooms for such a terrible cause in the Civil War, only to have their jewelry stolen from Jefferson and Varina Davis as they fled the destruction of the war.

She turned off onto Getz's back road again and parked behind a clump of bushes not far from where she'd let Bryce out. Hiding her purse under the passenger seat, she kept only her keys with her. She carefully slid her feet along in the snow just as Bryce had, which made for more slow and strenuous going, but she didn't want him to be angry—angrier than he might be when he saw she was back already.

Now where and however had he gotten in? She didn't see him, and his tracks glided past a lot of windows and even two doors. Darn. Maybe she should not have tried this.

Shading her eyes, she peered in a window and gasped. A room with hanging masks and costumes—Halloween in December! Biting her lower lip, she moved to another window. Should she knock to be let in? Go back to the truck to wait?

The next window had a shade partway down, so she nearly kneeled in the snow to look in. Oh! Flags and posters from Wasilla High School where not only Getz but Rina Witlow Galsworth had attended. They couldn't be too far apart in age—had they known each other?

She jolted when she saw a man walk by. She'd found him. Bryce!

She knocked on the window. He ducked, hid, then looked back. She was sure that she could hear him swear through the glass.

He came close, then unbolted and pulled up the window.

"I told you to come later."

"I did what I needed to in town. I came to tell you that Suze has not called me, so Getz is still at the lodge."

"Damn, Meg. All right, sit on the ledge and lift your legs in."

"I've been scuffing tracks, just like you."

"You're not staying," he said, closing the window once she was in. "This place gives me the creeps. I did find some old books on the American Civil War, but books on everything else too. One room is like a chaotic lending library. I'm going to look in a room that has jewelry hanging on pegs and on things like little metal trees. But you are going back to town or the lodge until the time and place I told you to come pick me up."

"Bryce, now that I'm here, I—"

"Now that you're here, I'll worry about both of us, so you're heading back, however much you could help. It's overwhelming in here for two people. I read that hoarding—"

"Which Getz calls collecting."

"—is actually a disorder that can be a symptom of mental illness. A form of insecurity, and you're making me really insecure right now, as much help as you've been, sweetheart."

"Don't 'sweetheart' me if you're tossing me out."

"Meg. For your own good—and my sanity. Please. Just wait a sec, and I'll be back to let you out that window. And call my cell if you see any sign of Getz outside of the lodge. Give me a little more time here than I originally wanted."

Disappointed, she waited for Bryce to come back. Imagine—pom-poms, old notebooks, the Wasilla High School newspapers stacked here. And yearbooks. Yes, it's very possible Getz was in school about when Rina was. Maybe a senior when she was a freshman or a sophomore and if so, there could be some kind of information about her in one of these yearbooks. Could she borrow it? Smuggle it into the lodge to look through it, then be sure he got it back somehow? Mail it to him anonymously?

She heard Bryce coming back. She'd helped him before with her hunches and research. If she could learn more about Rina's past...

She jammed it up under her thick jacket as he came back into the room, went straight to the window and opened it for her. He thrust something into her hand. "He threw this away in the wastebasket—yeah, a wastebasket in this place—by his cluttered desk. It was wadded up as you can see, a list of how much the mayor's been paying him for a while. Keep it safe. Now, get going."

He opened the window and helped her out. At least, she thought, since he took something from here too, even though it was from the wastebasket, if she had to tell him about the old high school yearbook, it might go easier for her.

"Be careful!" he told her and closed the window.

Same to you! she thought, but she quickly scuffed her way back toward the truck.

At the lodge, she smuggled in both the yearbook and the wrinkled paper to her room to examine later. So much was going on without her, all of it good, normal, happy. Getz was hunched over on a couch, going through what Suze told her were old magazines she'd said he could have. Meg could just picture another room at his place dedicated to them.

Rafe and Chip were building a pair of "snow people" out in back, and Meg waved at them through the back window. All three dogs were watching on the patio Rafe or Josh must have partly shoveled off. Both Bryce and Rafe were so kind to Chip and filled an obvious male-companionship gap in his life. And Bryce had filled one in hers.

Josh had just left after doing some repairs, Suze said, "And he was humming! That new girl is changing his life."

Meg sighed, wishing she could share everything going on with Suze. "I need to pick up Bryce in a little while after he does some errands. Let me fix an afternoon snack for Chip and Rafe—our guest Getz too, if he wants."

When she got some things together on the table and went to rap on the window for them—the Mr. and Mrs. Snowmen looked nearly done—she didn't see either of them, so they must be heading in.

Yes, she heard Chip's voice inside the front door, but had he and Rafe closed the dogs outside? Their wild barks seemed muted. Both Suze and Meg hurried past the reception desk to see what was going on.

Two men in horrid monster masks stood there, one holding a gun to Chip's head and the other pointing a pistol at them.

CHAPTER TWENTY-FOUR

Suze gasped, and Meg screamed. The man in the skull mask held Chip hard to his body with the boy's booted feet nearly off the floor.

Where was Rafe? This was a home invasion!

Getz came over to see what was going on and immediately thrust his hands in the air. He should have heard her scream and run to his room to call for help. Or had he walked out here to feign surprise?

"What—what do you want?" Meg cried. "Let him go. You have all of us here."

"So I see," the man in the second grotesque mask said in a gruff voice that might be faked. She could see his eyes clearly above the mask's smile with broken teeth. He held his gun on them. "What we want is instant and silent co-operation. Hands in sight, back up, all of you. We've been watching long enough to know you're the only ones here now. Cooperate and we'll be in and out soon."

"Darth Sidious, I'll hold the boy while you tie everyone except her," Skull Mask said, nodding toward Meg.

She had broken out into an instant sweat. Her pulse

pounded. The barrels of those guns looked as big as rain barrels. Chip, at least, kept quiet, though he was trembling.

"Please let him go and just turn your gun on me," she said to the man holding Chip. Her voice was steadier now. "I'll get you money or whatever you want."

The men, pushing Chip, came closer into the room while Meg walked backwards, hands in sight. "Mom," Chip said, "that's Darth Sidious and this is Supreme Leader Snoke. They're characters from *Star Wars*—bad ones. Better do what they say."

Suze spoke up. "Chip, where's Rafe?"

"They put the gun on me, so he let them tie him up outside. But he's got a choke kind of rope around his neck."

"Didn't shoot anybody yet," Snoke said, his voice cold and hard. His rubber mask of sunken skin quivered when he shook his head. "Everybody just shut up and do what we say. Now!"

The one Chip had called Darth Sidious had a mask not only with broken teeth but huge shadows under his eyes, streaks on his face and a cowl headpiece. It would be difficult to identify either of them by much other than their voices.

The next minutes were a terrible blur. Snoke's gun against Chip's head stayed there while Darth Sidious produced loops of rope and tied Suze and Getz sitting back-to-back on the floor, and then to the leg of the dining table. Meg was hoping they would tie Chip up and leave him behind too, but Snoke kept a gun on him as Darth Sidious shoved her ahead of him and Chip.

"Two things real quick," Snoke said. "We want to search Bryce Saylor's room, then your office here—the safe."

"What are you looking for?" she dared as she took the master key off the desk and walked ahead of them down the hall.

She had to work fast. Someone had to get to Rafe, and

she had to get that gun away from Chip's head. Perhaps these were the men who had sabotaged the sunken plane, so at the very least they were would-be killers. Were they looking for the lost jewelry or were they aware there had even been gold ingots and precious papers onboard?

Her hands trembled as she unlocked Bryce's door. This time his duffel bag was still out. Darth Sidious ransacked it, then tipped it upside down on the floor. He checked both pillowcases on the bed, rifled through the drawers and peered into the closet, skimming his hands along the empty top shelves. Meg assumed Bryce's laptop was under the bed where the man looked, but he came up with nothing. He stood again. He looked behind the curtains, then rummaged around in the bathroom while she and Chip barely breathed until Chip blurted, "Don't steal his diving stuff, 'cause that's his job."

"Chip, shhh," she said.

"But they hurt Rafe's neck and his hands."

"I don't want them to hurt you."

"All right, let's go," Snoke said, yanking her arm toward the door. "The office, the safe."

"Will you leave us alone then?"

"Shut up and do it!"

She had to hurry. Rafe could be injured, something about a rope around his neck. Were these the same men who had injured Bryce's first partner, Steve, given him a terrible head injury? And were they the would-be murderers who had blown up the unmarked plane and meant to blow up Bryce and his dive team?

Meg rushed past Suze and Getz, both still tied. She had not noticed until now they had been gagged. Was Getz in on things—had he told these men that Bryce was gone and Rafe was distracted? Or was he just an ignorant, innocent bystander?

Meg blocked their view when she dialed the combination for the safe. Her hands were still shaking, slippery with sweat so that she messed up her first attempt and started over.

"You stall like that again, you'll regret it," Snoke said. "We don't have all day."

Several sharp retorts came to mind, but she said nothing, just opened the safe and stood back, putting her hand on Chip's shoulder. Darth Sidious swung the door to the safe wide, leaned close and rifled through it. Meg racked her brain to place their voices, their mannerisms, anything, but nothing clicked. They must have been watching the lodge, seen Bryce was gone, and to them, Rafe would just be another visitor since he hadn't been in on things earlier. She had to get that gun away from Chip's head, get these men out of here, help Rafe and go for Bryce. If she didn't show up, what would he think or do?

"Here!" Darth Sidious shouted and he raked out a handful of what must be Suze's share of their grandmother's jewelry, because Meg had hers in her room. He shrugged at his accomplice, then turned to her and exploded, "Where's the damn rest of it?"

"That's all that's left of my deceased grandmother's jewelry."

He hesitated, his dark brown eyes glaring at her through the eyeholes of the mask. A gold filigreed necklace dripped from his fingers, and she noted he wore an onyx ring. It had a small gold shield in the middle of the onyx, like maybe a badge for a society or even a college or fraternity ring. His fingernails were clean and looked manicured. And for the first time she thought clearly enough to note that, besides a raspy voice, he had a slight drawl, though he was speaking so fast and harshly it wasn't pronounced.

When she didn't flinch but dropped her eyes from staring at him, he asked Snoke, "What do you think?"

"The rest is not something to leave out. Secreted else-where? Off-site?"

Meg knew she had to play dumb. "The rest of what?"

He threw the jewelry at her. She didn't try to catch it as it hit her chest, then slid to her feet.

And then, the sweetest words she'd ever heard.

"Let's go. No time to ransack the place or question them further. It's broad daylight. Let's go."

Meg grabbed Chip hard to her as the two men ran out of the office and slammed the door. "Are you all right?" Meg asked, smoothing back his hair, checking for injuries as she fought back tears. Those men had held a gun to her boy. "Does anything hurt?"

"I'm okay, Mom," Chip said. "But I'm worried about Aunt Suze and Rafe. It looks like they hurt him real bad."

Of course her brave boy would be worried about them. Had their attackers hurt anyone on their way out? She had to see what they drove away in!

Grabbing Chip's hand firmly in hers, Meg tore out past Suze into the hall and stared out the window just in time to see the two men, still masked, disappear into the thick trees at the side of the lodge with all three dogs barking at their heels, though, thank heavens, the dogs stopped at the tree line. No way she was going to chase them either.

"Chip," she told him as she grabbed a butcher knife from the kitchen counter, "get the scissors out of the top drawer of the desk and cut Aunt Suze and Mr. Getz's ropes. I'm going to check on Rafe."

She yanked open the back door. "Rafe! Rafe, they're gone. I'm going to cut you loose."

He was hog-tied hand and foot with his legs bent back nearly to his wrists behind his body. If he moved, the rope around his neck could choke him. He was awake, watching the forest where the men had run.

She also saw that he had managed to nearly saw through his ankle bonds by scooting toward the bare winter bushes and rubbing his feet back and forth against a hoe someone had left there. His hands and wrists were bruised, bleeding and purplish.

"They hurt anyone?" he rasped out as she kneeled to cut him loose—the rope at his throat first.

"No. They were looking for jewelry, I think."

"I—didn't see them 'til too late. Came from the forest. Then they had a gun on Chip. I screwed up, let you down."

"No one was hurt. And maybe we learned something. You've been such a help to Chip—just like Bryce. There's nothing more you could've done."

Suze, still with her wrist ropes hanging from her arms, darted out into the cold with Chip by her side.

"Suze, he's all right," Meg cried as Suze's expression broke with relief.

"Thank goodness," she said, helping Rafe to his feet.

"Getz?" Meg asked.

"A little shaken up, but otherwise, fine," Suze confirmed.

"Someone needs to tell Commander Bryce what happened," Chip said.

Meg and Rafe exchanged a look. "If I go," he said, "there'll be nobody here to guard—"

"You should go, Mom," Chip said. "I'll be okay. I've got Rafe and Aunt Suze."

Meg kneeled in the snow beside him. "Chip, no. I couldn't leave you—not now. Not after what happened."

"I'm okay, Mom. I promise. I'm brave like a Jedi."

Meg cupped his cheek and kissed his forehead. "Yes, you are. My brave Jedi. You go inside with Rafe and Aunt Suze and lock all the doors, do you hear me?"

Chip nodded.

"I won't let him out of my sight," Rafe promised. "Go get Bryce. And look in your rearview mirror."

"I will," Meg promised, then quickly ran back inside to grab a coat, her purse and the keys to her truck.

With another quick hug for Chip and a promise that she'd be back soon, she tore to her truck, grateful that no one was hurt. But danger and evil had come to their precious, snowy home and at holiday time.

Bryce was waiting for her, pacing behind the bushes near where she'd parked before. He was cold, stomping his feet, hugging himself. As far as she could tell, he had taken nothing else from Getz's place. She was grateful he didn't scold her about being late. Perhaps he thought she was angry with him for sending her away.

She was bursting to tell him, but the forest was closing in as the afternoon shadows grew longer and darker, graying the snow. She just wanted to get out of there and get back home to Chip. She was halfway back to town, ignoring his asking her if everything was all right.

"Meg, you're shaking. You're angry. What? At me?"

"Two men in horrible masks came into the lodge with guns, kept one to Chip's head the whole time, tied Rafe, then Suze and Getz. The intruders made me let them in your room to look around, then opened the safe in the office. Everyone is—is okay."

She stopped at the only light in town and turned to him, fighting not to burst into tears, so glad he was here to help.

He reached for her, held her hard despite their seat belts until the truck behind them honked, and she saw the light was green. She drove on.

"That changes everything," he said, reaching over to put a steadying hand on her shoulder. "But should I stay or leave the lodge to keep you safe? Were they after me?"

"Only wanted to search your room."

"Did they take my laptop?"

"They didn't see it, if it was under the bed. I'm thinking they were stupid about that. One guy dumped your duffel bag out, and I'll bet your laptop was right near that pile, so when he looked under the bed, it was in shadow—hidden, like when I looked under at first to bring it to you."

"Chip and Suze. They're really all right?"

"Shaken. Chip is being so brave."

"I'm not surprised."

"I supposed you'll need to question them."

"And Getz too. Did he seem to know them?"

"I couldn't tell but he sure came over and put his hands up fast enough. Bryce, they were in normal clothes but were masked like villains from a *Star Wars* movie. Chip knew the characters. I took some mental notes on them but I'm sure they were no one I knew."

He heaved a huge sigh. He twisted even more toward her. "I thought the lodge was safe, especially with Rafe there, even if Getz was maybe a Trojan horse."

"Rafe went down right away, cooperated since they had the gun on Chip. I—I don't know how this will affect him— Chip. Rafe too, they hog-tied him so that if he moved his feet or hands he'd choke himself. His wrists and hands— his artist's hands, as Suze says—looked bloody and beat up from the ropes. When I ran out to him, he was trying to saw himself loose on a garden hoe."

"So perhaps someone who works with horses or live-stock—skilled with rope."

"One guy, I think, faked a gruff voice—and had clean, great-looking hands and fingernails."

"Thank God no one was hurt. I'm wondering if some-one knew I was not just away but at Getz's. They must have not been after my laptop but the jewelry—which shows the

Confederate treasure is at the heart of all this. Someone stole it or hid it, or lost it and is desperate to get it back. Well, they won't get their hands on what we sent to the Big Man, but there must be more out there—probably around here."

They got out of the car and found the front door locked as Meg had directed. They rang the bell, both looking behind them and all around. Suze hurried to let them in.

"Is Chip okay?" Meg asked.

"I think the scare took a lot out of him. He's asleep in his room. I haven't called the troopers yet," Suze said. "Rafe said to wait for you."

"We'll have to contact them, but through the Big Man again," Bryce told Meg as Suze headed back inside. "We can't have the publicity. Maybe he can assign someone else incognito."

Once inside with the door closed and relocked behind them, Bryce pulled Meg to him. She hugged him back hard.

"We learned a lot more today."

"Learned it the hard way. The dangerous way, that will *not* be repeated. And here I sent you away from my assignment to keep you safe."

They went in arm in arm to see Suze rubbing some sort of healing ointment onto Rafe's neck since both of his wrists and hands were already bandaged. Meg thought of the day she had put the ointment on Bryce's neck for his diving rash, that day she had fallen a little more in love with him.

"Rafe!" Bryce called out and hurried over. "Sorry I wasn't here, man."

"Maybe that was the idea. I took a fall when they had the gun on Chip. Suze says he's exhausted, finally asleep in his room with the dogs. The whole thing was pretty well planned, *Star Wars* masks and all, as Chip will tell you."

Suze moved closer to him on the couch and kept putting Cortisone cream on his neck. "Glad I don't need the hospital like Steve did, because I've got a great nurse here," Rafe added.

"I'm worried about his hands," Suze said. "And that reminds me, Steve's wife, Jenny, called a few minutes ago to say he's better, being released from the hospital to go home. So—good news amid the bad. We do need to call the state troopers, don't we?"

"I'll take care of that," Bryce said. "Meg, let's go check on Chip."

They dropped their coats on the table and hurried down the hall to Chip's room. It was as if the three of them belonged together, were a family. *Look in the rearview mirror,* Rafe had warned when she went to pick up Bryce. She looked back at her life now: despite danger in the present and the future, she was moving on, however desperate she was to stop the invasion of evil in her beloved little piece of home.

CHAPTER TWENTY-FIVE

Chip was not asleep when Meg went in but was sitting up straight, wide-eyed in bed with the little black Scottie in his arms. The two other dogs lifted their heads from their beds on the floor and, seeing who it was, put them down again. Meg supposed Buff and King had come through this latest ordeal better than anyone.

"They didn't come back, did they? I had a nightmare about them."

"No, but Bryce is back and he's going to come in too, okay?"

"Oh, yeah. He's my friend, and I'm glad he wasn't here to get hurt like my other friend, Rafe."

It hit Meg again how isolating the lodge was for her boy. Sure, he had some friends at school, but he lived in a world of adults here—distressed adults.

She sat down on the side of Chip's bed and pulled him into her lap as if he were a toddler. "They were very bad people," she whispered. "They ran away. Bryce is going to tell the troopers, and they'll help keep us safe."

When Bryce peeked in, she gestured him over. He kneeled

on the woven rag rug next to the bed, his right shoulder pressed to the mattress and his left elbow across Chip's knees. "Hey, Chip," he said, "I'm proud of you for keeping calm and being so brave with those bad men here. And for recognizing their masks."

"I was glad when they let me and Mom stick together. But just in case they come back, I got up and put the soccer goal frame inside her bedroom door. Extra barrier to help keep them out."

"Good man," Bryce assured him.

"Thank you, honey," Meg choked out, her lips in Chip's hair as she kissed his head where those idiots had put the muzzle of the gun. Maybe he was too young to know what could have happened—she hoped so. "Besides, I can get into my room through our adjoining door here."

"But now that Commander Bryce is back, he can watch you close too," Chip said.

Her gaze snagged with Bryce's steady stare.

"Good reasoning, if you ask me," Bryce said. "I promise you, we will put up that goalie net, and we'll practice how to dodge enemy soccer balls that try to get past you. And if we get to go to my house in Juneau for a few days during your Christmas vacation, I have a big basement we can play inside, whatever the weather does."

"Can we, Mom?" he pleaded, not even waiting for her answer, but turning back to Bryce. "If it's just the three of us, would Mom play too?"

"Here's the deal," Bryce said, leaning closer and grasping Chip's shoulder. "If your Mom wants to play, she can. But I live real close to my friend Steve, who just got out of the hospital. He can't play since he hurt his head, but he has a son named Mark who could play with us—teach you the ropes."

"Okay, good. But did you hear those bad guys had lots of

ropes and tied almost everyone up but Mom and me? They hurt Rafe too, and he needs his hands to draw and paint."

"You know, the best thing you can do right now," Bryce told the boy, "is to get some sleep. In the morning, I'd like to talk to you about anything you remember about those men. Not *Star Wars* stuff, but anything real about them."

"Questions like you asked after the plane crash?"

"That's right." Bryce turned to address Meg. "I'll wait out in the hall while you tuck Chip in. We're all exhausted." He tousled Chip's hair, got up and went out, quietly closing the door behind him.

"If you have any more bad dreams," she told Chip as she kissed his bruised forehead again and tucked him back in bed, "you just come into bed with me."

Bryce was waiting for her in the hall, leaning wearily against the wall.

They hugged each other for a long moment.

"Meg, I want to keep you safe," he said, his chin on top of her head. "Chip too, all of you, but this is getting worse. I'm going to ask for a trooper, disguised as a regular guest, to bunk here for a few days for extra protection. I can swing it."

"Or the Big Man can. You know, considering he's got, like, the second highest security clearance in the country."

Bryce pulled his head back to study her face. He was growing more and more certain that Meg had puzzled out the Big Man's identity. Well, she could speculate all she wanted. He certainly wasn't going to confirm the fact that Samson Walters, the sitting Vice President of the United States, was indeed the Big Man behind the curtain. He let her comment lie where it landed, pulling her close once more before he spoke. "Anyway, I need to talk to him first thing when the sun's up in DC. I'm actually too beat to try to have someone wake him up so I'll email him some info now and talk to him later. Besides, I've been waiting to hear what was turned up in the search of Lloyd Witlow's house. More jewels? Gold, papers? Who knows what could have been there. No one will believe it—Confederate treasure squirreled away somewhere in deep woods Alaska by someone. But where and by who?"

At 3 a.m. the next morning—damn time zones—Bryce woke up to his smartphone alarm and called the Big Man.

"Great news about Steve being released from the hospital, sir," Bryce began.

"For sure. A victory for the good guys."

"I was going back to visit him, but after what happened here yesterday, I can't leave."

"I got your email. *Star Wars* masks, no less. The black ops folks are getting nervous—maybe they'll make another mistake. Meanwhile, I think you and your female noncom partner have a good excuse to attend the rather hastily planned funeral of Lloyd Witlow this afternoon at the Union Room in the sawmill near Wasilla."

"We haven't heard a thing about it."

"Maybe that's the idea. His daughter finally got his body back and is moving fast to bury him. But you two have every right to be there to pay your respects, even though you didn't know him. And yes, I'll pull a few strings to get you an incognito trooper like you mentioned in your email who knows the area. I'll have him move into the lodge for a while, keep his eyes peeled, et cetera."

"That will help. What time is the funeral today?"

"Visiting hour starts at one. Funeral at two, then a family entourage to the main Wasilla cemetery—ah, Aurora Cemetery, which will probably be covered with snow. Private graveside service, so I bet the calling hours and main funeral service should be large. The guy lived in or near Wasilla all his life."

"Sometimes they hold winter corpses in cold storage until the ground thaws. But I'd guess the fact we haven't heard about the funeral means Witlow's daughter, Rina, and maybe the mayor and their lawyer are still angry at us."

"The troopers who served the search warrant at Witlow's house say his daughter threw a fit about not only their search but a delayed burial, so they're going to carve a place for him next to his wife in the frozen ground. Bundle up and keep your eyes and ears open."

"Will do. Any more info from the examination of the Confederate loot?"

"Forensics found a strange clue on some old paper wrapping for some of the jewelry. It listed a long defunct jewelry store in Brooklyn, Michigan—second-generation jeweler dead decades ago. Damn, where did I put that? I'm drowning in the usual trivia, and each piece of it could jump up to bite me, as I never let a secretary in on these ops. Guess I'll have to send that to you. And watch out for possible pallbearers in *Star Wars* masks. Weirder and weirder."

"Yes, sir. I'll get back to you soon."

"Take good care of your partner in arms. Make sure you can trust her."

The so-called Union Room at the sawmill was at the rear of the sprawling building. The sawmill itself lay silent as if in mourning too, but family, staff and outsiders were gathering for the funeral service.

"Quite a few cars," Meg observed as Bryce drove her truck in and parked. "But Lloyd was the owner here and a hometown Wasilla boy, so obviously well-known. Yet no one seems to know who financed his flying lessons, plane or runway. Let's do a lot of eavesdropping here today."

"It scares me that you and the Big Man are starting to think alike."

She glanced out into the blinding snow behind the mill toward the dramatic rise of the mountains. She was pretty sure she could see where the private runway lay, a little less snow on it than elsewhere, though the sharp winds in this open area were slowly shifting that.

They went inside and left their coats on a rack with others. The room beyond looked quite plain. It was filled with rows of chairs and a speaker's dais in front. Several tables set around the side walls displayed large photos of Lloyd and his wife, other pictures with workers at the mill or people Meg could not identify. But none with his plane as far as she could see from here. Sad, if he'd loved flying so much, despite what had happened. She noted several shots of him with his wife and young daughter but none of Rina as an adult. Someone had brought in some swags of greenery for the bare walls, and at the door, there was a book to sign, which they did.

Meg and Bryce joined a line of people waiting to greet the family. As far as Meg could see ahead, that was just Rina and Todd. Farther inside the room, she could now see a cluster of guests chatting. Leaning to her left a bit, she saw the closed casket, and a quote about flying propped up on an easel. In large cursive writing, she could see it simply read, *They shall mount up with wings like eagles.*

Rina saw them first and frowned. Was she going to make a scene or ask them to leave?

She drew Meg a bit back from the reception line, and Bryce quickly followed. Todd was talking to someone, but he joined them too.

"Did you or the NTSB ask for Alaska State Troopers to search my father's house?" she asked them, her voice low. A frown crushed her features. She looked red-eyed from crying or lack of sleep. "I know you were at the mill, inside his—our house."

"A search warrant was not our decision," Meg told her.

Bryce said, looking straight from her to Todd then back again, "However, you do realize that when an unmarked plane with a pilot with no registered flight plan and no ID dies in an apparent accident, it's standard procedure to investigate."

"As if he was accused of something," Rina insisted, whispering, almost hissing. "They dared to take some things from the house and are promising us a list of their theft later. I'm not sure what and why. I am demanding my property—my inheritance—back now."

Leaning slightly toward Bryce, Todd interrupted, "My father, who is a Michigan senator in DC, albeit in a different jurisdiction, is looking into this too. We're grateful for what you did to recover Lloyd's body, Mr. Saylor, but we demand property rights and privacy. We do not want any more of this in the papers, and several reporters have called the mayor's house looking for us."

Did that mean they were still at the mayor's? Meg wondered. And if so, who had made that public knowledge? She certainly hadn't seen them at the birthday party. Keeping her voice calm, she said, "Will you be going back to Ohio or even Michigan soon or staying to oversee things here? Leaving might help to get the media off your back, but I imagine they might then pursue you in the Midwest—Ohio or even Michigan," she repeated, trying to drive home that she'd looked into their private lives.

Something had snagged in her mind at Todd's revelation about his father, but it was obvious Todd and Rina had to get back to their guests, so no more pursuing that right now.

Meg said, "We should all be on the same side in this tragedy."

Even that did not calm the waters. The Galsworths hurried back to their reception line, where the sawmill's foreman, Rencie, was patiently waiting. Most of the crowd inside were men—no doubt sawmill staff—but there were some women too.

"The father-senator connection is interesting," Bryce told her as he took her elbow and guided her to seats in a middle row, "though I'm not sure how or why. I'll have to ask you-know-who if he knows Michigan Senator Galsworth or what he knows of him."

"Technically, the VP of the United States is in charge of the senate, so he must know him or know of him."

"There you go, making assumptions about the Big Man again."

Meg shot him a sly smile. "I'm right, though, aren't I?"

Bryce met her smile, but ignored the question. "Let's just talk about the weather here, in case we're overheard," Bryce told her and squeezed her arm. "And speaking of that, let's do some listening of our own. Meanwhile, look around to see if you spot that onyx ring you said Darth Sidious wore, listen for their voices—anything."

Bryce had spent much of the morning interviewing everyone at the lodge—even Bill Getz. He had asked Getz not to tell anyone about the home invasion so the lodge would not be invaded again, by reporters and curiosity seekers this time. Getz had agreed, except for one person he had to tell—the mayor. "Look, Agent Saylor," Bryce told her Getz had said, "I got a good deal with the mayor. He's got me on salary, keeping an eye on things here in town, and I can't be keeping big news about his town from him—no way!"

Despite being annoyed at that, it did explain the list of payments Bryce had found, and he said he was feeling guilty about breaking into the guy's treasure trove of hoarded stuff, so he said he'd let that go for now, but still keep an eye on him.

At least Bryce said all their stories jibed. But they still didn't add up to decent descriptions of the intruders, so, even here, Meg knew she needed to study apparent strangers, which she did as more people came in for the service. She felt silly, looking down at hands for rings. She did see one man with manicured nails that stood out in this crowd of big-knuckled bruisers, but that was all. That guy didn't sound like the home invader, and the ring he wore was a plain gold wedding band.

She'd told Bryce that Darth Sidious had brown eyes, but didn't more than half of the population? She had approximated their heights and weights for him but that was nothing distinctive either. Both masked men had been muscular, but so were three-fourths of the men in this area.

She'd been so busy today she hadn't even looked at the Wasilla High School yearbook she'd "borrowed" from Getz, nor could she recall where she'd hidden it. Was it possible she had just tossed it on her bed?

A Wasilla minister conducted the service while Rina and Todd, as well as a few close workers and friends, occupied the front rows. Pastor Parsons praised Lloyd for remaining "a simple man," one who loved his workplace and its people, his family, his little getaway cabin and learning to fly. The pastor read a different Bible passage from the book of Proverbs that picked up on the theme of soaring high above the clouds and flying toward heaven.

Bryce reached over to squeeze Meg's hand. Did he think she was remembering Ryan's plane crash? Was he thinking of his own love of flying, or of Lloyd Witlow's crash again? Or about "the riches" the lost Confederate treasure would bring to anyone who could get their hands on it?

Before the service, they had overheard someone say that the pastor had known Lloyd well from "way back." There was a buzz that the deceased had come into money from somewhere. One woman behind them was certain that "His only child, Varina, finally realized she'd been wrong to run away from here and was trying to atone lately—or did she realize Daddy had come into some cash? Never did like that girl, treating her parents like that."

"Oh, yes, and I heard Todd's parents are well off," another woman had responded. "His father's an important something or other in the Midwest. Maybe Varina thought the airplane was a makeup gift and her father-in-law paid for it."

"Interesting way to research," Meg had whispered to Bryce in the shift to other topics behind them as they'd huddled close in the draft in the chilly room. "Maybe Rina and Todd did pay for the plane, but consider the source— hearsay. I'd rather research in a book or online, which reminds me I have a confession to make."

"Should we ask the pastor if he'll hear that confession?"

"Very funny."

"That you've fallen crazy in love with me?"

"How can you joke at an event like this?"

"I see it as a celebration of life, not death. The guy wanted to fly and, despite catastrophe, he did. Probably he died doing what he loved, at least."

"My confession is I took one of Getz's items out of that hoarder's nest, but then, so did you."

"Mine was in his wastebasket and directly linked to who he might have been working with. What did you take?"

"A Wasilla High School yearbook, that's all. And don't think I won't look up Todd's father online, though I can't see what that link matters even if the senator's money, which he gifted or loaned to his son and daughter-in-law, supported Lloyd's passion to fly."

"I'm seeing enemies behind every tree. But I am not going to have to arrest you for sneaking that book out of Getz's hoarding chaos. Remember even on our way out to keep your eyes peeled for anyone from the mill, from Wasilla—anyone—who might sound like or resemble the home invaders."

"I've been doing that. I'm wearing down."

"Me too."

He reached over to take her hand. She leaned her shoulder into his. Despite the danger and the fact they were at a funeral, she was so comforted by his closeness.

CHAPTER TWENTY-SIX

The next morning at an early breakfast with just the two of them, Bryce told Meg, "I've had a quick decision from you-know-who, for your and Suze's ears only. We will have a state trooper here in civilian clothes sometime this morning. I'm told he's familiar with the area, because he was around the tracking camp when there was a murder there. He's a skier, so that works out. He's going to say he came to ski but will pretend to sprain his wrist and decide to stay on for a few days anyway. He's going by the name Kurt James."

That name hit her hard. Here she'd been mining her memory for why Todd Galsworth's Michigan senator father's mention had hit a nerve and now this. Although the two of them were completely alone, she looked around.

"I bet I know him," she whispered. She leaned closer to him across the corner of the table and mouthed, "If Kurt James is really Jim Kurtz, he was also at Alex and Quinn's wedding."

Bryce's head jerked. He whispered back, "You're something. Glad you're helping me with this mess." He smiled, sipped more coffee but winked over the rim of his cup as his ankle brushed hers under the table.

As if their speaking of the trooper had conjured him up, they heard the front bell and Suze called from the front hall, "It's him, our new ski guest, I mean."

"When she sees him she might blurt out she knows him," Meg whispered. "Got to head that off."

Meg rushed to join her since Bill Getz had suddenly appeared, all ears and eyes.

"Suze," Meg whispered as Suze opened the front door, "we can't let on we know him."

"Oh," she whispered, then said louder, "Look, our new guest Kurt James is here."

They all welcomed him, helped him bring his ski gear in and shook hands all around, even Getz, which made Meg doubly nervous. Why had he suddenly materialized when the doorbell rang? Was he serious about saying he'd be leaving soon or would this keep him here, peering around corners, prying? And that reminded her again that the high school yearbook she'd borrowed had not been in her room, and she'd been so distracted and exhausted that she hadn't searched thoroughly for it. But she had to also warn Chip not to blurt out that skier Kurt James was really state trooper Jim Kurtz.

"I've got to go find Chip," she whispered to Bryce.

"In the basement with his soccer net."

She slipped away while the others were chatting. So how much had "Kurt" been briefed by the Big Man? Or had he only been assigned and filled in by local troopers, maybe those who had searched Lloyd Witlow's house?

She found Chip downstairs near the service and storage rooms with the soccer net propped up against the end of the hall. The net was heavy and unwieldy, so either Bryce or Rafe had carried it down. The three dogs had enough

smarts to sit way down at the other end of the hall to not be
assaulted with the barrage of kicked balls.

"Good one!" she told him when a ball slammed into the
net.

"I can't get good angles here, but Commander Bryce
helped me bring it down here 'cause of all the snow outside.
Temporary, he said, 'til we visit his house in Juneau."

"Listen, honey, I'm hoping you can keep a very important secret."

"You found out who those *Star Wars* guys are? Is one the
mayor?"

She gasped. "Why would you say that?"

"'Cause when he was here with those other people, I heard
him say you and Commander Bryce needed watching, so I
thought he might have sent those guys or come himself to
watch you."

From the mouths of babes, she thought. "No, but here's
the thing. Do you remember the state trooper and his wife
who were at Aunt Alex and Quinn's wedding reception
here?"

"Sure. He didn't wear his uniform that day."

"Since those bad men with guns came, we thought it
would be good to have a trooper help keep the lodge safe,
but not to have him in a uniform—no car out in front—a
secret. Like he's just a skier and a regular guest."

"Well, how can it be a secret if Trooper Kurtz is that guy
and a bunch of us know him?"

"Because it's okay if we know him, just not anyone else.
His new pretend name is Kurt James," she said and spelled
that out for him. "So you will call him Mr. James and never
let on you know who he really is or why he's here, not even
if you think no one is listening. That will really help and
make Commander Bryce very proud of you. Okay?"

"Sure. I know all about disguises, even ones without a mask."

"Good. No secret smiles at him, no winks or whispers. I knew you would be good at that."

Despite the extra security, the lodge still seemed to Meg like a ticking time bomb. It was not from being pretty much snowed in, though that kind of cabin fever got to her sometimes. But with "Kurt," Rafe and Bryce—not to mention Getz—all on alert for their own ends, she was going crazy.

She had searched but had not yet found the yearbook she'd put in her room when she was in a rush and distracted, so had someone been inside and taken it? The idea of Bill Getz being in there gave her the double creeps.

She had extra things to do like make more candy to maintain the stock for holiday gift sales, and she needed to harvest the wild mistletoe she sold seasonally too. Grandma had first propagated a breed of miniature mistletoe in a stand of yellow cedar a few miles away. Once a year Meg visited that stand of trees where the holiday plants had thrived. Though it was frigid outside, she wanted to do that. But today, she had an idea to find out more about Lloyd Witlow that could help their cause.

"Bryce," she said, pulling him aside when he joined Chip and her in the basement, "how about I take Chip into Wasilla and buy him a soccer jersey?"

"Maybe I should go too. After everything, I don't want you two out alone."

"Like it's been safe around here? A home invasion and he gets put literally under the gun? Truth is, I'm going to call to see if I can interview that minister who spoke at Lloyd's funeral. Remember, we overheard he knew Lloyd well from 'way back,' and the pastor quoted that verse about not running after riches or it can cause trouble. Of all people, I'd like to think he won't lie as so many others seem to be doing."

"Not a bad idea, since we're clutching at straws, and we have good security here. How about I go along and wait with Chip while you talk to the pastor? And let's buy all three of us the same jerseys if we can find them. Folks who play together stay together—or so I've heard."

She nodded with tears in her eyes. He was thinking of all three of them as a family—or at least a team.

From the back seat of the truck, Chip said, "I think you guys should put your jerseys on right now too. Mine looks real good."

"Your mother is going to talk to a minister for a few minutes while you and I wait inside the church for her."

"Is it about a wedding?"

"Chip—" she started to protest, but Bryce cut in.

"Not yet, pal. It's too early to talk about weddings when the three of us haven't even played soccer together yet."

"Oh, yeah," the boy said as they pulled into the half-cleared church parking lot, nearly deserted on this Wednesday afternoon.

Meg had been watching for cars behind them while Bryce drove. Since the home invasion, she'd had the feeling they were being watched—even targeted.

Bryce and Chip talked soccer in the foyer while the receptionist escorted Meg into the pastor's office. The smiling man rose from behind his desk and shook her hand. The woman went out and left the door open.

"Thank you for seeing me on short notice, Pastor Parsons."

"A minister who is both a pastor and a parson must do double duty, and you are most welcome."

She wondered how many times he'd used that line to break the ice. Smiling, she went on, "I don't know if you realize that, by accident, I was present at the site where Mr. Witlow's plane crashed, both when he went down and when his body was recovered at Falls Lake."

"Ah, yes," he said, steepling his hands before his calm face, which hid his mouth and much of his expression. "So I remember hearing, Mrs. Metzler."

"I understand from your remarks at the funeral and from things that people said there that you knew Lloyd Witlow quite well. It was such a mystery that he had no identification on him—nor did the plane have any painted on its exterior—and I could not help but wonder about the man, especially considering your choice of the funeral passage— 'Do not overwork to be rich,' and 'riches fly away.' I talked to people at the sawmill who greatly admired him but indicated his passion for flying and his reconciliation with his daughter happened much at the same time—and that he did not have his own funds for all those expenses. I hope he was content with Rina's return and that he—in your own words—can now fly away like an eagle toward heaven."

"In the wise book's own words. You have met Rina and her husband, I believe?"

"Twice. They visited the lodge I co-own near Falls Lake, and we spoke again at the funeral."

"Then, just let me say this to avoid breaking any private confidences. I meant those words for the living, not the dead. Especially for Rina, who went off track long ago and, at least, has been lately trying to make amends, but in the world's way, not by actually honoring her father."

Meg almost said, *I see,* but she really still didn't. She sat forward and decided to risk more. "In gifts and money, not time and affection? I know she fled here once, hated this place and her life here."

"We all go astray at times, Mrs. Metzler. You've perhaps heard the saying, 'You can't go home again'? The Bible says to honor your father and mother and all will be well. That's the only one of the Ten Commandments which has a promise attached to it and the implication of trouble if it is not followed. Now I never knew Rina as an adult but the two times I met her lately, I would think that curse clings to her. I do give her credit, though, for being protective of her father's goods. She and Todd are going through her father's house and office at the mill for keepsakes, though I doubt they'll be up for a trek to his distant, snowed-in hunting cabin."

He didn't think Rina was sincere! And maybe just wanted things to sell right now? If Rina was hard up for money, dared Meg dig deeper?

"At least, as you said, perhaps she is trying to atone for her past relationship with her parents—and here both are gone now."

"She got her waywardness from her mother, but her mother stayed true and 'stuck it out,' as they say. I'm regretful that's all I can add, but I thank you for coming to the memorial, for caring about a man whose death you witnessed. Sometimes it is an honor to witness life and death, but sometimes a burden. Let me call Madeline and have her see you out."

"So?" Bryce prompted in a whisper when they were almost home and Chip had fallen asleep in the back seat.

"He said some kind of cryptic things, and yet I think he was telling me that Rina was not really—well, repentant for deserting her parents. I've got to learn more about her, more about them. About her husband too."

"You've turned up a lot before."

"I've got to find that yearbook to research Rina at about the time she left here. I might get on one of those ancestry websites and see if Todd's related to that Brooklyn, Michigan, jeweler the Big Man mentioned to you. After all, the regiment who captured Jefferson and Varina Davis and all that gold and jewelry was from Michigan, but it's a big state. I'm clutching at straws again, but what else do we have?"

"Through all this, we have found that we have each other."

She gripped her hands together in her lap. "Bryce, it scares me how much I've come to need and care for you in so short a time, but so much has happened."

"And more to come. Suze asked me if I'd help decorate the lodge and I not only said yes but recruited both Rafe— well, she already had him lined up—and Kurt. It's going to be Kurt's excuse for spraining his wrist so Getz doesn't think it's weird when he doesn't go skiing, despite all that equipment he hauled in."

"Family time amid all this. I love that idea."

"If Chip wasn't asleep in the back, I'd park off the road, and we'd celebrate finding each other."

"Speaking of finding something this holiday season, will you strap on snowshoes and hike with me to harvest some mistletoe I can sell in town?"

"Harvest it and use some of it!"

She had to laugh at how he flirted and warmed her all over. "Bryce, I've been struggling to utter the words, not used to feeling this way since Ryan, but—I do love you. I want you to know that."

"I love you too, Meg. And I have every intention of showing you just how much every chance I get, but first, I need a blow-by-blow of what Pastor Parsons said. You never know what small or big piece of evidence is going to turn up where. Like we found each other, we'll find something— we have to."

CHAPTER TWENTY-SEVEN

The next morning, Meg was in her room, just starting an on-line search for Senator Galsworth. The first thing that came up was a picture of the handsome, silver-haired man with his entire name, Hanson Galsworth, but before she could learn much else she heard voices raised clear down the hall from the great room.

Locking her door behind her, as she always did now, she dashed out.

Oh, no, the mayor was here and yelling at Bryce. They stood only about six feet apart, and Suze had taken cover behind the welcome desk.

"You can't deep dive for an airplane that's not there any-more. I don't know why you're still around if you haven't turned anything up!" the mayor shouted. "Or if you have, you need to share it with the local powers-that-be."

"And that would be you?" Bryce countered, his voice calm and steady despite how on edge he'd been lately.

"It took you long enough to learn who the pilot was, and then you didn't come to me except accidentally when you were looking for a newspaper. I could have helped you all along."

"All along would have been good. But you chose to support a jewelry store owner and a woman who fled Alaska because she hated it here—and her husband and a lawyer you obviously recommended."

"Don't try throwing your government weight around here, Commander. I *am* the government in this bailiwick. Well, Meg," he said, noticing her at last. "Got to be careful, girl, as you can be known by the company you keep."

"Good advice for all of us, boy—that is, Mayor Purvis," she dared.

Suze gasped. Bryce bit back a grin and cleared his throat. Meg didn't look at either of them but jumped at the new voice behind her. Getz. She should have known if there was anything to hear or see, he'd be hovering.

"Tell them I work for you, mayor," Getz said, sounding nervous. "But on the up and up. I get some real looks around here."

"I've hired Bill Getz," the mayor said, "to keep an eye on and inform me about…you know, eyesores in town and its environs—private dumps, trash thrown in places where it should not be. That sort of thing,"

"That a big problem around here?" Bryce asked.

"It can be," the mayor said. "Not that that's why he's here at the lodge. Came into a little windfall, didn't you, and just wanted a short change of venue?"

At least, Meg thought, everyone had simmered down. Only Bryce had stayed the same, rock steady, even though he was now backed up by Rafe and Kurt, who had just come in. Kurt had said the mayor wouldn't recognize him—he was pretty sure—and he'd never seen Getz either.

"I just expect," the mayor said in a calmer, quieter voice,

"to be kept totally informed if there is anything happening here or anywhere else in my jurisdiction I need to know."

"On a need-to-know basis," Bryce repeated. "I can agree to that."

The two men stared—actually glared—at each other for a moment before the mayor turned and headed for the front door.

Getz went out right behind him, and Kurt went to the door, likely to keep an eye on them.

Bryce, Rafe and Meg huddled.

"Well," she said, "at least he didn't have a *Star Wars* mask on."

"You don't mean it could have been him?" Bryce asked.

"Chip suggested it, but no. I just mean he was about as welcome. But the thing is, would he come in here like that if he were guilty of hiding or fencing jewels and other precious contraband? Wouldn't he lie low—Getz too?"

"Or," Rafe said, "could it be reverse psychology? His idea could be 'Here I am throwing my weight around, so I can't possibly be involved or I'd know better.'"

"Exactly," Bryce said and motioned Meg over to the expanse of windows when Rafe went to find Suze, who had gone back to her office. "After that barrage, do you still want to go out in the truck, then hike to get mistletoe? I promise I'll behave, because I do not want to be labeled a 'boy.' You've changed, sweetheart, standing up to him like that. When I first came, you would have accepted that 'girl' indirect insult."

She sighed, not sure what to say, amazed at her own transition. "You know, I was just starting to research Todd's senator father. All I got so far was he's from Jackson County, Michigan, his first name is Hanson and he's good-looking, unlike his son. We can call him 'Handsome Hanson.' But yes, I'll get out the snowshoes, and we'll drive as far toward the stand of cedars as we can, then gather some mistletoe. I was thinking Chip might want to go, but that soccer net has worked wonders for his exercise and interest."

"Let's look up more on Handsome Hanson tonight, together. And if the Big Man tries to contact me while I'm out of the cell phone tower range, so be it. But I am taking my gun. Actually, I have a pistol and a rifle."

"I—I didn't know you had even one."

"I should have told you, but they're so hidden you didn't see them with my stuff when you packed for me, nor did our *Star Wars* invaders."

"Well, who knows? If that mistletoe is stubborn, we may have to shoot it down from the highest branches, and, if so, we'll be bombed with pine cones too. Kind of like life around here, lately."

When she stopped the truck in a snowy pull-off area down a side road on the far side of town, she gasped. About a quarter mile away on a foothill to the lofty Talkeetna Mountains beyond, she could see the stand of yellow cedars that some called Alaskan cedars. She'd been telling Bryce how they were prized for their golden-hued wood, which was both sturdy and decay-resistant—or so she thought. But what devastation in the year since she'd been here with Suze! The stand of cedar trees still stood tall but bare-limbed like giant toothpicks.

"What happened to majestic and mysterious?" Bryce asked, reaching over to grip her wrist as they stared upward through the windshield.

"I—I can't believe it. Last year I saw the foliage was a bit sparse, but I thought it was just the weather, maybe less rain for once. But this…"

She couldn't help tearing up. "It's like a ghost forest, a mass graveyard of trees. Damn climate change—that's what it is," she whispered, fishing in her coat pocket for a tissue to dab at her eyes. "I can't bear to see this, but let's get out and go closer. I think the little greenery we see may be the mistletoe clinging."

When the cold wind hit her, she felt her damp cheeks stiffen. The shrinking glaciers to the north were one thing, but she hadn't heard about this. The stand was small and not well known, which was why Grandma chose it for her mistletoe "farm." Thank heavens, she wasn't here to see it now, but Meg suffered for her.

She and Bryce steadied each other as they put their feet in the snowshoe hinges, then tightened their straps. Again, they were holding each other up in more ways than one, she thought. She reached over to hug him, however awkwardly in their big snowshoes. She felt his pistol pressed between them in his front pocket of his padded coat.

"I'm praying this is not a bad omen," she said as they started to trek on top of the thick snow towards the sad stand of trees.

At least, there, clinging to a few dry and dying branches were remnants of mistletoe with their greenish sprigs and white berries.

"See?" Bryce said, taking her mittened hand. "Even when things are bleak, there is new life. Let's get what we can by tossing sticks or I can use the gun, but with so much foliage gone, someone might hear it and investigate. Meg, I want to—I intend to—kiss you and not because of this mistletoe or even to comfort or distract you. We're a team now, one which has gone way beyond just helping to investigate a plane crash or long lost jewelry. Agreed?"

"Agreed," she said and lifted her face to him for a kiss, which she returned with her whole sad but joyous heart.

That evening after Chip was finally in bed, Bryce and Meg camped out in the workroom, where she had made more candy that was now cooling on racks. She'd brought her laptop in and was trying to research Senator Hanson Galsworth, while Bryce sat next to her to take notes, near enough to see the laptop screen and near enough to want to touch and kiss her. And to top that, she'd washed a good amount of the mistletoe they'd found and it was dangling from strings hung across the room or drying on paper towels in easy reach. He grinned at that.

As invaluable as she'd been, she did manage to scramble his brain, to distract him from what he should be concentrating on. He just hoped their few days together at his house over the holidays, away from here without other people and distractions, would prove to both of them—and Chip—that they were meant to be together. And he hoped her love for and loyalty to Suze would not keep her from moving there with him if he proposed.

"You won't believe this!" she told him, staring wide-eyed at the screen. "The *Detroit Free Press* said a few weeks ago that it's rumored Senator Hanson 'Han' Galsworth the Fourth may make a run for the White House in the next election. Or, the writer speculates, he may just raise his profile so he could be asked to run on the opposing ticket as a vice-presidential candidate."

When she looked up from the screen, Bryce tried not to look surprised or frown, but the ramifications of that could be far-reaching. Could the Big Man have an ulterior motive in continuing to pursue this investigation? Was he setting Bryce up to discredit someone who might run against his ticket? No, the Big Man had no more idea than they that Todd and Rina could have funded Lloyd Witlow flying historic national treasures to backwoods Alaska, of all places.

"Of course," she added while he agonized over that thought, "that would mean Galsworth would be in opposition to the president who says he's running again, so that would impact you-know-who too."

Damn, he thought. She was either with him or way ahead of him. Trying to convince himself, he told her, "A lot of politicians float rumors to test the waters."

"True. I still think I should get on that ancestry research site to see if any of the Galsworth ancestors were in that Michigan regiment that captured Jefferson Davis, Varina and their family—and all that treasure. What if men in that regiment stole or split up the loot? Or were rewarded with it, then hid it and passed it down through the generations? But the notes I took on which regiment that was are in my room."

"It was the Fourth Michigan Calvary Regiment."

She looked surprised again. "So you've been checking on it too?"

"Not checking your work, but realizing you had a point about it."

"So do you have names? More history of it?" she asked, turning back to type that in the regiment name followed by *American Civil War.*

He didn't answer but scooted his chair closer so he could look at the screen too. With his chin almost on her shoulder, he read aloud, "Union General James H. Wilson oversaw Lieutenant Colonel Benjamin D. Pritchard who commanded the 439 men of the Fourth. When they captured fleeing Confederate President Davis, one Union soldier said to him, 'Well, Jeffy, how do you feel now?'"

"It says here," she read from the screen, "that at least a million dollars of gold—the value at that time, much inflated now—was unaccounted for that day, as well as Confederate archives and jewelry donated for the cause."

"See what areas in Michigan the soldiers came from to make up that regiment."

He watched her scroll down, then go to another site. She was a beautiful woman. He loved to look at her, touch her. If this investigation came to a dead end, at least he'd found a new beginning with her.

She read aloud, "They were mustered out July 1, 1865, and went back to their homes and businesses. And here—see—many of the men were from Jackson County. That's where the Galsworths lived for several generations, and I think Todd is the first to move to northern Ohio to start his insurance company there. At least he doesn't have to live with the name Hanson Galsworth the Fourth!"

"I'd like to know what his agency insures and for whom."

"And," she added, turning to him, "could he be sending what his family inherited and insured long ago to Alaska? And stashing it where? No, I think I'd bet on the mayor and Melissa somehow getting their hands on that jewelry."

"But you said she was desperate for stock to sell and made you a big offer for the little you have."

"Maybe because she knows she doesn't dare sell the stolen goods right now—that we would be on to her. So she goes to the mayor for help…and they're having an affair. Reminds me of that poem—'What a tangled web we weave when first we practice to deceive.'"

"Exactly," he said, "but we are going to get to the bottom of this and get that national treasure back."

"Could the mayor have hidden things in Getz's place? Maybe if it was coming to the mayor somehow in cahoots with Lloyd Witlow, since Mayor Purvis doesn't have a Michigan connection."

"That we know of. Maybe his original roots are in Michigan," Bryce said. "Like maybe the loot was part of his heritage somehow. So many people in Alaska came from somewhere else."

"Or is the cache buried or stored near somewhere that

only a small plane like Lloyd's could land? Did he mean to land there and lost control of the plane or was he headed for somewhere else nearby when it crashed?"

"We may never know," he admitted with a huge sigh. "But I've got to keep poking around—riling people, which could be dangerous and why I want you to stick close to the lodge, research like you're doing, but no more field work. I swear I'm going to get this solved soon so we can get to whatever is normal—together."

He tugged her closer and kissed her. When they were together like this, safe, warm, he could almost convince himself that everything in this crazy case and between them would be all right.

CHAPTER TWENTY-EIGHT

Meg was astounded she'd managed to sleep almost seven hours, her best rest in weeks. But she still woke up early. She got ready for the day, putting on work clothes as she and Suze were going to decorate the lodge for Christmas. Bryce and Rafe were both going to help, so she was excited about that. Bryce had said since the Big Man was taking several days for his visit to beautiful Paris, France, he and Rafe could for sure take some time to decorate the lodge in beautiful Falls Lake, Alaska.

Since she had an extra hour, she grabbed a granola bar from her dresser and went immediately to her laptop. She researched Brooklyn, Michigan, in Jackson County, then looked for anyone in the Fourth Cavalry Regiment with the last name of Galsworth. Nothing, though a soldier could have been born on the maternal side and have a different last name.

The granola bar crumbled. Muttering, she had to blow pieces off her keyboard. She tried another tactic, going back to Brooklyn and scrolling through old pictures of the town. It was still small today, population 1,206 in the last census of

2010, even though it hosted a NASCAR speedway. It was in a lovely, hilly area with a lot of summer cottages on various lakes. The place was founded in 1832.

And then she found it. Not exactly what she'd wanted, because the name of the jewelry store and owners was not Galsworth, but here was an old black-and-white photo of the "downtown" of Brooklyn with a storefront window that read Fine Jewelry and Watch Repair. The owner stood before the store with his arms folded and was labeled as Mr. Starrs. Indeed the window was painted with that name with its extra *r* and a spray of stars.

Suze knocked and popped her head in. "Hey, busy day," she said. "And your favorite NTSB commander is having coffee alone and wondering where you are."

"I finally got some sleep, then had to check something out here."

Suze stepped in and closed the door behind her. "Guess what? Rafe insisted on buying one of the oil paintings I did of the lodge last summer. He's going to hang it in his apartment!"

"Great! But...where is that? I got the idea that wherever he is is home."

"Here and there, he says, but right now an apartment in Seattle. He likes it here better, he says."

Meg turned off the laptop and stood. Suze looked so happy and so—hopeful.

"Suze, you should listen to him about starting a local art club or artists' colony here at the lodge. Like he said, maybe have several weeks when you advertise it far and wide and people come in to draw or paint the scenery. You could have him visit to teach quick sketching."

She sighed. "Anything to get him back here...to hold on to him..." Her eyes misted. "Sorry," she added with a sniff. "It's just that Alex is so happy with Quinn, and they'll be back here for New Year's and be looking forward to a life together. You and Bryce—I know that's going to work out, I just feel it. And you know I love Chip and sure would like a chip off the old block of my own. Meg, I love the lodge, but sometimes—and the holidays make it worse—I just... I just wish..."

To Meg's surprise, Suze burst into tears, covering her face with her hands. Meg hurried to her, hugged her.

"I understand," Meg murmured. "Things will work out. The lawyer was a mistake, but someone like Rafe—"

She shook her head. Her words came muffled. "He'll be moving on soon. I'm married to the lodge—and I don't mean I'm not blessed to have it."

Meg reached over to yank a tissue from the box on her bedside table and gave it to Suze, who blotted her eyes and took deep breaths. Even if things worked out with Bryce— and that must mean a move to Juneau—could she leave Suze?

"You'd better go on out," Suze said and blew her nose. "I'll be out in a sec. Lots to do today, Christmas joy and all that, fa, la, la, la."

"Take your time here. See you in a bit, because I can handle things out there. At least for breakfast right now."

Feeling inadequate to comfort Suze more, she patted her shoulder and hurried out.

"We usually decorate a whole month before the twenty-fifth," Suze told everyone assembled once the boxes of holiday decorations were brought down from the attic. "But things have been so hectic that we're late this year. I want to thank Kurt and Rafe for going out with the sled to cut and bring in the tree Meg and I marked this autumn as well as the pine boughs for ropes and wreaths. I've put the tree stand right where it should go in front of the windows. Thanks in advance to everyone for your help, and we'll be sure a big lunch is ready for everyone right after."

Bryce noticed the Christmas spirit must be in full force here because the hoarder of all hoarders stepped forward with a string of bells in his hands. It was on a long, beat-up leather strap.

"I just want to say I did enjoy my days here," Getz announced. "I'm leaving today and can't help, 'cause I've got to decorate my own place. But I hope you can use these old sleigh bells, like on the mantel or some place. Or a door 'cause they sound really good if you shake them."

He demonstrated. The jingling, melodious sound filled the air, and everyone clapped. It was a rare come-together holiday moment, Bryce thought, and felt a twinge of guilt for already having seen Getz's place, even his room with jumbled Christmas decorations from who knew where. Maybe the guy was innocent, however suspicious. If Bryce could just clear the mayor and his cohorts, including the jewelry store owner the mayor was having an affair with. But no, no one in the clear yet.

After Getz left, everyone got in the spirit of things. The three dogs ran around with bows attached to their collars. The tree went up and was decorated, all six feet of it with a star atop. Everyone laughed as they untangled strings of lights. Out of the boxes and tissue paper, Meg and Suze produced beautiful ornaments and strings of blown glass beads that had been their grandmother's. Those reflected the lights, making the tree doubly glow as it got darker outside when snow began and the entire tree shone in the windows that acted like giant mirrors.

A crèche scene appeared for the mantel with wise men and angels. On ladders, Bryce helped Meg string ropes of fresh pine nearly to the ceiling. Rafe popped corn for a midmorning snack and to make old-fashioned strings of it for the tree. Eventually, they all sat down for lunch.

In the midafternoon, everyone went their own way until they gathered again for a pot roast dinner. Bryce felt the pull, the allure, of family then, the dream of having his own home with wife and kids. He smiled as he watched Meg and Chip together, happy, having fun. He'd like to think some of that was because he was here with them.

Kurt spent time on the phone before dessert and coffee talking to his wife, Janice, and family. Rafe called his parents, and Bryce overheard him praise Suze's art work—and she heard that too, smiling and blushing. Bryce called Steve, telling him he would be bringing Meg and Chip to Juneau for a few days soon.

It was all so holiday-ish, so Christmassy, and it wasn't any of that yet. Except in his heart. And in his fervent wishes for the future, a safe future for all here.

"Our Christmas tree smells good," Chip told Meg as she tucked him in that night. "Wish I had one in here, 'cause my three furry friends don't smell like that."

"That's one reason you and I are on give-the-dogs-a-bath duty. Soon there will be one less when Spenser goes back with Aunt Alex and Uncle Quinn."

"Yeah. His leash is under the bed, I think. I'll make sure he's looking real good when they get here for New Year's."

"I'll get it out now," she said, dropping to her knees from her seat on the bed and peeking under. "Chip! There's a ton of stuff here. Even books. You didn't shove your school books under here, did you?"

She pulled out the leash and several books came with it—including the Wasilla High School yearbook she'd been searching for and fretting about.

"Chip! This book—it's mine," she said, still on her knees, holding it up. "Did you take this from my room?"

"I didn't steal it," he protested, which made her feel guilty because she had.

"I mean, why did you take it?"

"Mom, when you were in your bathroom once and I was supposed to wait for you, I saw it on the bed and looked at the pictures and stuff. This school had a soccer team, really neat pictures of them and a game they played. So I just borrowed it to show Commander Bryce and then forgot it, I mean with all the crazy stuff going on around here."

"Yes. Yes, I see. Well, I need it back. I want to look through it too."

"I sure hope I can get good enough to be on a soccer team in high school in Wasilla—if we live here then, I mean."

She sat back down on the bed, scuffing everything except the leash back underneath the bed, while she cradled the book on her lap. She'd look through it and get it back to Bill Getz somehow without his knowing who took it. She knew Bryce felt guilty for breaking into the hoarder's house, and she did too. Would Getz realize someone had been there? Would he know who—why?

"Mom, you're not mad, are you?"

"I just wish you would have told me and given it back. But I'm glad you kept it in a safe place." In a hurry now to show this to Bryce, she leaned over to kiss him good-night. "Sleep tight, don't let the doggies bite."

Both frustrated and relieved, she ruffled Chip's hair, got up and went out into the hall, hoping Bryce was still waiting for her by the tree where she'd left him. Rafe and Suze were huddled at the other end of the great room, which smelled so wonderfully of pine.

Yes, Bryce was there, one arm along the back of the couch, one leg crossed over the other. His eyes seemed to glow in the reflected tree lights. He patted the place beside him, and she sat, holding up the front of the yearbook toward him.

"Where did you find that?" he asked, sitting up straighter.

Instantly, she regretted ruining the relaxed, special moment. Why did the dangerous outside have to keep impinging on the precious possibility here? She'd become part of it now, those developments, the danger.

"Under Chip's bed. He liked the soccer team pictures in it."

"Let's go in the kitchen so we can look at it."

They went into the cleaned-up kitchen, and she switched on the lights. They sat on tall stools at the work counter, and she looked in the back of the book index for Rina Witlow and Bill Getz.

"I'll check her out first," she said, frowning over the small print. "Yes, here's a reference. This is her sophomore year and his—ah, his junior year. Both have more than one page reference and, oh, I see one here where they are on the same page."

He leaned close as she riffled through the book. Bryce said, "Maybe they're still on the same page. Someone was working together and using Lloyd as a carrier pigeon to hide the goods. I'm betting the mayor and our antique jewelry store owner, but—despite the distance—I think you're leaning toward the charming Rina and Todd."

They hunched over the page as she found it and spread it out on the counter. "Bingo!" he said.

"But it still proves nothing but they used to know each other—maybe even dated? I can't believe it."

They stared at a photograph of a young Bill Getz and Rina Witlow. Grinning, dancing together at a school event, no less. It was on a page of random student life pictures with humorous titles. The one under this photo read, *Mr. Armstrong's worst nightmare: two crazy rebels in cahoots!*

"Mr. Armstrong's picture is over here—he's the principal," she whispered, pointing.

"Maybe those two together are Mr. Saylor's worst nightmare too," he muttered, frowning. "When we saw them both at the lodge, there was no sign they knew each other."

"Maybe, if they did date, she asked him not to let on because of Todd."

"Or if they were on the same theft team now, they didn't want to let on because of me—us. Getz would have warned her who I was, what I was there for—or someone did."

"The mayor's the one who's been pulling Getz's strings, had him on salary, and I have trouble believing it's just to keep an eye on things around town. Let's look at these other pages they're on."

"Okay. But whatever else we find, we're going to talk to Getz first thing in the morning. Not to tell him we've been to his place before or 'borrowed' this book, but to tell him we heard that he used to know—or even date—Rina. We'll just see where that goes. Again we're pulling at loose, tangled strings here, but remember after we untangled those strings of Christmas bulbs, the lights went on. That's got to happen for us too."

CHAPTER TWENTY-NINE

The next morning when it was barely light, Bryce drove Meg to Getz's long, patchwork cabin. She knew he hadn't wanted her to come along, but she convinced him it would be better, maybe keep the lid on if things got heated.

"This time we won't park behind the bushes by the frozen stream," she said as the truck bumped down the access road to the lonely site of the house. "But we'll still have to cross it."

The moment they got out, Bryce said, "Do you smell smoke?"

"A little. Not unusual, especially this time of year. Maybe it's Getz's chimney. A fireplace would be the only way he keeps his living quarters warm. That string of storage rooms in back were all chilly."

"Not only smoke but fire!" he said, grabbing her arm as they started to cross the narrow ice. "Behind those trees— with embers in the sky! Unless he's burning a lot of trash, that has to be his place. We've got to check on him. Besides, he could have made a bonfire to burn evidence if he thinks we're on to him. Look—his truck is here, parked farther down the stream."

They skidded across the narrow frozen stream, but then the snow impeded them.

"Look," she cried. "Fire through the trees. I even hear it."

When they tore into the clearing, they both gasped, then began to cough in the thickening smoke. The center section of Getz's house was on fire, easy kindling with all that stuff piled within. The section where Bryce recalled old papers and magazines were stored was ablaze with ten-foot flames.

"Call for help!" he shouted and put out his arm so she wouldn't go closer. "In case he's inside, I'm going in."

"No, you might get trapped! Those walls or roof could cave in. Surely he got out, maybe set it himself so no one could find things he had there. And I don't think my phone will work way out here."

"Drive until you get a signal! I'm going into the front where he lived. Go!"

She wanted to refuse, to argue more, to grab Bryce and not let him go. But she went back, slid across the ice and climbed the snowy bank toward her truck. She tried her phone. NO SERVICE IN THIS AREA.

She got in and sped down the bumpy road. Her tires crunched snow; her thoughts flew. Getz had just left the lodge yesterday. Surely he would not do this, but who would? Did Bryce insist on going in because this fire meant Getz knew something they had to know or because he feared the loss of any of the treasure in that inferno? Could this be an accidental fire—or not?

She knew one thing. Getz's passion for hoarding, his entire life must be going up in flames. She was scared for him.

She parked on the side of the main road and tried her phone again. It worked now—she punched in 9-1-1.

★ ★ ★

Bryce told himself he was not going past the first two rooms. Where had this fire started? He tried to break down the front door with his feet. Then, when it didn't budge, he used a big log from the stack of firewood on the front porch.

The door splintered vertically. He reached in to turn the lock and the knob. He had gloves on but he could tell the metal was hot.

"Getz! Getz, you in here? Call out, man!"

Small main room, beat-up leather easy chair with a quilt. Two hanging, unlit lanterns. In the kitchen Bryce wet his handkerchief in a plastic pail of water and held the wet cloth over his nose and mouth, but that didn't keep his eyes from watering, let alone trying to see through the gray pall of smoke.

Damn! If Meg came back like she did the other time he was here, she'd better not come in. He should have told her that.

Getz was not in here either, but the smoke was getting worse. He wished he was breathing canned air through his diving gear. One more room and he'd have to turn back. What if Getz wasn't here at all? What if this was a trap for Bryce? No, only Rafe and Kurt knew where they had been headed.

The next room—he thought it would be a bedroom, but it wasn't. Not even the office he'd been in before. He jolted to a stop. Two store mannequins and two straw scarecrows sat at a table as if they were real, and one of the scarecrows was aflame. Whoever had set the fire must have lit this one too. Could the arsonist still be here?

He saw one of the mannequins was Getz himself, propped up and sitting sideways in the chair!

Unconscious? Dead?

Praying for help, he grabbed a white blanket that was

lying nearby and stooped and yanked Getz toward him in what he'd been trained to call a fireman's carry, covering the man's head with the blanket in an effort to block some of the smoke. He nearly fell, staggered forward under the man's weight, then backed out toward the front of the long, narrow place.

As he half fell out the front door, gasping for air, he still couldn't tell if Getz was alive. Dead weight. His skin felt hot, but how would it not in that inferno?

He started for the stream, when—thank God—Meg tore at him across it. They nearly slid into each other, the blanket covering Getz falling to the ground.

It was only then that he realized Getz was tied hand and foot. So he hadn't started the fire by design or by mistake. And that meant—though the would-be killer could have run—they could be in danger too.

"The volunteer firemen are coming!" Meg shouted and started coughing in the smoke. "They're bringing the water truck, but I told them—" she gasped for air "—there's a stream here even if it's under ice."

He had a quick flashback to being under the ice the times he dove to Witlow's plane. He shook off the vision and laid Getz down on the snowy bank near her truck.

"Bryce, he's alive. I saw him blink. Bill!" she cried, putting her hands under his head when it sank back. "The firemen are coming and they can help you too."

The man was not burned, but he looked to be in shock. He opened one eye, looked at Meg, then closed it. He whispered something but his voice was raspy, and the crackle of the flames drowned out his words.

Meg bent closer to him. "Say it again," she said.

The man muttered something, then sighed and seemed to settle into the earth.

"Did you get that?" Bryce asked, his voice a raspy whisper.

"I think he said, 'Two men set timed bombs to start the fire and two more.'"

"Two more men or two more bombs?" Again, Bryce pictured the blast that destroyed Witlow's plane and nearly killed him and his dive team.

"We have to move back," he ordered Meg. "I'll bring him. Run!"

But she helped him lift the limp man into his arms, and they staggered through deep snow to her truck and laid Getz in the back bed of it to keep from jostling him more. When they got in and Bryce backed the truck a short distance down the road to escape the smoke, he saw the volunteer fire truck was coming right at them. He pulled Meg's pickup way over as the big truck raced by but didn't go far.

Though she hadn't said anything about it, in the pulsating lights on the fire truck, he saw Meg's gloves were slick with blood.

"From his head," she said, looking at them too. "I didn't want you to stop and look, but his head is soft in back—bashed in."

"Stay put. I've got to warn them about possible bombs in the fire."

But she ignored his order—par for this course, he told himself. As two of the firemen hurried up to them, starkly illumined in the big truck's headlights, Bryce saw Meg get out and wash her red gloves, then her hands off in the snow.

He told them, "Bill Getz is in the back of our truck, hurt or worse. He said two men planted incendiary bombs in his place to start the fire, but there may be two more, and I don't think they have blown yet, so—"

As if to prove his words, the woods and sky reverberated with two massive blasts that shook the earth under their feet. Flaming debris shot overhead and rained down amid shuddering trees.

Bryce hit the ground with Meg beneath him, nearly bury-ing her in the bloody snow. They held tight to each other as the trees seemed to sway, the very ground to shake under them. He looked back to see that the fire truck was intact and its crew had hit the ground too. Several fir trees had caught fire, though the snow heaped on their branches soon snuffed it out as the inferno beyond roared louder.

He knew the place was gone and feared Getz was too. One of the firemen, a medic, went to check on him and came back with a shake of his head while they all huddled there waiting, hoping for the fire to burn out.

As the noise subsided, Meg stirred under him and he rolled his weight off her. She said in his ear, "I must be crazy to love a man who keeps coming so close to death."

He sensed she was thinking of her husband. Would his own dangerous occupation keep her from saying yes to him? But she'd become so daring and brave, right in step with him, helping him, even urging him on.

"I'll take the love part," he told her. "And, I promise you, once I manage to move on from this, I'll cut back on deep sea dives."

"But you'd still be flying."

He helped her up as all four firemen reappeared, two of them dragging a hose from the back of the truck. They broke the ice in the stream to access the water below to smother the fire. One man checked on Getz again, then covered him with a folded tarp, leaving him in the back of Meg's truck.

Bryce knew one thing: the fire in his belly to solve this case, to find the two men, was not going out. Did the same people blow up Witlow's plane? They were skilled at what they did—who had hired them, or was this their fight too? Could they be the same men who had invaded the lodge and held Meg and Chip at gunpoint, searching for—for what?

More jewelry? Who the hell were they and who were they working for?

First guess—the mayor, who had maybe decided to silence Getz because he knew too much or was a loose cannon. Second guess—the Galsworths, to keep Getz quiet that he knew Rina from years back, that he had been working for her and her Michigan husband, maybe for her treasure-running father too. That could have been Getz who Meg and Chip saw waiting for Witlow's plane to land that day before everything went wrong. The distinctive smell in Getz's home—before all that smoke—had been like that blanket piece, and wouldn't it have been like him to put an old white blanket he'd picked up somewhere over himself for camouflage the day he went out to meet Witlow?

Then it occurred to him—the blanket he'd used to get Getz out of the house! He ran back to retrieve it from where it had fallen and saw that, though damaged with smoke and stained with blood, it had probably once been a white blanket. It was singed in places, but there was no mistaking the tear at the corner, where a piece of the fabric had been ripped clean off. Snagged on a tree branch? He lifted the blanket to his nose, but all he could smell was smoke.

"Is that the mystery blanket?" Meg asked.

"Could be," he said. "Hard to tell now, but we should hang on to it just in case."

He felt damn bad for Getz. The guy knew his own treasures were going up in flames. He'd been such a loner. He must have known too much about something—or someone.

One of the firemen approached them, his voice steady as he spoke. "The coroner or his delegate from Anchorage will have to pronounce him officially, but he's gone. The guy was an eccentric character—a monument—around here. I'm gonna call the state troopers and the squad right now even though he's gone."

"Poor guy," Bryce muttered as they stood, brushing snow off themselves and each other. "And this means more damn questions from the mayor coming. If anything precious for our case was in Getz's house, it's gone."

"We have to hope whoever was pulling his strings was smart enough not to keep the lost treasure there. If those two bombers were trying to find it, surely they looked around there before setting the place on fire."

"And maybe tried to beat some answers out of him. It could be more than his head was hurt, the way he was carefully tied. I didn't look close, but, once again, I think we're dealing with two men who are very skilled at ropes and knots. And they have a sick sense of humor to put Getz at a table with scarecrows and a mannequin. Oh—didn't tell you that yet.

"Listen, when you're questioned," he went on, clearing his throat, "leave out everything about our earlier visit here. I've already stashed the note about Mayor Purvis hiring him, and as for that yearbook photo—"

"Getz hadn't written his name in the book, not that I saw, so maybe it wasn't originally his. But it could be useful if we can link him to Rina—to get her to talk to us or in court someday."

He just shook his head in utter disbelief of this woman. She was thinking like an agent, maybe not even NTSB, but FBI or CIA. For one crazed moment, he wondered if she was somehow involved, if she'd been waiting for Witlow's plane to land when it crashed. But no—no way. He was just losing it. And he'd lost all self-control when it came to her.

"You're trembling," she told him.

"So are you. Cold. Nerves. We're stuck here until the authorities come. I don't care if you-know-who is being wined and dined by French President Macron, I'm calling him as soon as I can. Not for reinforcements this time, since he's sent us those, but to ask him why in hell he hasn't emailed documents and pictures of what I sent him in those first underwater boxes from Lloyd's plane. How long does it take so-called forensic experts to dry out and look at stuff like that?"

"Maybe they were water damaged as well as fragile."

The firemen were spraying cold water on the dying flames. Bryce sighed and looked at the shrouded form of Bill Getz as they walked past her truck. For a moment, he thought of the Confederate and Union soldiers shrouded like this who had died for their causes in the Civil War. This was a kind of war too, one over the historical treasure the rebel president had sought to escape with, a priceless, elusive fortune that now seemed a deadly curse on all who tried to hoard or hide it—or find it.

CHAPTER THIRTY

After answering questions from the state trooper who showed up before Getz's body was taken away, Meg and Bryce leaned wearily against the hood of her truck. They had not told the trooper that his fellow officer Jim Kurtz was on assignment at the lodge, though they used the officers' phone system to patch through to tell Suze what had happened and to talk to "Kurt."

"To top off all that tragedy," Suze said when she got back on the phone with Meg, "guess who's here, making what she calls a final, fair and fabulous bid for our old jewelry? And she says she's not leaving until she talks to you, and I couldn't tell her where you were. Meg, it's just one awful thing after the other," she added with a shaky voice and a single sob.

"I agree. But we can't just hide out and hope it all goes away. We have to stop it—somehow. We'll be back as soon as we can. If Melissa doesn't want to wait, fine, because I'm not selling her my things either."

"She has her husband, Jordan, with her. You think she throws her weight around, you should see him. Twice he's said he was in the Marines. He's clearly used to giving orders. At least Rafe is talking to him, because Kurt's lying low since he thinks he's met *Semper Fi* Jordan McKee before. Meg, it's just a terrible day and now poor Getz. Oh, got to go. Chip's making a mess washing the dogs."

Meg sighed. Could things get worse today? Maybe it would do everyone good if she, Chip and Bryce could get away for a few days—that is, if she could get their friends Sam and Mary Spruce to come in to live at the lodge while they were gone. Josh, who was Sam's brother, would be around off and on, and Rafe and Kurt were here for a while.

Bryce was still coughing from the smoke and his rough voice broke into her agonizing. "Any news from the lodge? Is Suze okay?"

"Melissa McKee is there with her husband. Bryce, despite the fact we're focusing in on the mayor or the Galsworths, we can't forget her. And Suze is really wrung out."

"So are we. You're right about Melissa McKee, but she's a long shot. I think we're done here. We did—" he coughed again "—what we could. The invitation is still open for you and Chip going home with me, whatever we can manage. If the Big Man can take extra days in France, we can afford a couple."

Her eyes, sore from smoke, watered with more tears. She nodded and took his sooty hand. Bryce raised his other to the officer in charge, who nodded.

They turned toward her truck, which, thankfully, no longer had Getz's shrouded corpse in the back. His body had been taken to Anchorage for an autopsy.

"We know where to find you," the trooper called out.

Bryce said to her, "Maybe they know where to find us— but maybe they won't. Let's see if we can clear two days in Juneau. We can work from there. I know I won't need to convince Chip, only his mother."

"I'll go. I'm ready."

They smiled into each other's eyes, and she noted again how gray his skin was from the smoke. Even his hair looked powdered, maybe a bit singed too. Several pieces of ash were caught in his hairline, and she brushed them away.

"I can drive," she told him and held out her hand for the keys.

"Sweetheart, in more ways than one, you are already in the driver's seat." He handed her the keys. "Let's get home and clean up."

"Despite who's waiting for us, sounds good to me," she said as they got in and she started the truck.

"You know," he went on, "maybe it's not such a coincidence that Melissa and her husband are there waiting for us. If they expected us to be at the lodge, maybe they meant to show us they were nowhere near this fire. They may not have been, but maybe they used their hired goons to question and threaten poor Getz, then to send him and that place up in smoke—with their specialty remote-detonated bombs. If so, I'll bet they were shocked if Suze told them we were there to see it happen."

"And maybe that's why Melissa is being so obnoxious about wanting to buy our small amount of jewelry—to convince us that she doesn't have a huge cache of it to sell."

Everyone except Kurt, who was still making himself scarce in case Melissa's husband would recognize him, gathered around Meg and Bryce after they washed up. Chip was downstairs kicking balls into the net so he and Bryce could have a "basement game" later in the day. Meg had decided she'd tell Chip in her own way about Bill Getz's death and the fire, but she was impressed that he always obeyed Bryce without hesitation or question.

Why Melissa might be having an affair with the mayor was beyond Meg's grasp when she saw Jordan McKee close up, because he was good-looking, seemed protective of her and generally friendly. But this initial impression soon segued to a more aggressive and dictatorial one, and Meg saw what Suze had meant. But why would Melissa gravitate toward the mayor, for he was much the same way, unless that was the kind of man she really liked? And, if so, could Jordan be forcing her to help with the stolen treasure?

Wishing they were just explaining Getz's death to Suze, Rafe and Kurt, Bryce went over what had happened, leaving out any suspicions they had about Getz being a spy or being linked to the Thanksgiving Day plane crash.

"Poor guy," Jordan said, shaking his head. "Someone must have wanted something from his collection of stuff, then maybe they argued. But bombs detonating, then turning into a bigger conflagration? Wonder if they were timed to go off or the fire ignited them."

Bryce shot Meg a quick look. The words *detonating* and *conflagration* coming out of this man's mouth so easily just sounded strange, but Meg knew they were both on edge, probably overreacting.

"Jordan worked with explosives in the Marines," Melissa said.

This time Bryce's eyebrows lifted—until he managed to hide his interest with a frown. "So did you ever work on underwater demolition? I had some experience with that in the service."

"Not really, not directly."

"One great thing about the service is making lifelong friends," Bryce went on. "I still keep in touch and work with some of my old buddies. Even living in Alaska, hope that's been one of your long-term benefits too."

"Yeah, now and then, but you're right about living here, since most of them are in the Lower Forty-Eight," Jordan said and changed the subject.

As exhausted as she was, Meg realized that Bryce was wondering if Jordan had some old friends who had specialized in remote demolitions. But no one would blurt out questions about bombs if he were really guilty—would he? Or was this man, who obviously shared his wife's interests, actually trying to attract them, get them to consult him?

After being turned down by both Meg and Suze about selling their jewelry again, Melissa huffed out the front door, and Jordan more or less swaggered out behind her.

Meg and Bryce collapsed at the dining table as Suze hurried to her room, and Rafe and Kurt huddled in the front hall, talking. "What do you think?" Bryce asked her. "The McKees are baiting a trap for us? Or else Jordan's just a blowhard and has nothing to do with anything but being part owner of his wife's struggling jewelry store and it just so happens he used to work in demolitions?"

"I think my brain's going to implode, but now I have Jordan McKee to research—when I can see straight again."

"I've got to go downstairs and make good on my promise to Chip, but I'm exhausted too."

"Let's both go and tell him more or less what happened, tell him the truth, that we're mentally and physically bushed."

"Can we tell Chip we're going to my house in Juneau tomorrow, for at least one night, maybe two? The Big Man just responded to my email, giving me the go-ahead."

"If Suze can get someone else in here to help that soon. It's Josh's day to work, so that will help."

"Besides, don't you think Rafe would scrub floors for her?"

Meg smiled and shrugged. "I'm afraid he'll be hitting the road when this is over."

"Kurt too—even me," he whispered, covering her wrist with his big hand. "Unless you and Chip can find a way to go with me for longer than a couple of days. Can you envision living the school year in Juneau, the summers here? Could Suze run this place during the colder months without you?"

Her pulse pounded. "Let's take this one step at a time."

"We are, but it makes sense to look ahead so we don't stumble on the next step. I admit it's been nonstop fast and insane danger since we met—not exactly conducive to a loving relationship—for most people, at least. But this is us."

She nodded and smiled, lost in his intense gaze. As exhausted as she was, she felt desire for him clear down to her chest, lower belly, even her toes. If she and Chip went to his home, if she spent that kind of time with him, she would be lost in love.

But with Bryce, maybe lost and found.

"Boy, it took you guys a long time," Chip protested when they joined him in the basement. "My foot hurts from kicking this ball in the net."

"We're pretty tired too," Meg put in before Bryce could say anything. That wasn't the direction he'd meant to take this conversation.

"And you guys smell like smoke. Even Mom's hair when she hugged me."

Deciding to ignore that, Bryce said, "Remember what I told you about how a goalie sometimes has to save the team? It's not easy, is it? Sometimes goalies get blasted with the ball, get hurt falling down and stretching out to keep that ball out of the net. It takes hard work and can be really exhausting, but it's worth it to win with your teammates."

Chip came closer and looked up at Bryce. "I remember that, what you said before."

"Okay. My job is sometimes like that. Like I feel that I got blasted today, missed the ball and the bad guys scored. Mr. Getz's house, where your mom and I went to see him, had a terrible fire. I went in to be sure he got out, but he was already hurt. He died right after I got him out where your mom was waiting, because she called the fire truck."

"Oh!" Chip said, wide-eyed. "He was kind of a weird guy, but I'm sorry he died. At least he didn't burn up with all his stuff. I'll bet some magazines and stuff he took from here got burned up too."

"Meg," Bryce said, "do you have anything to add to that?"

She told Chip, "You're right that Mr. Getz was kind of different from other people at the lodge, but that's okay as long as they don't hurt others. And, remember, he gave us those sleigh bells before he left."

"Yeah, that was good."

"So here's the deal," Bryce said with a nod at Meg. "I'd like to invite you and your mom to visit my house in Juneau for a couple of days, where we can relax and have enough room to play soccer instead of in this narrow hallway. I'd like to show you two my town and neighborhood, and there's a kid in the area for you to play soccer with, even though he's older than you."

"Which prob'ly means he's better than me, but I could learn some stuff from him, I bet."

Meg put in, "We're all learning things every day, not just you, Chip." She looked directly into Bryce's eyes.

At least, Bryce thought, he had this glimpse of normality—of maybe building trust for a new family. He was totally frustrated with this case and the fact that the Vice President of the United States of America was off being feted in Paris and hadn't sent him the damned evidence he'd asked for twice. Not the right move on the Big Man's part, so he hoped this was the right move on his.

He put one arm around Meg and tugged her close, and with the other he pulled Chip into their embrace.

Meg hugged them back. Chip did too. Whatever happened in this case, he prayed that private, precious time with Meg and Chip would, at least, work out.

CHAPTER THIRTY-ONE

Loaded with Chip's soccer gear and wearing their over-sized jerseys on top of their winter jackets, Bryce, Meg and Chip drove Meg's truck to Anchorage to get Bryce's plane. Though today was Sunday, Chip did not have school the next two days because of teacher meetings, so it was a perfect time to get away.

"I bet a lot of kids in my class haven't been to the state capital," Chip said from his back seat. "Juneau's bigger than Anchorage, right?"

Bryce told him, "Not in people, but in size. It covers such a large area among some tall mountains that the average population figures out to only about ten people per mile. But in cruise ship season up to six thousand people visiting can make some places really crowded."

"I already read there's great big glaciers, like thicker ice than even Falls Lake."

"Right. And if you and your mom would like to visit again in the warmer weather, we'll go up to see the one called Mendenhall Glacier. There's a really neat cable car ride called a tramway too, but it's not open in cold weather."

"Good thing we have the soccer stuff with us then."

Meg's smile warmed him so much that Bryce turned the heater down a bit. He was praying all of this would work out, for Chip. For her too. And him.

"Bryce," Meg said when their things were loaded on his plane in the hangar in Anchorage and they were ready to board, "I hope you don't mind that I still don't sit in the co-pilot's seat. Not with the mountains we'll be flying over. Besides, Chip would love to. I didn't tell him yet one way or the other, but we can when he gets back from the bathroom."

A shadow flitted across Bryce's face with a hint of frown. He was no doubt sad that, despite all they'd been through, she was still not ready to totally conquer Ryan's death by looking out at the mountains and cliffs. Of course, he had no idea she had faced the very place once before where Ryan had died—and that was enough. She'd kept it a secret for so long now, it felt impossible to talk about, the emotions too big, too personal. It wasn't something she wanted to revisit.

"Hey, no problem," Bryce told her. "Chip will love that, and I want him to love this trip." He lowered his voice. "I want both of you to, and, if you do, I'm really hoping we will make it more than once in the future, a shared future—ours."

She blinked back tears. This man could be rough and single-minded, but his words and voice—so tender and sincere.

Chip's voice shattered her reverie and their mutual gaze as he ran back to them: "Okay, I went to the bathroom, so I'm ready!"

"Bryce says you can have the copilot seat. But don't you talk too much if he's busy flying."

"Great! I've got to learn a lot, so I can fly someday too."

Meg managed to nod, but her stomach flip-flopped. In such a short time she'd come so far, because she would have stopped that kind of talk merely a month ago. But, she thought as she sat in the first passenger seat again, when it came to small planes she still had a long way to go.

Once on the ground at the Juneau International Airport, Bryce had his car, which had been parked in the long-timer's lot, brought to the hangar, and they transferred all their goods once again. Not that Bryce had protested when he saw how many things she'd brought, because most of the baggage was soccer gear.

She'd included the only new-looking fleece robe and slippers she had and a floor-length nightgown she loved but never wore—black with lace insets. And some nicer day clothes that she almost never wore around the lodge. With Bryce, she had gone back to caring what she wore, how she looked. He had helped her to reclaim her womanhood and herself.

Now he kept up a steady stream of narration about what they were seeing as he drove from the northwest part of town toward his neighborhood in the sprawling northeastern foothills.

"It is a pretty funny place for the state capital," Meg said. "I mean with no roads in or out of it."

"It has the sea, and that's what mattered when the city was founded and chosen as the state capital," Bryce told them. "Of course, it was also closer to Canada and the US than other 'southern' cities like Anchorage, and the Klondike Gold Rush coming through this area helped build it up."

Chip said, "I know some about that. I mean we studied about some crazy things the spectators—"

"I think you mean prospectors," Meg put in.

"Yeah, that's it. Like our teacher said people do some really bad things for gold and money."

Bryce turned to glance at her before looking back at the road, which wound up into the spruce-covered, snowy hills toward his house. "That's for sure," he told Chip, but Meg knew they were on the same wavelength, thinking of Pastor Parson's cryptic words at Witlow's funeral, not to mention a plane crash, a fierce fire, bombs going off aboveground and under the ice. Had people done all that for the Confederate gold and treasure?

"Okay, look up and you can see my house from here," he said, craning his neck and looking up, so Meg did too. "It looks like it's perched on the hill but there's plenty under it with a great view, trees, a stream—frozen now—and the valley below the hills."

He kept saying "hills," she thought, but really they were the beginning of mountains. This man knew her well, knew that she was still afraid of high peaks and sheer cliff faces. And he was right.

Meg and Chip loved the house Bryce's father had built and had left him. Despite the dramatic view—especially from the wraparound patio—she could imagine living here. Eagles soared at this height, and the clouds seemed like neighbors. And there really were neighbors not far down the road, closer to the valley, including Steve, Jenny and Mark Ralston, whom they were going to visit later. Meg would be glad to see Jenny again, now that her husband was recovering. Mark, though he was nearly seven years older than Chip, had seemed like a very nice kid.

After they unpacked and Bryce dug frozen pizza out of his refrigerator to microwave, they set up the soccer net in the basement. Bryce and Chip played away at that while Meg wandered back upstairs.

This was a lovely three-bedroom home with not only a den but an office. How she had missed having a home. The entire place had clean lines and was filled with light, even on a wintry day. Bryce had quickly opened the vertical blinds and turned up the furnace. The decor was minimal and modern, but some new furniture and special touches could make it warm and homey. And the views were spectacular.

She spent some time looking at framed photos of his family in the living room and den. His father had been handsome too. His mother never quite smiled, but looked strong and determined as any Alaskan woman should be. Was she? Meg felt she was becoming that way again.

"Hey, Mom, I blocked a couple of balls Commander Bryce kicked at me real hard!" jolted her from her reverie. "He's says if it's okay with you now, we're going to visit his friends down the mountain, but he calls it a hill."

She had to laugh. Bryce coming upstairs behind Chip did too, looking like he was a kid who had been caught at something.

Bryce grinned and ruffled Chip's hair. Meg smiled, really happy and excited, feeling as though she was flying high from deep within.

Steve was sitting in a reclining chair when they visited, but said he was walking now with a cane. Jenny beamed to have them all here, and their son, Mark, still looked a bit shy but pleased too. For their differences in ages, Chip and Mark seemed to hit it off, and Mark soon took him to look at his own soccer setup in the basement. So maybe that's where Bryce had gotten that idea.

After initial small talk over hot chocolate and cookies, the two men spoke at the other end of the living room. Some of it Meg could overhear as Jenny showed her around. After the tour, Jenny and Meg sat in matching club chairs in the next room. The view from here was good, but other houses were in sight, and the place didn't seem to be perched in the heavens as Bryce's was. Several photos were on the spinet piano. Meg had to smile at how traditional, almost old-fashioned

Jenny looked in them, always next to her diver husband with his ponytail and neck tattoo of *Semper Fi*.

After they'd corralled Chip to leave, Meg whispered to Bryce, "So could Steve know his fellow marine Jordan McKee?"

"I can't get ahead of you. I asked. He's only heard of him—doesn't know him or about him," Bryce said, keeping his voice low. "Another dead end."

"Don't say it that way," she blurted. "I mean—I'm not superstitious, but with Getz and Lloyd, it just scares me."

"That's why you're here, safe and sound," he told her, then turned back to say his goodbyes.

"Mom," Chip said as they started for the door, "they asked me if I can come back and stay with them tonight. Mark's soccer setup is bigger than mine—which is okay, Commander, 'cause I really love mine," he added, turning to Bryce.

Putting his hand on Chip's shoulder, Bryce told everyone, "We have created not only a soccer fan but a future goalie. It's up to your mother—and Mrs. Ralston—to decide."

"We'd love to have him," Jenny said, turning to Meg. "Mark has to go to school tomorrow—unlike lucky Chip—so you boys will have to promise not to stay up too late."

"Can I, Mom?" Chip asked.

"Of course, that would be so kind of you, Jenny. We'll bring some things for him when we drop him off."

"We'll bring him on the way to dinner in town," Bryce put in. "Not fast food, not up to his standards anyway, so he won't miss a thing."

Everyone smiled, even Steve, who had gotten up with help to walk them to the door using his cane.

"Steve," Bryce said, shaking his friend's hand yet again, "I'm so glad to see you better."

"We'll work together again someday, once you get this

case off your back. At least this danger and destruction reminds us what's really important in life, right? I mean, protecting people, guarding the country, even the nutty government, but friends and family most of all."

Bryce nodded and hugged him with one arm, still holding Meg's hand with the other. She blinked back tears, especially when Chip leaned on her a bit.

Friends and family most of all? Yes, whatever the cost, she wanted that with all her heart.

CHAPTER THIRTY-TWO

"Kind of quiet, isn't it?" Bryce told Meg after they'd left Chip at the Ralstons' and headed down the mountain to have dinner in town. Then, like a married couple, they were going to stop at the store for breakfast groceries.

"Once in a while it's nice," she admitted and reached out to put her hand on his knee as he often did hers.

Bryce could swear, with her, normal things like this were exciting, so he could almost imagine giving up the rush of adrenaline that spiked so often in his current career. If she balked at the danger he sometimes faced, he would almost consider consulting work or starting his own underwater kelp or algae farm instead of being part owner in one where he was totally hands-off. But this evening, night, next morning, he'd forget business, for this time could be the most important of his life.

"I want so much for this to be a normal first date," he admitted. "When really did we have anything in the beginning that approached normal?"

"No meet cute for sure."

"Not cute at all. Deadly and dangerous, but from now on—I swear it—different. I think you'll like this restaurant. Big menu, modern decor, great service. It's called Salt. Despite how spread out and diverse Juneau is, once you get downtown, you feel what a tight-knit community it is. Actually, I have to 'fess up that this place has the reputation of a date night spot. I don't want us to start all over again, since we've come so far, but, like in the old days, I'd like to court you."

"Maybe that rough start is what I needed to jolt myself out of my doldrums, my rut, as much as I love the lodge, as much as I dote on Chip and rely on Suze. It was a crazy, even dangerous beginning for us, yes, but it woke me up."

"Glad to hear that, because sometimes with you, I think I'm dreaming."

Over dinner, they talked of silly things and important things. Of families they grew up in, of childhood likes and dislikes. Of their years of schooling, career victories—she had a degree in elementary education but had not taught since she became pregnant early in her marriage. They sipped local craft beer and lingered over crab bisque soup. She ordered a small filet and he the big rib eye steak. Too full to each get a dessert, they shared a vanilla crème brûlée and lingered even longer over coffee.

"I'm not really good with too much evening caffeine," she told him. "I'll be awake until all hours."

He grinned. "Sounds good to me."

She thrilled at that. No, she was in a constant state of "thralldom" with this man. Not the kind when they'd been in trouble, but an ecstatic, emotional—erotic—excitement. If she did make love with him tonight, if she did marry him, surely it would not always be this way. But she was willing to find out.

★ ★ ★

Back at Bryce's house, she told him, "I can't get used to how quiet it is. Time for just the two of us, no Chip, no lodge guests, no Suze, no responsibilities—not even dogs."

Settled on the couch in front of a lovely fire he'd made, he tried to shake everything else off too. But it was hard to forget that other fire that had killed Getz and incinerated his hoard of treasures. Treasures—like the historic treasure they sought, and the treasured moments and memories they were building together.

He poured them goblets of chardonnay. They clinked the crystal rims, sipped and looked into each other's eyes. He asked his Alexa for some slow dance music and pulled her up into his arms when the old Sinatra tune "Fly Me to the Moon" began.

Tight together, they swayed, turned a bit. It seemed they fitted together well this way, and he longed for another way. Patience, he told himself. If they didn't sit down again and chat, he'd move too fast, make love to her standing right here, so he broke their embrace and tugged her toward the couch again.

"I saw online while you were packing up for Chip and changing your clothes that there may be a burst of aurora borealis tonight," he said. "Heavenly fireworks to remember on this night. I want to make love to you and spend the night together. I want you to consider marrying me. I want you, my sweetheart. I supposed it's fast on earth time, but we're not running on that, are we? We found each other late and in a shocking way, but we can make up for that on our time."

Wide-eyed, she nodded. "I want us to try. I do love you— how you treat me, how good you are with Chip. Let's drink to that."

"Forever," he whispered as they clinked the rims of their goblets.

After a few sips, he took her glass from her unresisting hand and set it down by his on the glass coffee table. He reached for her, and she came into his embrace willingly, even eagerly. Whatever had happened in his life, the crises, the near misses, his love of diving deep and flying high— this was the very best thing.

Meg watched as Bryce tamped the fire down a bit and put the screen in front of the hearth. Leaving their goblets on the coffee table, holding hands, they went down the hall-way toward the bedrooms. His was at the end of the hall, an eternity away, she thought. She was floating and did not feel her feet on the floor.

He did not turn on the bedroom light, but left the hall light on, which threw a pale golden shaft across his bed. A king-sized bed for a single man? Tonight she would help to fill it, and maybe ever after—if she could find a way to leave Suze, to move Chip, and to help Bryce survive this all-con-suming case of his—of theirs.

They kept kissing, kissing. Caressing. Despite the chill in the room, she felt flushed as they shed their clothes and climbed in under the covers he ripped back.

She was suddenly afraid, but then not. This was Bryce, and she loved him, trusted him. Just as she had loved and trusted Ryan. Loving Bryce now didn't diminish the love she'd had for her husband. This was something new, and while new could be strange and even a little scary, there was something about Bryce that felt comforting and familiar. She felt as though she'd known him for much longer, as though they fit well together because they'd somehow been made to do so. Yes, being with Bryce was new and scary and thrilling, but it also felt incredibly right.

Hands, lips, even his tongue whispered promises along her skin. She held on to him, dazed, ecstatic. She felt needy and so hot she kicked the covers off and met him halfway, touching, stroking.

He fumbled in his bedside drawer—he was prepared for this—then tugged her under him. Again she was ready, trusting, but so eager she didn't know herself.

They came together beautifully, perfectly. She cried out at the wonder of it.

"Too fast?" he spoke at last.

"No—fine. More than fine."

"You are that. So perfect. Perfect fit—us."

She spiraled up, up. Flying. Not afraid. The view, the feeling, the sky and this man, so awesome.

He collapsed beside her, panting. She lay tight to his side.

"Look," he gasped, pointing, and she saw what he meant.

The curtained window of his room with its dark, lofty view had turned greenish gold. At first, she thought of the night they'd been close to making love at Alex's house and that screaming, bright-light helicopter descended. Not here! Not again!

But no. She saw what he meant, remembered what he had said before about the gift—the good luck—of perhaps seeing the aurora borealis together tonight.

A random thing right now, a special thing, a gift and blessing.

He dragged a blanket from the bed and wrapped it around both of them as they went to the window and he pulled the curtains even wider open. The glow poured in to shimmer everything to life. Luminous, unearthly colors pulsated, pale green gold, dark blue with streaks of upward light. It was as if they were standing under shimmering water.

"Good luck for us," he whispered, holding her close.

"I've seen it before, but never like this."

"And I've never been in love—really in love before. Meg, the truth is, in the time I've known you, I've quickly found it impossible to imagine my life without you. What do you think about the idea of getting married again?"

Her stomach fluttered with butterflies. "Married…to you? Are you asking?"

He smiled. "I am. Will you marry me, Meg?"

She surprised herself by her lack of hesitation. "Absolutely." This wasn't moving on—this was moving forward. With Bryce. It's what Ryan would have wanted. For her to be happy.

He leaned forward and kissed her softly before he spoke. "Now, let's get back in bed and watch this light together. Tomorrow, I'm going to ask Chip if he'd be okay with us getting married."

"If soccer's in the deal, he'll probably say yes."

He laughed. She did too. They hurried back to bed and reveled in the glory of the lights and of their love.

"Me and Mark talked really late, after his mom turned the lights out," Chip told them the next midmorning when they picked him up and said goodbye to the Ralstons for now. "Then his mom said it was late and stop fooling around, because he had school coming up even if I didn't."

Meg and Bryce's eyes met before he looked back at the road as they drove into town again, this time to show Chip the Last Chance Mining Museum and where the Mount Roberts Tramway began.

"So why is this place called 'the last chance'?" Chip asked when they parked at the museum.

Bryce told him, "The men panning for gold could run out of money—or good weather—before problems came along. But some of them stayed on, desperate to make their fortunes. Some did get rich, most didn't."

"I'd like to be rich someday," the boy told them as they went inside. "But I'd rather be good at soccer."

"If you're good enough at soccer someday," Bryce said, "that might mean being rich."

The three of them went through the displays, which included a lot about mining for gold without a stream and metal pan. Later, they'd stopped for hamburgers when Bryce's cell phone rang.

Meg saw him punch the screen and frown at it.

"Email coming in from the Big Man," he said. "More than one. Yes, I think it's what I've been waiting for at last."

Chip piped up, "Does it mean we have to leave? And who's the Big Man?"

"My boss. Just a nickname. Yeah, let's finish up here and head on back to the house."

His intense gaze met Meg's. His eyebrows nearly met as he frowned. For some reason, fear stabbed her. That this precious time might be over. That Bryce would go away, be called to Washington, the NTSB office at Anchorage, at the least. That he would be in danger again and she couldn't help him or go with him. That she might lose him. She feared the light of the glowing aurora she'd been living in right now would turn into a single shooting star and disappear.

She got Chip in bed, listening to his tales of being with his new friend Mark. Surely it would be good for her boy to have more friends here than he did around the lodge or even at school since he immediately rode the school bus out of town after classes.

Finally, he wound down. "I do miss the dogs, though," he admitted. "But if we live here someday, one of them could come too or we could get a new one—if they just had puppies, but you said they got fixed and can't."

"Go to sleep, honey. We'll talk about all that tomorrow."

She wondered if Bryce would still ask Chip if he could

marry her, or had business slammed back in now and that would have to wait?

She left Chip's door ajar in case he called her, but went to Bryce's office, where he was staring at his laptop and printing what looked like reproductions of grainy photographs.

"Old pictures were in the boxes in Lloyd's plane?" she asked, seeing one emerging from the printer.

She moved closer to Bryce and looked over his shoulder at the screen.

"Those boxes in Lloyd's plane had a lot more jewelry," he said. "And some old papers—a manifest in shaky handwriting of what Jefferson Davis and his troops carried. But the reproductions of some of these photos are not of that era, not tintypes or anything like that. Much more modern. That's what I'm printing now. And they seem to be Alaskan scenes. Could Lloyd have added these photos to what was already in the boxes? I'm hoping that seeing these printouts will be better than on this small laptop screen."

"Should I not be here for this?"

He turned to look at her. "You've been with me all the way. And if these shots that look like they could be taken in Alaska—or hell, Russia, for all I know—are Witlow's, maybe you'll recognize something you've seen that I don't know. Let's spread them out on the couch since my desk is a mess. Sorry to have this ruin our last night here, but I'm convinced we'll make up for it, once this is over."

But he said that matter-of-factly. Not teasing, not with intensity. All business now, obsessed with the puzzle of the treasure again. He was on his knees by the couch, laying them out.

She kneeled beside him, scrutinizing one picture, then the next. Some were aerial views, but some were taken from ground level of a small cabin in a vast expanse of grassland and then several of the small building in the snow. Now where had she seen a cabin like that before, one with two huge caribou racks nailed over the front door?

"This is slightly above the tree line, way up somewhere," she told him. "Look, there's the shadow on the snow of the person who took the picture. It looks like someone in a parka with a big hood, someone with a small sled loaded with goods—with something."

"Right," he said, nodding.

"No clue where it is, of course. Either vast expanses of grass or snow, snow, snow. Oh, here's one with some geographics in it, that might help us identify where it was taken," she said, reaching for another printout as Bryce leaned closer.

She held it up to study it. If she had not been kneeling, she would have fallen to the floor.

She couldn't believe her eyes. She—she knew this place, the distinctive height and angle of this mountain, its sheer rock face without clinging snow and ice in this shot.

Granted, she'd seen this scene just once and not in the dead of winter, but she was sure. She had vowed she would never be there again, but this was it for sure, including the small, elongated frozen lake where Carter had landed his plane. The distant herd of animals. The—the mountain itself.

"Meg. Sweetheart?" came a voice from a distance, as if it were being ripped away by the howling wind.

Her hands started to tremble so hard that the paper rattled. Bryce put an arm around her waist.

"This is the Caribou Mountain and lake area," she said, her voice not her own. She slammed the paper down on the couch and stabbed it with one finger. "It's about sixty miles northwest of Falls Lake. I only saw it once but I even remember that cabin at a distance and the skinny lake. And that is Caribou Cliff," she said, slamming the piece of paper with her fist. "Which killed Ryan."

CHAPTER THIRTY-THREE

Bryce held Meg on his lap until she stopped shaking.

"I can't believe it, but I know that place," she told him.

"You were there once, before or after he died? And you just flew past it? How can you be so sure? Or were pictures in the newspapers when his crash was covered?"

"Yes, it was in the papers, but I was nearly comatose—wouldn't look at any of it, asked Suze to keep it all away. But then, later, about three months, I decided I had to see it, just once and that would be it. I guess I wanted closure, but it didn't really work. Anyway, I asked Carter Jones, an old friend of Ryan's, to take me up there to see where he'd died. I—I didn't even tell Suze and for sure not Chip. I can't believe it. What are the odds he'd have pictures of this place? What does this mean?"

He held her tighter. She was still trembling, but her voice became more steady as she talked.

"Maybe nothing. Maybe something," Bryce said. "I don't normally believe in coincidences, but sometimes that's all it is."

He could call it a coincidence—to Meg, it felt like fate.

"So you had Carter fly past the site?" Bryce asked.

"Yes, but we decided to land at that little lake you can see at the edge of a couple of the photos. It was a nice day. I sat in the back, not the copilot's seat. Out the side window I saw it all. The lake didn't allow a long water runway. We landed on it, got out and trekked maybe a quarter mile to the cliff where Ryan's plane—where he had hit the solid rock face in the fog or storm."

She sat up straighter, pulling away from Bryce's embrace, fumbling for a tissue in her pocket. She blew her nose, then sighed so hard she nearly slid off his knees.

"You don't have to tell me more if you don't want to— or can't," he said, steadying her with a hand on her back. "If you didn't tell anyone else…that was a private time for you. It's okay."

"But the thing is, we discovered there were little caves in the rock at ground level, maybe going in ten to fifteen feet where the ice or wind must have eroded—carved them out years ago. So I left a little lantern I'd brought with me, a special one, lit—though, of course, it must have gone out quickly. That entry to that cavern led clear around to another entrance. But the other thing is, besides the fact those little caverns might make good hiding places, we could see a little cabin, the one in a couple of the photos. But we didn't go near it."

As if all business now, she slid off his lap to her knees again and riffled through the papers on the couch. "Here, this one and this. See the cabin?" she asked, thrusting them at him. "Of course, it could be one of numerous hunter cabins, even an old prospector's place. But it—or those caverns—could be a great place for someone to hide a cache of—of whatever."

"And with all these photos of it here, it could have been Lloyd Witlow's cabin, or at least one he used. But your point is, used for what?"

"Used for another piece to the puzzle, for all we know right now. When we were in Lloyd's house briefly that day, we focused on the photo and inscription of him with Rina, but there was that other photo on the wall of a small cabin with caribou racks—maybe this cabin! It meant something special to him—it might have been his getaway—his secret storehouse."

"Another long shot, but that's all we've had. I'll fly there. If you can tell me exactly where it is, where to find that little hidden lake—and then those caves. I'll take Rafe."

Still with papers in her hands, she turned to him.

"I should go too."

"Sweetheart, you can't want to face that place again. I can't risk that for you."

"You're risking yourself and Rafe. You'll need someone in the copilot seat to help you navigate, spot that cabin or lake in that vast snowfield. It was in the summer when I saw it, but I can help. I can sit in the copilot seat. I haven't wanted to—just couldn't, but I'm ready. If I'm with you."

"I still say you've done enough. And just because Witlow had some of the jewelry outside of the boxes and more inside his plane doesn't mean he siphoned some off for himself—or for Rina."

"That's it!" she said. "He could have been in the boxes and was hiding some of it for himself. Or he felt the mayor, or Melissa and her husband—or even Rina and Todd—were not leveling with him. Like maybe whoever is behind this was holding back, just using Lloyd and poor Getz too. And then got rid of them when they took some of the priceless goods or became some sort of liability, threatening to expose the treasure."

"I'm still not sure about the plane being sabotaged. The way you and Chip described its lame duck landing, the problem could have also been malfunction or novice pilot error.

You could be right about your theory, but not about going with me. As I said, you can't risk that and I can't either. I'm drawing the line here. Absolutely not."

The next day at the lodge, even as Meg packed her duffel bag with food and a warm change of clothes, they still argued.

"See," she said as he ended the call to the Big Man, "he thinks I'd be invaluable. He thinks I should go." She turned to Bryce, hand on her hip. "Even if you get the exact coordinates in those mountains and land the plane on that small frozen lake, you should not search for the caves or the cabin alone. You need a guide—someone who's been there before. Great that Rafe agreed to stay with the plane to guard it, so you wouldn't be trapped there if someone was around and tried to sabotage it. Chip's back in school tomorrow, so he won't be fussing that we're gone.

"So, I'm going," she went on, zipping her bag. "We can be there, look at the caves, hike to the cabin and search it together. We're getting good at breaking and entering, aren't we?"

"Yeah, and the place goes up in flames. But the fact Lloyd had so many pictures of that cabin in the middle of nowhere, even a picture in his house…"

He sighed and sank onto the edge of her bed. She sat beside him.

"Look, Commander Bryce Saylor. We have been in this together from the first, and you—and you-know-who—have said I helped. We'll have Rafe along for security and you said you'd go armed. We're going to work together on this again, get whoever is at fault, or at least find out who they are. And recover whatever of that old treasure is still salvageable and not in the hands of someone—well, someone evil. We then need to move on with our lives, together."

He sighed and put his arm around her shoulders. "To-gether," he said. "That reminds me—Chip said it was all right with him."

"You asked him?"

"Man to man, while we were unloading the soccer gear when we got back. We decided Ryan will always be his 'Daddy,' as he calls him, but he'd like to call me 'Dad.' And his best friend, he added."

She blinked back tears. Bryce's eyes watered too.

"So that's all set," he said. "As soon as I get back from Caribou Lake and Mountain, how about we get an engage-ment ring in Anchorage? And not at Melissa McKee's shop."

"I will love that and I will say I do. But I'm going with you, and I don't just mean to choose a ring."

"Let's not have our first fight even if it would be fun mak-ing up. You're not going."

"I am, or I'll tell the Big Man I know who he is and ask about this special covert task force you're a part of."

"I'll tell you so you don't need to talk to him. There are details I can't reveal—classified information—but what it boils down to is, the administration thinks—fears—that Alaska is being used as a conduit to smuggle people into the country. Spies. Maybe even saboteurs. Our intel tells us it's a long-term plan by the Russians to bolster and supplement their growing use of global internet technology."

"What, like trying to rig elections?"

"Right, but they're being pretty hands-on, and we don't know why. Apparently, these 'people plants' are flown in across the Bering Strait in small private jets but are picked up on the coast by smaller unmarked planes."

"But what does that have to do with Lloyd Witlow?"

"Nothing as far as I'm aware, but the moment that Con-federate treasure turned up, the Big Man wasn't about to hand this assignment off. It may not be a matter of international security, but it's certainly a matter of national concern. The truth is, there's nobody at the NTSB with clearance to handle something like this. So it's fallen to the special task force to expose those involved and recover what we can."

Russian spies. She couldn't believe it. It felt like something out of a movie. "Can't these spies or whatever just get in legally under some guise—as an exchange student, a visiting scientist, a tourist, for heaven's sakes—and then they could just go rogue?" she asked.

"They could," Bryce said. "But then they could be on the US radar. This way, they're in black ops—hidden, as is their mission. Finding Lloyd and that plane and its contraband has opened up an entirely new problem—one that you helped solve. Not smuggling people but that historic treasure anyone would like to get their hands on. Sadly, since Lloyd's plane was blown up, we'll never know why it crashed. I have a sinking feeling the Big Man is going to be expanding the parameters of the task force's mission after this. The Confederate treasure sure got his attention—but so did the mention of Senator Hanson Galsworth."

"I suppose it's not surprising he wouldn't want to let this one go. He definitely won't want to let you go anytime soon either. I know I don't want to."

He smiled down at her. "I definitely don't have a problem with that."

"Well good. I'm glad to hear that," she said, then got to her feet. "And now, you'd better get ready, because I'm already packed. Bryce, I am going with you and Rafe."

"You're doing what?" Suze demanded when they were both in the kitchen.

"As soon as it gets light tomorrow, I'm going for a flight from Anchorage with Bryce and Rafe—"

"Rafe too? To where?"

"I can't exactly tell you."

"Because you don't know or won't say?"

"Suze, please, trust me on this. I know you trust Rafe. And I'm going to be sitting in the copilot's seat, just to get over the hump. I'm ready for that now."

"I know you've been okay back in small planes since Bryce, but sitting up in front is a big step."

If only Suze knew, Meg thought, *where* she was going, she'd really have a fit. She worried that if something did go wrong—like they got stranded or even if they did find more clues to locate the treasure—Suze would be deeply hurt that Meg had kept big secrets from her.

But her biggest worry was that, despite all they'd been through together, Bryce at the last minute still might absolutely refuse to take her. Or he could try to sneak off with Rafe to Anchorage to get in his plane without her. But, taking a tip from Chip, she was going to make sure that didn't happen.

CHAPTER THIRTY-FOUR

Meg was grateful for once that they had no guests, if you didn't count the three-man security team of Bryce, Rafe and Kurt, sent by the man she was now certain was Samson Walters, the Vice President of the United States of America. She knew she risked making a fool of herself by putting Chip's soccer net in front of Bryce's bedroom door and spending the night in Chip's sleeping bag in the hall nearby. She was too psyched to sleep anyway, so no way was Bryce getting past her.

She lay on her side with her head on her packed duffel bag for a pillow. She was fully dressed, even had her shoes on. Absolutely, she had to do this, to help Bryce check Lloyd's cabin. And, though she had not told Bryce or even Suze, she had to be at Caribou Cliff once more, with Bryce this time, to really say farewell to Ryan. He was gone but her life must move forward.

Suze came padding down the hall in a robe and slippers.

"What in the world are you doing?" she demanded, bending close over Meg and keeping her voice down. "You said you intended to fly with Rafe and Bryce to see a wilderness cabin, but are you supposed to meet them out here?"

"Shh! It's a long story."

"One you haven't really told me—not even chapter one. I know you said you've accepted his proposal, and I'm happy for you and Chip, but you and I are going to have to have a serious conversation about all of this and soon. I loved Bryce's idea of the three of you spending the summers here, but we have a lot more details to work out, young lady, so don't think for one second that I'm letting you off the hook."

"I know. And we will, I promise. As soon as this is over, we will find some time to work out the details. The last thing I'd ever want to do is leave you in the lurch. Leaving you will be hardest of all."

"Well, I appreciate that, but it doesn't explain why you're lying here in the hall."

Meg sighed, feeling ridiculous. "I'm camping out here because I want to go along tomorrow, and he doesn't want to take me."

"Because you'd be in the way? It's a secret trip?"

"I can say one thing, but you can't tell anyone—*anyone*."

"I promise."

"The place we're going is near where Ryan died." Meg took a deep breath. She could do this. "Suze, I went there once before, secretly. To see it, to face it. I'm sorry I didn't tell you. I meant to, but then the more time passed, the harder it was to bring up. Going there just felt so…personal. Too personal to discuss. I think I also didn't want to have to admit that I hadn't found closure there—that I wasn't okay. And then somewhere along the way I convinced myself that not talking about it made what happened to Ryan feel less real. It was comforting somehow."

Suze gasped, then seemed to recover. "Oh, Meg, I'm sorry you went through that alone. I wish I could've been there for you, but I do understand why you kept it a secret. I won't tell anyone, hon, and I hope that this time, you find the closure you're looking for. I'm always here if you need me. But you know what scares me? Not only that I sometimes think I don't know you anymore, but that I don't know myself. As dangerous as working with Bryce sounds, I think if I were you and it was Rafe going, I'd go with him too."

She sat cross-legged on the hall floor beside the sleeping bag, and they held hands as if they were kids again, scared by owl hoots outside or the haunting cries of a lone loon on the lake when they first came here to visit Grandma years ago.

After Suze went to bed, Meg did fall asleep and was jolted awake by Bryce shaking her shoulder. She sat up instantly.

"You are damned stubborn," he said, bending over her. "Let's grab something to eat, get Rafe and get going."

Her pulse pounded so hard it was like a drum. He was going to take her? He realized how important it was to her! When he walked off down the hall, maybe to wake Rafe, she darted into the bathroom, then, hefting her duffel bag, rushed to the kitchen and fixed cereal, toast and orange juice for the three of them. No time to even perk the coffee. Adrenaline would have to keep them going today. And she'd asked Suze to cover for her with Chip when he got up. Never mind the conversation she owed Suze about their plans—she planned to more than make up for lost time with that kid when this was over.

They did not talk much at breakfast nor in her truck en route to the Anchorage airport. Had he been planning earlier to take her truck and leave her behind? No, because she had the key and he hadn't asked for it, so maybe he meant to take her—if she proved to him how badly she wanted to go. And she had. Or something during the night had made him change his mind about her going.

"Frosty in here despite the heater," Rafe finally said. "And I thought I heard congratulations are in order."

"True," Bryce said. "We just had a disagreement about my fiancée coming along today. The site where we're going—do you want to explain it, Meg?"

"Not to mention that Bryce thinks this trip is dangerous, Caribou Cliff is the place where my husband was killed in a plane crash in bad weather. I've been there once before. I recognized it from some photos, and I thought I could help."

"I hear you've been invaluable all along," Rafe told her. "And yes, Commander Saylor is the one who told me how you helped."

Both Meg and Bryce let out audible sighs as some of the tension of their disagreement and what they were doing lifted, at least she thought so. But facing that place again, even for a good reason, still scared her more than she could say.

When daylight came, Bryce was grateful the weather was clear. Great visibility, although the glare of the miles of pristine snow would blind them if they didn't all wear glacier glasses, which were much stronger than sunglasses.

"You okay?" he asked Meg as they left the Anchorage area behind and banked toward the north. "Rafe can come up here if you'd rather go back like you used to."

"No more 'used to,'" she told him from the copilot's seat. "This is now, and this is something I have to do. Besides, I can't be married to a man who loves to fly if I can't completely share that."

"You've come a long way—but so have I. We do this, learn and find what we can, and head back."

"I saw you brought some tools that make you look like an old-time prospector, or rather, like someone who is getting adept at breaking and entering. Maybe the place will be open."

"I doubt it. Entering a small, well-built cabin in a snow field with subfreezing temps will be a bit different from lifting an unlocked window at Getz's—poor guy. These deaths, people being injured—it has to stop."

"As terrible as things have been, we found each other. And Suze found Rafe, though she's scared he'll just leave and that will be that."

"Maybe you and I can work to keep them together," he said. "Not meddle, but—I think we've been a fantastic team. More than anything, that makes me hopeful about today. Answers have to be out there somewhere, somehow..."

His voice trailed off as he rechecked his instruments and then gazed out into the white vastness of what some called "The Great Alone." But he didn't feel alone, and from now on he couldn't imagine how he could live without her.

Rafe came up into the cockpit and held on to the back of their seats as Bryce made one circle of their target area. The vast stone face of Caribou Cliff frowned out from one side of the tall mountain.

"See that little lake down there?" Meg asked. "Is it long enough to land this plane on? Carter had a smaller plane when we were here, and it wasn't iced over then."

Bryce said, "I see it. Or we could land on that snowfield that leads up to the cabin. But who knows what's under some of that snow—we could lose a pontoon. Wonder how long that cabin's stood there. We may have to dig it out. Either landing spot, Meg and I are going to have to snowshoe to it while you guard the plane, Rafe."

"Smart you brought a pair of walkie-talkies," he said. "Or else we'd be using signal flags and binoculars out here. You and I can keep in touch."

"Okay, I say we'll try this end of the lake that's closest to the cabin and the caverns Meg described," Bryce told them. "I'd really like to search those caverns too, but we may not have time on this trip. Still a needle in a haystack, but it's possible Lloyd was siphoning off some of the treasure, maybe at his daughter and son-in-law's request, and hiding it here. Or his working for them—or the mayor and Melissa—was a quid pro quo for someone paying for the plane and flying lessons.

"Rafe, better buckle up. I'm going to take us around and in. Meg, you okay? You've been doing great, but you look a little queasy."

"It's just seeing the cliff again. But it's not going to stop me. I'm going to conquer it. With your help and support."

"That's my woman," he said as Rafe patted both their shoulders and went in back to take his seat again. "Notice I didn't say 'girl' so I don't get a takedown like you gave the mayor," he added, obviously trying to bolster her spirits. "Okay," he called back to Rafe, "we're going in!"

Massive Mount Caribou and its cliff face looked even larger to Meg this time, a hulking monster with snow on its head and shoulders. As Bryce took the plane close to the wall of rock to make a pass at the far end of the frozen lake, her stomach cartwheeled and seemed to go into free fall.

She gripped her hands together, closed her eyes. Dizzy, but just for a moment.

He dipped the left wing to come around to use the entire length of the frozen lake. She saw a herd of the animal that gave the place its name, straggling along the edge of the lake, probably annoyed they had to move to get away from the buzz of the plane—and to stop eating whatever they were getting from the meager stands of trees. The thirty or so caribou, some sporting huge racks of antlers, headed out toward the open area where the cabin stood, half buried in snow. She remembered that, in the photos, there were caribou racks hung above the front door of the cottage, so hunters had obviously been through here for years. Yes, she was glad that Bryce and Rafe were both armed but they weren't hunting these majestic animals.

Bryce put the plane down smoothly, powered off early, but they still nearly slid into the snow bank at the far end.

"Whew," he said. "Even shorter than it looked. Hope there's a decent wind for a good lift when we take off."

Once they landed, it was all business. Rafe had packed their backpacks with some food and more layers of clothes. Eating snow would do for water. The wind outside whined and stung and sent loose drifts skittering across the surface of the ice. They trudged off the lake ice onto the snowy bank. Rafe went that far too.

The men tested their two-way radios, then checked their long-range rifles. Rafe helped them snap on their snowshoes. She and Bryce adjusted their knitted face masks so they could see out and breathe. Hers was knitted in dark blue and his in dark green. It made her think of Halloween masks, but that reminded her of the terrible invasion of the lodge.

Finally, Rafe strapped Bryce's "break-in" tools on the back of his pack next to his rifle. Across her backpack, Rafe had tied their lone snow shovel, in case they had to dig their way into the cabin.

Rafe hit Bryce on both shoulders and gave them a double thumbs-up. Before he headed back to the plane, he pointed to his watch to remind them to pay attention to the time since the days were extra short up here. Meg realized if they had to take off after dark, it would be like Ryan flying in bad weather so close to that monster of a cliff.

They waved at Rafe and set a good pace on their snowshoes toward the cabin. It was fairly easy to spot, although it looked half buried in drifting snow. She saw the herd of caribou had moved to a site around the cabin and hoped that would not cause them any problems. It looked like they were stripping the bark from it to eat, and no wonder with scarce food sources up here this time of year. They would surely migrate farther down for food, but the continual snowstorms might have delayed them.

The cabin grew larger as they trekked toward it. Meg was sweating, out of breath, but she kept up. To think they'd have to do this in the other direction, hopefully carrying something they found within. But if Lloyd had buried things, the ground would be frozen solid, though she couldn't imagine their finding contraband just sitting there, like in some Aladdin's cave.

As they reached the cabin, she saw snow hovered under its broad eaves. Icicles like crystal daggers hung from the roof. At least the drifts were taller against the back of the cabin, not the front that had the single door. Peeking out above the snow was the top of a single small window—maybe they could get in that way. Someone had carried a pane of glass clear up here, then covered it with a crisscross of wire to keep bears from breaking in—or humans.

Bryce shrugged off his heavy pack and, using the snow shovel she'd carried, dug down to the latch on the door, then dug the entire door out. She helped by shoving the pile of snow he made away with her feet. He tried to lift the latch, but it was locked, frozen or both. He reached for the thin ice pick tied to his backpack.

"Okay." His voice came muffled with a big puff of his breath in the cold air. "One way or the other, we have to get in. Stand back so I can use this pick to loosen or break the lock."

He pried with it, then scraped with it, then hit with it. He pressed his shoulder against the door, then banged and shoved.

With a screech of its hinges and a little avalanche of snow from the roof, the heavy wooden door creaked and swung slowly open before them.

CHAPTER THIRTY-FIVE

Bryce shuffled into the dim cabin and Meg followed, looking around, wide-eyed. Several boards stood on end leaning against the lone window, so the only light was the open door behind them. It threw their muted shadows across the floor. The only furnishings were a tiny table, a single chair and a low built-in bunk bed across the back wall. Several dusty cans of beans sat on shelves in a crude open cupboard on the right side wall.

"Damn," Bryce muttered as he reached back to bring her in. "A dirt floor. If anything is buried under there, the ground should be frozen solid."

"Look how thick the walls are to keep it warm in here and make the building sturdy in the winds. Shall we close the door for warmth or keep it open for the light?"

"I'll close it in a minute."

He lifted the boards away from the window, dragged his backpack in, then closed the door and dug out a big flashlight. After helping her take off her backpack, he played the beam under the wooden bunk bed, in the corners, even under the eaves.

"Nothing visible," he said, "but you're right about the walls." He moved around the twelve-foot-square cabin, knocking his gloved fist on the walls, then tore off his glove and did it again bare-knuckled, midway up, then high and low. He lay on his stomach and reached under the bed to knock against that wall.

"Mice," he muttered as she heard something skitter away. "I think this wall under here does sound different—not as hollow."

A strange knocking sound echoed on the door. She startled, and he jerked and hit his head on the bunk. He whispered, "No one could be out there this fast."

Meg looked out the wired window. "The caribou are still here, maybe eating bark again. It must have been one of their antlers. I guess since we're inside they think it's all theirs again."

"Get that pick I opened the door with and hand it to me. I've got to knock a hole in this side of the wall. It may be nothing, but unless there's a false roof above or something buried under this frozen ground, this may be all we have."

"Unless there could be something in those caverns," she said as she grabbed the pick and got on her knees, then her stomach to scoot it under the built-in bunk to him.

"If we have time, we'll glance inside them," he said, grunting now as he reached out with the pick. "This whole thing is a long shot, but that's better than nothing. The Big Man's going to recall me soon, at least send me to the unit in Anchorage, I can tell."

"Now you tell me! But I knew you couldn't stay at the lodge forever. Hopefully, for Christmas."

"You got me, babe. And I'm hoping we can visit my family over the holidays or get them to the lodge. But to serious business right now, my dear greatest distraction. Hold this flashlight for me so I can see what I'm doing."

He had trouble, she could tell, from not having space to swing the pick at the wall under the bunk, but he did get through. A grinding crunch, then another followed.

"Here, I'm shoving some wood pieces back to you," he muttered and pounded again. She took what he pushed at her back from their tight space.

She crawled closer under the bed, out of breath, still holding the flashlight for him. Wood groaned and splintered.

"You know," he grunted out, "there's nothing here at floor level, but down farther I'm digging into a space hollowed out below the permafrost in a pocket of wood. Yes, something's down here!"

She twisted around next to him and aimed the flashlight, but he took it from her and shot it down into the hole.

"Things wrapped in plastic," he said, sounding completely breathless. "Papers. And something bright!"

She heard rustling. He scooted even closer to the wall so he could reach below ground level.

"Jewelry," he shouted. "And gold!"

He hauled out three—no, four—thick plastic sacks and thrust them back toward her. She saw a golden gleam too and gasped as she dragged the dirty sacks out into the room. A gold bar, then two of them, heavy, gleamed in the beam of light he now shot at them. Did that mean, in this dark, tight, cold place, a victory?

"A good hiding place," Bryce said, breathless. "Even if this cabin got knocked over or burned to the ground, these would be safe."

Once they had scooted backwards from under the bunk, like prospectors who had found the mother lode, they shouted for joy.

"I'll bet that got the herd away!" he crowed as they hugged each other hard. "Let's divide it for our packs, then get out of here."

She was so excited that, like a little kid, she clapped her hands. "Lloyd probably liked to think he was sleeping on top of it to guard it. The day he crashed, maybe his cargo was en route to this cabin. So he was headed for Caribou Lake, but he had a problem and tried to land on Falls Lake."

"This loot may not be all of it—of course, we know there was at least a second load on that plane—but I bet it's all that Lloyd hid here. I'll call Rafe to expect us earlier than we thought and visit those caves another time. We've done it, and now to trace who Lloyd was working for, finally get the Feds involved. We've done it!"

They left their tools behind to lighten their packs so they could carry out the extra weight. Bryce took both gold bars because he didn't want Meg to have to lug more than the papers and half the jewelry. He was flying high, didn't even need his plane to get back to civilization, he kidded himself.

"With this haul, we could open our own jewelry store and put Melissa out of business," he teased.

"She may be out of business anyway, if she's at all mixed up in this scheme. I'm betting on Todd and Rina, but maybe also the mayor or Melissa—who knows? They'll all be grilled now."

"I'm so happy I could kiss the first caribou I see, but I'm saving all that for you. I didn't look to see if they're still out there," he added, bending to snap on her snowshoes and then his.

She leaned carefully toward the window since her loaded pack made her top-heavy. "Yes, they're still out there but they look skittish, shifting around funny. Be quiet a sec. Do you hear something—like a distant whine?"

He froze, tilting his head. "Yeah, a plane, I bet, hopefully just passing over. No, it doesn't quite sound like a plane. Stay put and let me look."

In his snowshoes, he clomped over to the door, cracked it,

then opened it farther and leaned out. The whine—a double whine—seemed to be louder, closer. Outside the herd quit eating and looked around.

And then he saw it—them. "Meg, two snowmobiles in the distance, to the south. One person on each. We can't be caught here. Let's go."

"We can't outrun snowmobiles! We can't even outrun these caribou, which look like they're going to take off."

"That's it. We only have to make it to the caverns. If we get near the cliff face, can you find an entry—even one? We'll never make it back to the plane in time, and could get trapped here."

"The herd!" she said. "Let's try to go with it at least for a ways. We can keep low, make a break for the cliff that way. Yes, I can find the caverns if they're not snowed in."

He closed the door behind them but they had no time to cover up what they'd done inside. He actually hoped the two people on the snowmobiles were heading for the cabin and that would stall their looking for them. Dread and anger nearly swamped him. He had the strangest feeling the two coming closer over the snow field were the ones who had hurt him and his men. And now, he'd been stupid enough to risk Meg's life, however defiant she'd been about coming along.

"Keep low and hope the caribou ignore us!" he said. "If it's too much, I'll carry your pack too."

"I'm all right," she insisted, and he loved her all the more. They headed for the lake via the cliff that had claimed her husband's life. Hunched, moving with the shifting herd as camouflage and cover, he could only hope the two men fast approaching were not hitmen adept with guns, bombs and maybe fire too.

Meg was instantly out of breath, but adrenaline kicked in. If only she could move faster than these snowshoes let her. If only the herd weren't moving at a pace that would soon expose them. Could she really locate those caverns? She dared not lift her head to try to spot them from here.

The caribou, though merely trotting, passed them by, heading for the lake. At least they had covered her and Bryce's mad dash for a ways and they were near shelter. As the animals moved away, she noted the huge curve and shape of their antlers ending in what looked like hands raised in the air as if in surprise or surrender.

Again, the solid weight and mass of the cliff face that had killed Ryan loomed over them, now friend instead of foe if they could just reach it in time.

Once they were completely exposed, Bryce looked back. "They stopped at the cabin," he yelled, panting hard. "Got to make it to shelter. Too far to the lake, and they'll see our tracks, caribou trail or not."

"The cave I remember was to the left of here," she told him. "It was one that went back in and curved, then came out another entrance." Her heart was pounding so hard she could hardly hear herself, and the frigid air stung clear down into her lungs. "Hang left!" she shouted, and her voice came back as an echo. "The entry's not too far."

She prayed it would not be snow-filled or iced in. Thank heavens, she saw it, or thought she did. Yes. Yes!

"There!" she cried, pointing despite how her arms ached and the weight of the pack cut into her shoulders. "I think I see the dark entry, under that hanging shelf of ice and snow."

They hurried to it. Yes, a cave entry, hopefully the one she recalled. It was partly blocked by boulders, definitely under an overhang with a half curtain of ice and snow that could crash down. But when she'd left the little memorial lantern inside, she and Carter had walked deeper in and had come out another way—if this was that cavern.

They both looked back. The snowmobiles were already roaring their way.

"Was going to call Rafe for help—his gun," he gasped. "But no way I'll get him on the two-way inside the cave. Still, let's go in. Got to hide this stuff and you, then dig my rifle out—I might have to make a stand."

They dropped their backpacks, and Meg helped Bryce untie his rifle. While he kept watch, hidden near the cave entrance, she dragged the packs back in a ways and shoved them behind a pile of loose stones. The wind whipping into the cave whined and then seemed to scream—or was that her own fears?

She was tempted to see if this area led to the other cave entrance she remembered, but it was so dark back here she could hardly see and the flashlight was packed. She wished they had time to explore their options.

Walking back up behind him and peering out over his shoulder, she asked, "Do you think those men—if they are men, can't tell from here—knew the treasure was in the cabin and came to stop us or retrieve it? Or could we have been followed by someone watching your plane? You know, maybe in another plane they landed somewhere nearby. Maybe Lloyd or someone had two snowmobiles stashed somewhere near here. What if they're the same men who've been after you—or who invaded the lodge?"

"Stay back, Meg. I may have to use this rifle and I don't want you in the cross fire."

But she didn't budge at first, peering around him as the two men—they walked like men—killed the motors, got off their machines and came closer. They were looking up. For sure, they had seen where they had gone.

"Bryce, listen to me. The way they walk, the swagger,

their body builds. I swear it's the men who broke into the lodge."

"But who hired them? Get back in, I said," he repeated and pushed her away without looking at her. "Meg, whatever happens, I love you and always will. Go!"

That terrified her. The fight went out of her. Her legs started to shake and her teeth to chatter. They were near the place where Ryan had died. His crumpled, crashed plane had fallen right outside. His body...

She realized then that the lantern she had left to symbolize his life snuffed out was gone. Probably some hiker had taken it, thinking it was a historic relic or just plain needing it. But she liked to think it had gone with Ryan's spirit. Maybe that was the closure she needed. That and knowing she now had someone else she refused to lose in Bryce.

She went back as he had said and, praying silently, kneeled by their backpacks. Then she recalled that she'd been told Ryan's plane crashing into the cliff had brought down several shelves of rock. If only there was some way to do that again, right on top of those men. That might block her and Bryce in, but there was that other way out—assuming it still existed.

"Bryce," she called quietly to him, "remember I said there used to be another way out of here? You could go around, hold the gun on them from behind."

"And leave you in here? I heard you about another exit, and I hope you're right because I have another idea to stop them. That entrance to this cavern is not under the Alaskan ice for nothing. Get way back, I said. Meg, for once just do it!"

As the two men who had stepped to the front of the cave took shelter behind boulders, no doubt in case they'd meet gunfire, to her horror Bryce walked, hands up, his rifle in one hand, angling the muzzle toward the ceiling above the entrance.

"All right," Bryce called out, his voice echoing. "You've got us trapped."

"Drop that gun and hand the goods over—with the girl!" one man ordered.

Then to her amazement, Bryce fell to his back on the cave floor as he fired his rifle *bang, bang, bang* upward at the entrance ceiling. Or had he been shot? Though she was behind a boulder, she flattened out too when the men tried to return fire. But with a crash and roar, the world caved in.

CHAPTER THIRTY-SIX

It took Meg a moment to realize the ceiling had not caved in, that Bryce had not been shot. He was pulling her to her feet as the rumbling stopped, the thin overhang of jagged ice that had previously sheltered the opening to the cave now settled in a massive pile, nearly blocking the mouth of the cave.

It had also done as Bryce had intended—burying the men.

A crooked smile of daylight poured in above where the now taller mouth of the cave had not quite filled up. But it would take them a while to scale it without gear or dig a path out below, all the time worried they might set off another avalanche of snow and ice.

"Sweetheart, hope you're right about another way out of here, or we'll have Rafe going crazy," he said, still out of breath. "I hated to do that because I don't want those two bastards dead so they can't answer questions. I've got to try to dig them out. Let's get my walkie-talkie, and we'll use the flashlight to hopefully find your other entrance. We'll try to save and tie up those guys, then call Rafe. We'll have to lug our backpacks with us, and the snowshoes in case they didn't leave the keys in their snowmobiles."

"How did you know you could block them, bury them?"

"Not my first time trapped under the ice. I knew if I shot on an angle, I could bring down just the outer overhang of ice, making a clean break. I had to time it just right, but the broken ice did exactly what I expected it to do. Now we just need to make sure we find that other exit."

Their flashlight had been knocked around and its beam was sporadic now, like her strength, she thought. Lugging their packs again, they set a good pace around the curve of the cave.

After they fumbled and stumbled around a big turn, a pinpoint of wan light loomed ahead. Bryce fell down once on uneven stone ground, but his heavy pack padded his fall. Their fading flashlight finally went out.

"Take my hand!" he said. "We'll slow down now that we see the light."

Both were sweating, panting. She wanted to rip off her knitted face mask, but she kept it on.

They stopped just inside this entry to the twin cave mouths, and Bryce looked around outside, then came back to her. "I don't see them anywhere—they must be under the ice and snow pile. I'm going to dig for them. We need them alive."

He took off his pack, then dug and clawed like a madman at the rubble of ice and snow. Meg helped too, lifting chunks of ice away, kicking snow aside. No rocks as far as she could see—Bryce really had known what he was doing—but good old Alaskan ice had done them in, buried them the way they had tried to do to Bryce and his men.

"Here," he shouted. "A hand and a gun!"

He passed the gun to her. She took it but stared at the

bare hand that had held it. Fingernails nicely manicured and an onyx ring.

"This is one of them," she told him. "One who came to the lodge in a mask."

They dug him out, still breathing but unconscious. They tied his hands behind his back with his own belt. Meg stared at his face. It seemed vaguely familiar, but it wasn't until Bryce found the other man, who wasn't breathing, that she knew where she'd seen them.

"Bryce, is he dead?"

"No, has a carotid pulse—and I think a broken leg. It's unlikely he'll get away, but be ready so we can tie him up with his belt too. I'm going to try CPR first and I need him flat on his back."

She helped Bryce count compressions on the guy's chest by singing the Bee Gees' rhythmic song "Stayin' Alive" as she'd been taught in a CPR class ages ago. When the guy choked back to life and they quickly bound his hands with his belt, she knew for sure where she'd seen them.

"Bryce, these are sawmill men—swampers. They were at Lloyd's funeral! They would have known him, worked for him, maybe for Rina and Todd too!"

"Rina, is she here?" the man they'd rescued first choked out. His eyes were dilated, and he blinked in the setting sunlight. "That crazy, paranoid bitch owes us big-time."

"Is she the one who put you up to this?" Bryce demanded. The man seemed reluctant to answer, so Bryce reminded him that whomever they were working for stood to be in a lot more trouble than they were—assuming they cooperated.

"It was her and that moneybags husband of hers," the second man said. "But Rina's the one who couldn't seem to stick to the plan, demanding that we blow up her father's plane and then set fire to that crazy loner's house. But hey,

I'm no stranger to cop shows. I'm not saying any more without my lawyer present."

Meg's wide-eyed stare slammed into Bryce's. They were both out of breath, exhausted but triumphant.

"The state troopers will need to investigate in full, but it sounds like the answers we need are forthcoming," he said with a weary smile. "Todd and Rina." He blinked back tears to match hers. "We'll celebrate later. Right now, as beat up as they are, you'll have to hold that one's gun while I get our packs on their snowmobiles. Then I'll come back for them. Hope there are keys in their pockets," he added, checking pockets in their parkas and coming up with two of them.

"And, gentlemen," he announced, "the lady is very likely to shoot if either of you so much as move."

Both men looked dazed. The guy with the ring and great fingernails—and a bloody face—actually nodded.

"I'll be right back with our packs, and then we've got to get them to the plane. I think you'll get a big promotion for all this, sweetheart, not only from me but from you-know-who."

She was so screaming exhausted she almost couldn't smile back at him. But she did.

CHAPTER THIRTY-SEVEN

Ten days later

"But do you have to go that far right before Christmas?" Chip protested. "Why can't I go to a party in Washington, DC, too? You and my soon-to-be dad aren't going to—you know—antelope, are you?"

"I think you mean elope, but no way! Never without you," Meg said, putting her arms around him, which wasn't easy since he was holding his ground behind his basement soccer net. "You're going to walk me down the aisle, remember, and that's not until next year. This is just a party for grown-ups, and I'll tell you all about it."

"Too much is just for grown-ups," he pouted, not hugging her back. "But someone's got to stay here with Aunt Suze, 'specially with Rafe gone, 'cause she's sad."

"You're right," Meg said, setting him back a bit. "She will really miss him."

"She cried after he left. I heard her in her room. And I bet not just because he's a good painter."

Although she wiped away a tear at how sad Suze had been

to see Rafe leave, she was happy Chip really cared about people and was so observant.

"Hey, you two!" Bryce said, coming down the basement steps to "soccer net alley," which didn't look like much after Bryce's big basement and Mark Ralston's setup in Juneau. "Does Chip have any questions about our going to DC?"

"Just that he's going to miss us and wants to hear all about it, right?" she prompted.

"And to say, be sure you don't get in any more trouble. No more *Star Wars* guys chasing you with guns in a cave until you bury them with snow. I still love *Star Wars*, but only when the bad guys are pretend, like in the movies."

"Me too, buddy," Meg said. "And I promise we'll be careful."

They left Chip to play so they could talk in private, Meg anxious to hear what Bryce had found out after the call he'd just had with the Big Man. Rina and Todd Galsworth, along with Todd's father, Senator Galsworth, were now all in custody, along with the two swampers who'd caused them so much trouble.

"So? Any news?" Meg asked, her voice hushed in case Chip could still hear them.

"Big news," Bryce reported. "Rina's been singing like a canary in exchange for leniency. Turns out the whole thing was Senator Handsome Hanson's master plan for the next federal election. Remember how we'd discovered he was thinking about a bid for the White House?" He paused and Meg nodded for him to continue. "Well, it turns out, he was planning to fund his campaign with a portion of the stolen treasure while also making a big public show of the fact that he and his associates had tracked down the long-lost Confederate documents and artifacts."

"Nice election strategy. A real national hero," Meg

sneered. "But how did he find it in the first place? And how did Rina and Todd get involved?"

"We're still working on the original source of the lost treasure, but apparently the senator is a big Confederate history buff."

Meg's eyes widened. "Like Rina's mother?"

Bryce nodded. "A crime committed on common ground. Apparently, he'd been looking into the mystery of the lost treasure for a while, even hired a hacker to see if he could track anything down on the dark web. Evidently, they found it and he hired someone to steal it, but to pull off his plan, he needed somewhere to hide it."

"Aha. Enter Todd and Rina and Rina's father, who just so happened to own a remote cabin and wanted to become a pilot."

"Precisely," Bryce said. "Rina reached out to Lloyd Witlow under the guise of wanting to make amends, and then they paid for his plane, flying lessons, the whole shebang. Before he knew it, they'd brought him into the plan—with promise of payment of course—and even asked him to find two of his most corruptible men at the lumber mill to help out."

"So that explains the who and the why, but I still don't understand what happened to Witlow's plane. And why did the swampers say it was Rina's decision to blow up the plane and take out Getz?"

"According to Rina, the plane crash was an accident. When she heard her father had been killed, her loyalty to the senator started to waver. She ordered the swampers to plant the bomb that blew up the plane to destroy evidence before sending them to the lodge to collect whatever we'd already salvaged. As for Getz, when Rina felt her ex was sniffing around too much per the mayor's instructions, she confronted him and I guess it left her feeling uneasy about what he may have witnessed, so she had the swampers set the explosions at his place too."

"Wow!" Meg exclaimed. "She really was paranoid."

"Despite her strained relationship with her father, I think his death must've hit her pretty hard. Maybe her guilt pushed her over the edge. She certainly had no problem confessing when it came down to it."

It was sad, really, Meg thought. Rina had lost her mother, hated Alaska enough to leave it behind, only to fall in with a corrupt family who brought her right back to the very place she'd escaped. Not to say she was a victim in any way—but it was always sad when life pushed desperate people to do desperate things.

"I suppose this means we were wrong about Melissa's involvement," Meg said. "I guess she really was just looking to build up stock for her jewelry business. Maybe to pay for a divorce?"

"Very likely." Bryce shrugged. "But even if she does leave her husband, I'm not sure the mayor plans to leave his wife anytime soon. It seems he's been doing everything he can to keep his affair with Melissa under wraps, keeping a close eye on the town and what people are saying. He has little birdies everywhere, protecting his interests—those guards he volunteered after the crash, Mason Nowles, Bill Getz..."

"Poor Getz."

Bryce sighed. "He really was just trying to do the job the mayor had hired him to do. And speaking of jobs, are you all set for our trip to DC?"

Now that was something Meg could feel excited about. She smiled. "All set. As long as I'm by your side, I'm ready for anything."

Everything seemed so good now, so right, so happy. That is, except for Suze. This spring, Rafe would be sent to Moscow. Probably similar weather to here, but surely he would miss the lodge—and the woman who was falling in love with him.

"Suze, you just never know," Meg said, leaning against her sister's painting bench while Suze just stared at a blank canvas, ignoring the prepared palette of paints at her side. "I could tell Rafe cares deeply for you too."

She sighed. "So he says. But duty calls—calls me too. It's fine for you to live with Bryce most of the year in Juneau and Alex to move to town with Quinn—but it just isn't going to happen for me even if I'm sure I've found my man at last. I don't mean to be jealous or—or negative about you and Alex. You are both doing the right thing.

"And," she said, turning toward Meg, "don't worry about Chip the two days you're in DC. He's good company for me, really he is. But, you know," she went on as she tossed her turpentine-smelling paint rag against the blank canvas, "I just don't feel I can use painting to calm down right now. Got to go work on fixing lunch for just the three of us, since Jim Kurtz has gone home to his family too."

Meg wanted to say something else to comfort or encourage her, but talk was not enough. Surely there was something she could do to help.

The vice president's official residence was just the sort of Victorian-style home Meg loved, but she didn't say so as they were driven through security-guarded black iron gates in an official car. She would love Bryce's contemporary-style home—or anyplace he lived.

On the grounds of the US Naval Observatory about five miles from the White House, the three-story home they pulled up to was white with a gray roof, a single round turret and a broad, curved veranda that wrapped around half of the house. Christmas wreaths hung below each second-story window, and a lit tree gleamed through a downstairs one.

A dinner party for ten, they'd been told, and her presence had been specifically requested. Bryce had joked that the Big Man was going to hire her for undercover work in the hotbed of crime in Falls Lake, Alaska. Then he had laughed and said the only kind of under-the-covers work he himself had for her was in bed.

A sailor opened their car door, and they got out. Nervous, she took Bryce's arm as they went up to the front door, which was opened by a naval officer. And, to her amazement, since she had the idea this was going to be an ordeal, out spilled warmth, conversation and Christmas music played by a live harpist in the large round hall.

There was no reception line, but the vice president and second lady greeted them warmly and chatted for a moment. Darned if they didn't both look like their pictures, she thought. But this was happening. She was really here.

"Good work from both of you," Samson Walters said, then pulled Bryce aside. "Bryce, I'll have to update you on the latest regarding the illustrious senator from Michigan who had his eye on the White House…"

Their hostess, Samson's wife, Katherine, indicated that Meg should come with her, and the men's voices faded, though she yearned to hear more. She had to get over that, being a part of dangerous events. She had to think about Chip and now Bryce—and she was thrilled. Maybe she'd try using her degree to teach elementary education in Juneau someday, but more covert or black ops, as Bryce called them? No way. She also had her candy business, which she had no plans to abandon. She'd just have to work out the logistics of shipping her candy to her clientele in Falls Lake— and maybe find some new buyers in her new hometown.

The gracious woman showed her the downstairs of the

mansion, while they drank a glass of wine they were offered from a silver tray. So far away from the lodge and yet not so far in other ways, though the reception hall, library, dining room, living room and sitting room were each so beautifully decorated. The grand piano held family photos—and, modestly, the second lady pointed out several framed pieces she had painted.

"I love that one of the bright red cardinal perched on a pine branch in the snow," Meg told her. "So perfect for Christmas too."

"I like that one, though I more often do buildings. I stick to watercolors rather than oils. I have a minor in art from my college days, and my big cause now is art therapy for ill children."

"My twin sister paints, mostly in oils," Suze said. "She has a friend—actually one who works for the NTSB as Bryce does—who suggested she host an art camp at our lodge, but perhaps that could turn into some sort of therapy—for her too."

They chatted on about the decor of rooms, about Christmas traditions. Although she was honored and enjoying herself, Meg's mind went into full fight mode. First, had this kind woman whisked her away so the men could go over some new plan—something that might take Bryce away like Rafe?

And second, dared she ask for a favor?

She steered their conversation back to Suze, but she knew she sounded nervous. "It would surely help my sister's art project, especially if it could incorporate art therapy too, if her inspiration and encourager, Rafe Coffman, could be pulled from his coming assignment in Moscow to stay a bit longer in Alaska. Hopefully by next spring at least, so they could plan a summer artist's therapy retreat."

Katherine Walters gently grasped Meg's upper arm. "We

artists stick together even if we don't know each other," she said, her face so serious and her voice in earnest. "I can do one thing, and that's put in a word to my husband, play up the Alaskan outreach for art therapy. The Lord knows, we all need some sort of therapy, and love is the best, right?"

"I can't thank you enough. For listening. Understanding. For your hospitality."

"I must tell you that my husband says you were very brave and helpful in—well, whatever you have been through. I promise you, there will be engraved invitations for you, Bryce, your sister—and perhaps this other artist—when we open the exhibition of the stolen, hidden Civil War treasures at the Smithsonian next year, featuring never before seen documents and Confederate artifacts."

"Already this is such a lovely evening, thank you for listening—for everything."

"Now, don't cry or the two of them will suspect something before I waylay 'the Big Man' about this Rafe situation. I have to choose my causes carefully. Let's join the others now and enjoy our meal. You know," Katherine added as they walked back toward the library where new arrivals were gathering, "I think an outreach to Alaska with two artists heading things up there might just be an excellent new project for me too, though I'm going to chair the Lost Civil War Treasure exhibit. Yes, nothing like coast-to-coast therapy of one kind or the other!"

"What I think!" Suze screamed over the phone when Meg called to tell her the next day what had happened. "I think I'd vote for her for queen of the world! Rafe called and his assignment has been changed already but he didn't know why. He can even come for Christmas, but won't be free from some desk job in DC until April. I can't believe this all happened so fast, so perfect."

Meg heard her cover the phone, or at least her voice was muffled, talking to someone.

"I know I screamed, Chip, but I'm all right," Meg overheard.

"Suze, are you two getting along okay?"

"I made the mistake of saying I'd guard the net while he took shots. He's getting quite good, and my shins are sore. Meg, can't wait until you're back because we have a lot to do. Besides Rafe, I got a call from Alex that they will be here not only for New Year's Eve but a few days before, so I told her we'd have a double holiday celebration when they get here. What was that Tiny Tim said in *A Christmas Carol*? 'God bless us, every one.'"

"We all need that after what we've been through—Alex, you and me. And speaking of Rafe getting reassigned, I think our luck is changing. So much good news. I mean, what could possibly go wrong now?"

CHAPTER THIRTY-EIGHT

The second holiday celebration at the lodge was even more special than the first on Christmas Day. Alex and Quinn were back with tales to tell and happiness to share. Rafe had flown in despite a storm delay for his flight in Chicago. Bryce had been testifying before a closed-door NTSB congressional committee, but he'd been here for nearly a week while they made wedding plans.

Chip and the dogs seemed on their best behavior, and Suze was ecstatic but trying not to act as if her relationship with Rafe was a done deal, because really it wasn't. She and Meg were picking up on vibes from him that—despite the fact he did not want to spend months in Moscow—he didn't like his career and life being "tampered with."

Suze had decided it was best not to take him on over that, not now at least. Didn't he realize that anyone who worked for the government as he and Bryce did was going to have his life controlled? And hadn't the Big Man's wife controlled even her husband in a way?

Meg was disappointed there was tension between Rafe and Suze when Alex was happily married and Meg herself engaged. Compare to that, Suze and Rafe were still trying to find their way, and who knew what would happen?

But now, snow was falling outside, silent and beautiful. No longer were they nervous about the dark woods beyond, for the two sawmill men who had worked for Lloyd but had been recruited by Rina and Todd had been arrested and were being questioned, as were that dynamic—and criminal—duo from Ohio. Even Meg might have to testify against them later, but, as far as she and Bryce could tell, it would be in the Big Man's best interest to bury some of what had gone on so it didn't appear he had worked hard to target a political opponent's son.

"A toast to all of us and to the new year and new lives to come!" Bryce announced and took a glass of champagne from the tray Suze had just brought out and placed on the coffee table. Meg saw there was 7Up for Chip, but in a goblet too. What would she ever do without her thoughtful, dear sister? But then the turnabout of that was true too.

"And to a new school for me in Juneau next year," Chip added. "I heard when I get to seventh grade, they have an indoor winter soccer team and a regular outdoors one too."

"Go, Chip! Go, Chip!" Bryce began a cheer the others echoed.

After they drank their toasts, Bryce sat back down next to Meg on the couch. She tipped into him on the soft leather and settled there against him with his arm around her shoulders. Tears blurred her vision as she looked around at the faces lit by firelight while the cold winds howled outside. How happy the newlyweds looked and how far they had all come. Only Rafe and Suze seemed a bit tenuous, but surely any problems would be settled soon, now that they were all Alaskans at heart. And all safe, at least for now.

★ ★ ★ ★ ★

AUTHOR'S NOTE

My husband and I loved our trip to Alaska, partly because it was not in the dead of winter! When we returned, I was so inspired by the stunning scenery and the can-do people that I wrote a novel set there, *Down River*. Several years later, I'm happy to return to the "last frontier" and "Great Alone" state in this story.

I have been published since 1982 and have written many novels. I'm grateful to have a supportive editor—thanks, Emily Ohanjanians—who lets me give her a general idea of where the story will go, because, unlike earlier books when I mapped most things out, I now write differently. I have a bare bones idea of plot, but I let the characters and situation guide me more as the plot evolves. I am sometimes surprised by the storyline, and I hope my readers are too.

For example, in this novel, I had no idea at first that what Lloyd Witlow was carrying in his plane that crashed was going to be tied to an actual lost historical treasure. I stumbled on the fact that the American Civil War Confederate president fled final defeat with a fortune in gold, women's donated jewelry and important papers. When he was captured, most of it was missing. So I stopped and researched that—and the plot thickened.

I did know about Victorian mourning jewelry and had found that fascinating, so I stopped to look into that too. If this interests you also, I would recommend *In Death Lamented* by Sarah Nehama (2012, Schiffer Art Books.) Perhaps if you have antique jewelry, you possess some of that.

There are several books about the flight of Confederate President Jefferson Davis, his wife, Varina, and family. I especially enjoyed William Rawlings's 2017 book *The Strange Journey of the Confederate Constitution* (Google Books.) Numerous articles have been written about this treasure—with, of course, searches and claims concerning where it ended up. One group insists it is still on a sunken ship at the bottom of Lake Michigan. If any of this interests you, you can take a look at www.history.com/news/confederate-gold-jefferson-davis. Also, Wikipedia has articles on Confederate gold.

I read several articles about the effects of global warming in Alaska. I knew about melting glaciers harming polar bears and warming waters displacing seals, but I was interested to read that the precious yellow cedars, some hundreds of years old with their valuable, strong wood and cultural importance to Alaskan Indigenous people, are dying by the hundreds. Scientists are looking for a solution to this cedar tree problem.

As ever, I want to thank others besides my support team of editor Emily and literary agent Annelise Robey. My cousin Barbara Baldwin, who lives in Sylvania, Ohio, where the fictional Galsworths live, was helpful. And thanks to neuro nurse Nancy Armstrong for information on head injuries.

I hope you enjoyed the story.

Best wishes,
Karen Harper